What on earth?

Something had happened to her pillow.

Audra turned her head. It felt as if she was lying against someone's shoulder.

Her eyelids flew open to discover a pair of gray eyes only inches away from hers. They were studying her features intently.

"Don't scream and spoil the moment. It's only 11:00 a.m. I'm not ready to get up yet."

She swallowed hard. They were lying side by side. "I must have had a terrible nightmare."

"Yes. You asked me not to leave you."

"I'm sorry you had to come to my rescue again."

"I'm not. When I told you I'd stay right here, you went back to sleep—and you've been peaceful ever since."

Audra forced herself to sit up and reach for her crutches. Without looking at him, she said, "If I'm hungry, you must be starving."

"Frankly, food's the last thing on my mind. It would be nice just to lie here and talk."

Too nice, Audra's heart cried. *I could make it a habit.* A minute-by-minute, by hour, by week, by month, by year, by lifetime habit!

Dear Reader,

I went to school in Switzerland and France between the ages of seventeen and twenty-two. I remember one year in particular, when I returned home for Christmas. I walked into my family house in Salt Lake City, a place of love and familiarity. One of my favorite Christmas songs was playing on the stereo, the smell of cloves and cinnamon wafted through the air and the Christmas tree held the same ornaments I'd loved as a child. Mother looked so beautiful, and Dad so handsome. Everything was perfect.

It suddenly hit me how blessed I was to be able to return home year after year and find everything the same. I was thinking about this when the stories of the Hawkins brothers came to me.

Their dangerous careers have sent them around the world, yet (like me) they take for granted their wonderful, loving parents and their home in Colorado full of cherished memories. They assume that home and those people will always be there waiting. I wondered what would happen to them if tragedy struck at home while they were away. How would they handle it?

I searched my soul to write their stories. *Home to Copper Mountain* is Rick's story; you'll find Nate's story in *Another Man's Wife*, released in February 2003. Get inside their skins as they deal with their grief and find enduring love with the strong women who come into their lives at exactly the right time.

Enjoy!

Rebecca Winters

P.S. If you have access to the Internet, please check out my Web site at http://www.rebeccawinters-author.com.

Home to Copper Mountain
Rebecca Winters

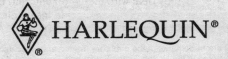

HARLEQUIN®

TORONTO • NEW YORK • LONDON
AMSTERDAM • PARIS • SYDNEY • HAMBURG
STOCKHOLM • ATHENS • TOKYO • MILAN • MADRID
PRAGUE • WARSAW • BUDAPEST • AUCKLAND

ISBN 0-373-71133-6

HOME TO COPPER MOUNTAIN

Printed in U.S.A.

Home to
Copper Mountain

CHAPTER ONE

"SHALL WE GO over to my desk and get the paper-work done so we can put you behind the wheel to-day?"

Until early this morning, Rick Hawkins hadn't in-tended to buy a car. But an unexpected phone call from his father, who knew that Rick was on his way to Arizona to sign some racing contracts, had been the lifeline Rick was looking for. He had grabbed for it with both hands. It was decided—he would visit his father in Texas on his way west.

Loath to suffer through hours of airport lines, se-curity checks, plane changes and rental cars, he de-cided to do himself a favor and arrive at the Jarrett Ranch outside Austin on his own power.

The black BMW M3 two-door coupe with the eigh-teen-inch wheels, 350-horsepower engine and six-speed manual transmission sitting in the middle of the showroom floor would do fine.

He turned to the young salesman. "If you can put me behind it in ten minutes, I'll take it."

"I think we could manage that. My name's John Dunn, by the way."

"John." Rick shook his hand, then followed him

inside his office to answer the inevitable series of questions about his finances.

"Who's your employer?"

"I'm out of work at the moment, but don't be alarmed. I plan to pay cash for the car. Check with my bank."

The salesman blinked before getting up from the desk. He handed him a brochure from a pile sitting next to a desk calendar.

May eighth. Spring had been here for a while. Rick hadn't noticed its arrival.

"While you're waiting, you might want to look through it. I'll be right back."

Rick didn't need to see any literature. If he hadn't felt such a strong loyalty to Mayada for signing him at nineteen, he would have switched to BMW when they'd offered him a racing contract two years later. Their engineering was unequaled.

But his drive to Texas wouldn't be like circling the track. This trip would be open-ended. And he would be driving his own car.

After another hellish night like last night, he decided to leave immediately and drive the whole distance in one shot. It would be a different race than any he'd run before.

Instead of outdriving the competition, he'd be facing his own worst enemy—an enemy chiseling away at his sense of self, his confidence, his happiness, his virtual raison d'être. Himself.

Many times in his racing career he'd been subjected to near-death experiences that had tested his grit and resilience.

This was different.

His mother, with her eternal spirit of optimism, was dead. The only home he'd ever known was gone. He had no woman to share his life. The thought of going back to racing didn't set him on fire. For the first time ever, he could see no sure path before him. And this thought terrified him.

Preoccupied by his demons, he hadn't noticed Mr. Dunn had already returned, accompanied by a smiling middle-aged manager. The manager carried a camera.

"Mr. Hawkins? I'm Lewis Karey. It's a great honor to meet you, sir."

"Thank you." Rick stood up and shook hands with him.

"John didn't realize he was dealing with *the* Lucky Hawkins, one of the world's most famous sports celebrities."

"Hardly."

"Wait till I let Munich know the three-time winner of the Laguna Seca purchased an M3 from us."

"This is a red-letter day for me, too," Rick murmured. "I'll tell you a little secret. I've never owned anything but a motorcycle to get around. This will be my first car."

"You? One of the greatest Formula One drivers in racing today and you've never owned your own car?" The manager looked and sounded incredulous.

Rick chuckled. "That's right, but when I decided I needed one, I knew exactly where to come."

Lewis Karey beamed. "I hope this business of your being out of work is temporary. This is the first I've heard you've left the racing circuit."

"Only time will tell what the future holds. Since no one outside of Mayada and my former sponsor knows the situation, I'd appreciate it if you wouldn't say anything."

Mr. Karey looked at John. "Our lips are sealed. Before we move the car out of the showroom to get it ready for you, could I take a couple of pictures of you standing by it?"

He had been through this experience hundreds of times before, why not once more? No one owned him yet. He was still a free property.

"Sure."

Until his father's severe depression had caused him to retire early from Formula One racing, his motorcycle had accompanied him on the racing circuit and had been the only transportation he'd needed.

Before returning to his family home in Copper Mountain, Colorado, to help his grieving father run the family ski business, he'd given his bike to the college-age son of his crew chief, Wally Sykes. Rick saw no reason for keeping it when he knew he could rely on the company Blazer or his deceased mother's car to get around.

But in a shocking turn of events, he'd arrived home to discover his father had overcome his grief enough to be married again. Furthermore, he was selling the ski shop and the Blazer, and was moving to Texas.

Believing his mom's Nissan would still be available to him while he decided whether to try to get a new sponsor and return to the racing circuit, Rick underwent a second shock.

His older brother, Nate, a former F-16 fighter pilot

who'd resigned his commission to fly home and help their father, too, suddenly decided to get married and become a flight instructor for the air force academy.

Nate, Laurel and the baby from her first marriage were now living in the Hawkins family home while they waited to move into their new house in Colorado Springs. Since they needed two cars, it was decided Laurel would keep the Nissan.

Everyone had somewhere to go, someone to be with. Except Rick, who felt totally displaced.

Since Nate's wedding, Rick had been staying in Denver with Laurel's sister, Julie, and her husband, Brent, just trying to hold on. But he couldn't impose on the Marsdens any longer. It was time to go.

The question was, after Arizona, *where?*

He felt like a man without a country, a man who belonged nowhere. It was a lonely experience, foreign in ways he couldn't describe. The nights were the worst, when he had no choice but to lie in a cold sweat and tough it out until morning.

"Okay," the manager said. "Now let's get a couple of pictures of you sitting in the car. I think we'll leave the door open for the full effect."

Rick obliged. Once he slid behind the wheel, he could smell the new tan leather upholstery. Nice.

By now every salesman, lot attendant, receptionist, cashier, mechanic and client in the building had materialized. There was quite a crowd assembled. Mr. Karey wasn't the only one taking pictures.

Rick ended up signing autographs on brochure after brochure while dozens of questions were fired at him by those who followed the sport.

"Mr. Hawkins is here to buy a car," the manager spoke above the questions. "He was kind enough to let us take pictures and sign autographs. Let's not stampede him."

Rick appreciated the man's intervention before questions were posed that he couldn't answer. It was better not to say anything that could be misquoted to the press.

A racing contract with everything he'd asked for and more had been drawn up by the attorneys of Trans T & T Communications. The megacorporation for whom Brent worked had shown a flattering eagerness to sponsor Rick.

Mayada, the Japanese manufacturer that designed the Formula One cars Rick had been driving for eight years, had also drafted a new contract. Both were in the hands of Neal Hasford, Rick's attorney in Arizona, awaiting his signature.

According to Neal the terms of the contracts looked good, but Rick had yet to put his name on the dotted line.

He shook everyone's hand, then turned to Mr. Karey. "I have to leave, but I'll be back within a half hour to sign the papers."

"Fine. We'll have everything ready for you."

After leaving the dealership, Rick headed for Aurora, a suburb of Denver where the Marsdens lived. His suitcases were already packed and waiting in the trunk of Julie's car. All he had to do was honk and she'd come out of the house to run him back for his new BMW. Then he'd be off.

"It's a good thing Brent isn't here to see this!" she

exclaimed as they drove into the parking lot of the
service department thirty minutes later. The gleaming
black car stood waiting. "We're trying to save up for
our dream home."

Rick turned to the lovely raven-haired mother-to-
be. She was kind and generous to a fault, just like his
new sister-in-law, Laurel. "In the end it's just a vehicle for transportation. What you and Brent have together can't be bought. You're the lucky ones."
She'd never know *how* lucky.

He jumped out of the car and she moved to take
her place behind the wheel. He tapped on the window
so she'd lower it.

"Tell Mike and Joey, the next time I come to Denver I'll take them out to Pike's Peak Raceway to
watch the junior stock-car races. My friend Chip Warner, a former racer who works out there, will show
them around."

Her eyes filmed over. "You'd better keep your
promise. We all wish you wouldn't leave. Phone often, please. Brent's really going to miss you."

"I'm going to miss all of you, too." *More than
you can imagine.*

If it was this difficult to say goodbye to her, he
didn't dare put himself through the gut-wrenching experience of paying his brother one final visit in Colorado Springs on his way to Texas.

He kissed her cheek. "Give me a moment to get
my bags out."

Julie nodded.

After he'd put them on the ground and closed the

trunk, he walked back to her. "Take care of yourself."

"I will. I guess I don't have to tell you. If we find out we're having a boy, it's unanimous—his name's going to be Rick."

She shouldn't have told him that. "I'd be flattered and honored."

With a wave of her hand, she took off. Her glistening blue eyes were the last thing he saw before Mr. Dunn approached. "If you want to step inside the building, someone will put your bags in the trunk."

"Thanks."

Rick followed him into another office where Mr. Karey was waiting. Once he'd written out a check and put his signature on everything, Rick glanced at the younger man standing by. "You're a good salesman, John."

His smile was sheepish. "I'm afraid I didn't do a thing to sell this car, Mr. Hawkins."

"That's what I mean. You left me alone to make up my own mind. That's the best kind of salesman."

Both men looked pleased. It was the manager who said, "Well, you're the dream customer." He handed him the keys and the leather kit containing all the papers and instructions. "Dare we make the pitch you'll never want to drive anything else again?"

"Dare away." He flashed them a smile. "I'm sure you're right."

They shook hands again and walked out to the car with him. The driver's door had been opened in invitation.

A flick of the ignition and the engine purred to life.

He adjusted the seat and the mirrors. They'd filled the tank. All systems were go.

''We'll look forward to seeing you when you come in for your first scheduled oil change.''

When that time came, Rick had no idea where he'd be, but they didn't need to know that. ''Thanks for the excellent service. I've appreciated it. So long.''

He drove out to the street and joined the stream of traffic. The car could travel from zero to sixty in four point eight seconds. He'd test it out as soon as he reached the freeway.

Later, when he came to those long, lonely stretches of road devoid of traffic, he'd find how well she traveled at a hundred and ten miles an hour.

What he needed right now was a map of Texas. Though he'd been around the world many times, he'd never raced there or had an inclination to visit.

At the next full-service station he bought the map, a six-pack of cold cola and a large bag of potato chips. That would hold him for a while.

Once back in the car, he opened the map and began estimating distances. Denver to Austin was approximately nine hundred miles. En route he'd phone his father for details to reach the ranch.

He glanced at his watch. Eleven-thirty. If he averaged a hundred miles an hour, plus or minus, he'd be in Austin by eight or eight-thirty that night.

FOURTEEN HOURS LATER, after stopping and starting for near-constant road construction, he turned on US 290, leaving Austin behind him.

The salespeople at the dealership wouldn't recognize his bug-spattered, mud-splattered car. He needed a shower and a shave, but that wasn't going to happen until he arrived at his destination.

According to his father's directions he needed to continue west a half hour or so until he came to Highway 16 where he would turn south. At exactly one point six-tenths of a mile, he'd see the entrance to the Jarrett Ranch on his right.

How in the hell did people live in a place where there was no sign of a mountain? After driving through this endless state, surrounded by a flat world of dust and heat, he couldn't comprehend how his father was surviving.

Clint Hawkins was a remarkable athlete who'd skied to many victories, including an Olympic gold medal. How did a man who loved winter and had spent his whole married life in the Colorado Rockies at ten thousand feet stand it?

No wonder so many Texans flocked to the towns of Copper Mountain and Breckenridge during ski season. Anything to get away from this miserable wilderness they called home.

Rick and Nate used to laugh over their visitors' funny accents and inability to stop talking for a single second to let someone else get a word in. Today he'd met the same type on the road when he'd stopped for gas and food.

As far as he was concerned, the Texans could keep Texas. He'd come to see his father, then he was out of here!

For the dozenth time he flicked on the radio hoping to find a station that played something besides rock or country. After leaving Colorado, he'd been hearing the same songs over and over as he drove through New Mexico and Texas. Was there no such thing as a classical-music station beyond the Rockies?

Before he'd left Denver he should have stopped at a CD store and bought some symphonic recordings to keep him company. Rick's mother had taught him to enjoy everything from baroque and classical to modern.

On the morning of a race, there was nothing he loved better than to listen to Vivaldi or Brahms or Mahler while he ate a big breakfast. Any of them brought structure and order to his mind, helping him to focus on the task ahead.

Aware his nerves were frayed from a combination of fatigue and a growing inner anxiety he couldn't throw off, he pressed the scan button to tune out the heavy-metal music blaring from some rock station out of Austin.

The next couple of stations were phone-in talk shows about politics or UFOs. He was about to shut off the radio for good when he came across a station where he heard a female vocalist backed by a terrific guitarist. It sounded like country music, but she sang with such a great voice he pressed the button to keep the tuner there.

You invade our space,
You drink our beer,
You pollute the place,
You shoot our deer,
You build your castles,

You do as you please,
If it's worth the battle you change the course of
streams,
You grow Bermuda grass,
You even plant hay,
Then you can't figure out why the wildlife went
away.
You fly down for weekends
To your twenty-acre spread,
Then you wonder why,
Your cattle all lie dead.
You're the dreaded windshield rancher invading
the Hill Country,
You wanted a part of Texas,
And by golly,
You destroyed habitat and birthright during a
bad economy.
You came, you saw, you conquered,
You took my legacy.
Because of you, you, you, you,
This happened to me, me, me, me.
I'm an uprooted bluebonnet,
I no longer have a home,
Do you hear me, windshield rancher?
Thanks to you I'm alone.
The light has now gone out,
I can't see in front of me,
There's no home to go back to,
Fear is my destiny.
The past is gone forever,
It walked out the door.
What once excited, excites no more,

The song ended, jerking Rick back to cognizance of his surroundings.

Damn. He'd been so mesmerized by what he'd heard, he'd overshot the turnoff to the ranch by four miles. Since no one was around, he made a tire-squealing U-turn in the middle of the road and flew back down the highway.

"And now for all you night creatures like me who can't sleep because your demons won't let you—oh yes, I've got them, too—shall we have a change of pace? I've had a lot of requests for Gounod's *Ave Maria* for voice and harp. Enjoy this last number before we say good-night."

Rick almost missed the entrance again because the female disc jockey had started to play the next recording. The second he heard the voice, he realized it was the same vocalist who'd performed the amazing country song. This time she was singing to an exquisite harp accompaniment.

Why didn't the disc jockey give out the name of the singer?

Whoever she was, she had extraordinary talent to be able to perform such diametrically opposed pieces of music with equal ability. He wanted her name so he could look for some of her records.

Parts of the first song resonated with him.

The light has now gone out,
I can't see in front of me,
There's no home to go back to,
Fear is my destiny.
The past is gone forever,

It walked out the door,
What once excited, excites no more.

Rick could have written those lines himself. Whoever the composer was had to be a native Texan, considering the subject matter. It sounded like life had dealt them a hard blow.

Realizing someone else out there in the cosmos was going through the same disquieting experience helped him to understand he wasn't the only person who felt as if they were losing their mind.

Absorbed in his painful thoughts, he was slow to process the fact that the white three-quarter-ton pickup truck moving toward him came to a stop as Rick passed it. He blinked, then reversed.

His father's familiar half smile had never been more welcome than in this back of beyond. They both put down their windows at the same time. The air still held the earth's warmth. He could smell skunk.

"Dad—" His throat swelled with unexpected emotion.

"It's good to see you, too, son. You told me you'd be driving a new M3. For a moment I thought I'd come upon James Bond. So…how did your first car handle?"

Rick's lips twitched. "A lot better than my first homemade go-cart."

"That's reassuring. I'll turn around so you can follow me the rest of the way."

Beyond tired, he was grateful to be led down the dark, dusty road. When they reached the ranch house three miles from the entrance, Rick regretted having to turn off the beautiful voice with the harp accompaniment. He wished her music could have kept him company all the way from Colorado.

He got out of the car eager to feel Clint Hawkins's famous bear hug.

Silhouetted against a night sky partly obscured by clouds, the Queen Anne–style house loomed behind his parent. The two-story structure had many gables and a tower with a conical roof. For a ranch house it looked totally out of place and unlike anything Rick had been imagining.

"IT'S THAT TIME AGAIN, ladies and gentlemen. We're coming up on three in the morning. I'll be taking your requests Friday at midnight on KHLB, the Hill Country station out of Austin at 580 on the AM dial. Thank you for listening to the *Red Jarrett Show*, where I aim to bring you a little bit of the best of everything."

The line-board operator back at the station in Austin turned the switch, and Audra Jarrett was off the air. Her boss had arranged for her to do her program from the ranch while she was recuperating from her accident. Several technicians from the studio had come out to the house to set up the mixing board, stands, plug-in mike and Telos digital sound system. So far everything had worked perfectly, but it seemed she had a ways to go before she was fully recovered.

She let out a groan of exhaustion and ran her fingers through her hair, which was damp at the roots from exertion.

After eyeing the short distance from her table to

the bedroom doorway, she felt for her crutches and with superhuman effort, grabbed them from where they'd been leaning against the wall. She stopped long enough to turn out the lights, then moved out into the hallway and into the bedroom next door and lay down on the bed. The night was warm enough that she didn't need a blanket to cover her.

There was no way she'd be getting up again any time soon to brush her teeth or change out of her top and cutoffs. They were the only shorts loose enough around the legs to slide up and down over her cast.

The strain of perching on the stool with her left leg in a full cast had been too draining. Whatever had possessed her to think she could transfer from her guitar to her harp between commercials while operating her own mixing board at the same time? Tonight she should have relied solely on recorded music.

She'd been home from the hospital almost a month. By now she assumed it wouldn't be a problem to perform some of her own music live during her radio show, broadcast from the bungalow on her uncle David's property.

It was a small three-bedroom home. With a few steps, everything was in easy reach. No stairs, no basement. But Audra hadn't counted on the weakness that assailed her body through the simple act of singing into the microphone again. It may have just been her leg that was broken, but this seemed to affect her whole body.

The car accident that had taken Pete Walker's life could have done a lot more damage. But it hadn't been her time to go.

No. Destiny's plan had been to kill her off in increments. She figured when her uncle found a buyer for the ranch, that would be the final blow.

Her eyelids fluttered closed from sorrow and fatigue.

What would she do without her music? Thanks to Pam, who'd started her on the piano in grade school, Audra had found her muse. Not even Boris, the talented French conductor she'd fallen in love with at the Paris Conservatory of Music, had been able to stamp out the solace when he'd rejected her.

As she settled back against the pillows her cell phone rang. That would be her cousin calling from the main ranch house three miles away to make sure Audra was okay.

Pam…the wonderful woman who'd been mother, sister and best friend rolled into one since Audra was a little girl.

She reached for her phone. After checking the caller ID to make sure, she clicked on to talk to her cousin. "It's 3:15 a.m., Mrs. Hawkins."

Audra loved calling her that. Clint Hawkins was the best thing that had ever happened to Pam. Audra was half in love with him herself.

"Your new husband is going to resent me if you keep this up. I've been out of the hospital for some time now, yet you're still hovering!"

"That's because I listened to your broadcast tonight. You were fabulous, but you overdid it."

Audra couldn't hide anything from her. "I found that out as soon as I was switched off the air."

"I'm mad at you, honey. The doctor warned you to be careful."

"I wanted to start performing again. It'll be easier next time."

"Why not wait till the cast comes off before you go back on the air, period?" Pam urged.

Because I can't stand the nights.

Memories of the crash wouldn't leave Audra alone. Her guilt—that she'd escaped death and Pete hadn't—continued to haunt her.

"I'd die of boredom, but I appreciate your phoning. I'm in bed, so stop worrying about me. Now, hurry and hang up before Clint discovers you're awake and talking to me again."

"My husband isn't here."

She frowned. "Has he flown to Colorado on another family emergency?" Audra hoped everything was fine with his recently married son, Nate. That marriage almost hadn't come off.

It didn't seem as if Clint and Pam were ever going to get the time alone they deserved, no thanks to Audra, whose accident had ruined their honeymoon.

"He's out in the truck looking for his son who should have arrived by now."

Audra blinked. "I didn't know you were expecting his family."

"He didn't either until earlier in the day."

"Which one is it?"

"Rick."

Ah yes, the famous race-car driver, Lucky Hawkins. The speed-loving son he'd secretly worried about for years. The one Clint feared would end up a statistic.

Audra refused to entertain the thought that he might have been in a collision on the highway driving down here. She didn't want Pam thinking bad thoughts either.

"It would be a hoot if he's lost."

"Now, Audra..."

She chuckled. "Well, it would. Can't you see this living sports legend whizzing around to the various ranches asking, 'Does my daddy live here?'"

"Be nice," her cousin murmured, but Audra could tell she was on the verge of laughter. "It's easy to get lost in the Hill Country after dark, and lest you forget, he's no boy."

Her cousin was right about that. An image of the good-looking male with black hair she'd seen in some of Pam's wedding pictures filled Audra's mind. Clint and his sons were more attractive than any three men had a right to be.

"Is this to be a quick visit?"

"Yes. Clint's so thrilled Rick agreed to come here on his way to Arizona, he's been restless all day waiting for him. I put him to work helping me cook. We're going to have a big lunch at noon. Sleep now and I'll be by for you about quarter to twelve."

"No, no. This is your first chance to show his son around *your* turf for a change. There's no way I'm going to interfere with that!"

"Audra—Uncle David wants everyone to meet. The cousins and their families are coming from Austin. He insisted."

"Oh, no."

"I'm not too excited about that myself."

Their uncle probably had to threaten leaving them out of the will for them to agree, but Audra didn't say the words out loud. Their bitterness over his handling of the Jarrett family finances since their parents' deaths years before had turned them into angry men.

After the loving care Pam had always shown their cousins growing up, Audra couldn't believe how mean-spirited and ungrateful they were. When they'd heard she was marrying what they considered to be some old geezer from Colorado, they'd mocked her and laid bets the relationship wouldn't last.

To their shock, she'd returned to Texas with her new husband following their honeymoon in Hawaii. Despite family emergencies that required Pam to leave Hawaii early to be with Audra after her accident, and Clint to fly home to Copper Mountain to talk some sense into his son Nate, who was hurting from a broken engagement, it appeared their marriage was thriving. Clint would be a permanent fixture around the ranch from now on.

Tom, the oldest of the three boys and their spokesman, had given their uncle David an ultimatum. They wanted Clint out of the main house. Until he was gone, they would no longer come out on weekends to help keep the fencing in good repair, a neverending project.

That kind of cruelty pained Audra, who was still hampered to a large extent by her broken leg. Her unexpected accident had brought Pam running to her síde to wait on her when Pam should have been enjoying precious time with her brand-new husband.

As it turned out, Clint Hawkins was anything but an old geezer.

Audra didn't know such a wonderful person existed anywhere. She'd shed tears of happiness he'd come into Pam's life. Already she sensed that beneath Clint's mild-mannered nature lived a highly principled man and a force to contend with. He protected Pam in so many subtle ways, their male cousins would be no match for him when they did meet.

As for Uncle David, Audra could tell that Clint had won him over when he'd agreed to fly Pam's husband to Odessa in the middle of the night.

There'd been some family emergency that required Clint's getting on a plane back to Colorado. Their uncle wouldn't have gone out of his way like that if he hadn't respected Clint a great deal.

When Audra really thought about it, lunch with the whole family ought to be downright interesting.

"I'll make sure I'm ready when you arrive. Thanks for checking up on me, Pam."

"As if I wouldn't. Get a good sleep."

I won't. "You, too."

Audra clicked off, then lay back against the pillows. The time she dreaded every night was here once again.

No longer on heavy painkillers that blotted out consciousness, when she closed her eyes, her mind replayed the horror of the accident.

Refusing to let it happen tonight, she turned on the

lamp and reached for the spiral notebook she kept by the bed. She could almost hear the music as she pulled the pencil from the coil and started jotting down the words to a song formulating in her mind. She'd already entitled it "Racetrack Lover."

Hey cowboy, can you hear me?
Better hold your sweetheart tight.
There's an exciting new man.
Coming into town tonight.
He's lucky on the track and lucky with the women,
He'll mess with your gal,
Consider that a given.
Tall, dark and sexy,
Handsome as sin,
He's the racetrack lover
Who's about to drive in.
If you don't want a broken heart before daylight,
Keep your gal out of sight and locked up tight.
Better put her in the barn,
And throw away the key,
Don't let him get near her,
Or believe you me,
He'll take her for a ride,
And rob you blind,
Before he spins his wheels,
And leaves her behind.
He's a charmer,
He's a talker,
He's a no-strings guy,
He's the racetrack lover in town on the fly.

Hey cowboy, can you hear me?

Better hold your sweetheart tight.

There's an exciting new man coming into tow—

"I'm so cold. Are *you* cold, Pete? *Pete?* Talk to me! Oh no! Oh please God, no.

"Don't let him be dead! Help him! Help him!" She pounded her fist against the glass.

"Why doesn't someone come?" She pounded harder. "Help! So much blood. He's not moving.

"Someone help! What am I going to do?"

"Audra?"

"Oh thank God. Get him out. Hurry!"

"Audra? Wake up," an alarmed voice sounded from the murky haze engulfing her. "Wake up! You're having a nightmare."

She felt a hand on her shoulder. "Come on. Wake up. It's all right. You're home in bed. It was just a bad dream."

"Pam?" she cried, clutching the hand that gripped her upper arm to force her awake.

But it wasn't small and feminine. This hand felt solid and male. Her eyelids flew open.

A man with black hair stood over her bed.

CHAPTER TWO

AUDRA SCREAMED bloody murder and threw off his hand while she tried to reach the nearest crutch. To her horror, her bad leg pretty well held her anchored.

"Forgive me for frightening you, Ms. Jarrett," he said in a low voice. "I'm Clint Hawkins's son Rick. I told Pam I'd pick you up for her."

Rick Hawkins?

She fought to catch her breath and waited for her heartbeat to return to normal. Her mind began to clear now that the threat of bodily injury had passed. Audra recognized him from Pam's wedding photographs. In those pictures his tall, well-honed physique had been dressed in a formal suit instead of a black T-shirt and jeans. He was even more attractive in person.

"When I got out of my car, I could hear screaming. It gave me the chills," he explained. His compassionate gaze let her know her nightmare must have been a beaut.

Audra moaned while she willed her body to calm down. To think he'd heard her carrying on from clear outside.

How awful! How humiliating!

"I thought you were being attacked. Your front

door was locked, so I got in through your bedroom window, which had been left open.''

Last night she'd been too physically exhausted to check the window. Her driving need had been to reach the bed before she collapsed.

To her chagrin the clock radio by her bed said five after twelve. She hadn't thought to set it because she rarely needed an alarm to wake her up. Normally she only slept seven hours.

"It's a-all right," she stammered. "If you would please wait for me in the living room. It's down the hall on your left."

"Would you like some help getting up first?"

"No— I can manage, thank you."

The concerned gray eyes staring down at her from between heavy black lashes made a sweep of her five-foot-five figure. They started with the toes peeping out of her cast, and ended with her dark red curls, missing nothing in between. She felt as if he'd just sucked all the air out of her lungs.

"So *you're* the cousin who almost lost a limb." His voice had a faraway sound, yet his gaze was all too personal as it took in her other leg, which was bare to the fringe of her denim shorts. "Thank God it didn't happen."

Thank heavens she hadn't changed out of her clothes before she'd finally drifted off. He could have found her in her underwear...

Audra had never felt so embarrassed in her whole life. Heat poured into her cheeks.

"So," she mimicked. She was attracted to him yet his presence in her bedroom made her feel violated, though she knew he'd meant her no harm. "*You're* the son with the death wish. The Hill Country's a little far out of your way for a pit stop, isn't it?"

Avoiding his eyes, she waited until he'd disappeared out the door before reaching for her crutches.

That's when she saw her spiral notebook still open and lying on the bed next to her hip. The pencil had fallen to the floor.

"*Racetrack Lover!*"

Oh no! Had he read what she'd written?

Audra closed the book and put it on the bedstand. In a few clumsy moves she eased herself off the mattress and was able to grab fresh underwear from the drawer.

No way was she going to wear another pair of shorts in front of him. Snug jeans were impossible to put on. A blouse and skirt would be easier to manage than a dress with a zipper up the back.

She pulled a light-blue blouse and denim skirt from the hangers in the closet, then moved to the bathroom across the hall as fast as she could.

Since she was unable to shower with the cast on, a quick sponge bath would have to do for today. The small bathroom left little space for her cast and the crutches, too.

She applied a dusky pomegranate shade of lipstick and flicked a brush through her curls. There wasn't anything she could do about the shadows under her eyes.

"Did you close and lock your window?" he asked as she entered the living room a few minutes later.

"It's a little late for that, don't you think? Until a few minutes ago we've never had a break-in."

She hadn't meant to sound sarcastic, but it must have come out sounding that way, because he grimaced.

"Then you're damn lucky."

"According to your father, so are you," she drawled.

The room was charged with tension, which broke as he moved toward the hallway. Audra made a half turn with her crutches.

Over her shoulder she said, "If you're determined to be a Boy Scout instead of an intruder, you might as well put the screen back on while you're at it."

After that reminder she opened the front door and started down the porch steps. There were only two of them. She managed without difficulty.

It didn't surprise her to find a new, gleaming black BMW parked in front of the bungalow. The kind of car she was seeing more and more of these days on the back roads...

Rich trespassers were raping the land with their easy money and didn't know a gelding from a stallion. Did the racetrack lover know the difference? It would be interesting to find out.

RICK STARTED UP the car without saying anything to her. He backed out of the driveway, past the mailbox, to the road leading to the main ranch house. When he'd offered to pick up Pam's cousin as a way to help, all he'd known about her was that she was recovering from an automobile accident in which the driver had been killed. Apparently, the man had worked at the same radio station she did.

Though he was armed with that much knowledge, he couldn't have imagined what awaited him at the bungalow. The screams he'd heard coming from inside were so bloodcurdling, he still hadn't recovered.

Ms. Audra Jarrett had come as a big surprise to him in more ways than one.

She was in her early to mid-twenties. For some reason he'd had the erroneous impression she was much closer to Pam's forty. He'd never been partial to red hair, but then he'd never seen a shining mass of dark-mahogany curls before. They danced above a pair of blue-gray eyes so close in color to his mother's, he was taken by surprise.

While he'd tried to wake the writhing woman on top of the bed, his gaze had been drawn to the curves of her slender body, making it impossible for him to look anywhere else.

Right now she didn't appear to be in the mood to talk. Who could blame her for her silence?

No doubt she'd been plagued by horrific dreams since the crash. They had to be disorienting and probably stayed with her even after she awakened from them.

He'd known several racers who'd had to be cut from a wreckage. While he'd watched and listened to Audra fight her way out of her nightmare, it was evident she'd been trapped in the car accident that had broken her leg.

Neither his father nor Pam had shared those details

with him. His breaking into her bedroom couldn't have helped the situation any.

"I'm sorry a total stranger had to be the cause of more distress," he apologized again. "You were in such a highly agitated state, my only thought was to get to you and wake you up so you wouldn't have to suffer any longer."

"I realize I sounded like a soldier back from Vietnam, so you're forgiven," she said without looking at him. "Last night Pam told me your father had gone out looking for you, so I can't say you came as a complete surprise. Otherwise I'd have cracked your head open with the end of my crutch."

"Ouch," he teased.

"Obviously he found you," she replied without a hint of warmth. "How far off the beaten track were you?"

His hands tightened on the steering wheel.

Audra Jarrett didn't like him.

Rick wasn't such a vain man he had to conquer every woman in sight. Still, her hostility had gotten beneath his skin.

Intrigued, he intended to learn the reason for her demeanor. He suspected today's events had little to do with the fact that she wished herself anywhere but in his car.

"We discovered each other on the ranch road about two miles from the house."

Her only response was to turn her head and stare out the passenger window. The gesture caused him to wonder if she resented his father for taking Pam away

from her and couldn't help disliking Rick for being
his son.

Rick's thoughts harkened back to a conversation
with his brother. Nate had found out that the men in
Pam's family were laying bets on how long the marriage to their father would last. That was why she
hadn't invited any of them to the wedding.

It was possible that no one in Pam's family, male
or female, was happy about her recent marriage.

Then again, maybe Audra's antipathy toward Rick
had nothing to do with his father. Perhaps after such
a terrible nightmare, she was just lashing out. The
accident had killed a man she loved, and Rick happened to be a handy target.

"I heard you calling for Pete over and over again,"
he said quietly. "He was your fiancé?"

That brought her head around. She studied him as
if he were a species she'd never come across before.

"Your father may have married my cousin, but that
doesn't make us related or entitle you to information
that's none of your business."

He saw her hands curl into fists. His attempt at
sensitivity wasn't going over well.

"Why don't we start again, Ms. Jarrett?" he suggested. "Since my father and Pam's happiness is of
the utmost importance to both of us, shall we try to
be friends while I'm here?"

His father intended to use the money from the sale
of the ski business to help Pam establish a bed-and-
breakfast on the ranch. Apparently, the idea had been
a dream of hers for years and would bring in much
needed income. Rick didn't want to see anything go

wrong with their plans when they both seemed so excited about it.

He pulled to a stop in front of the ranch house where there were a half-dozen cars and trucks assembled.

"I have a better idea," she replied.

His lips twitched while he waited to hear the rest of her remarks with an eagerness that surprised him.

"Let's agree to stay out of each other's way. It shouldn't be too difficult. Inside of twelve hours, boredom will consume you. By nightfall we'll be breathing the dust from your tires when you peal out of here for heaven knows what race with death you have scheduled next."

Her withering comment brought to mind a conversation he'd had with his brother a few weeks earlier.

When I saw Laurel's joy as she held her daughter in her arms, I knew what Mom and Dad felt when we were born. Since that moment, I've asked myself how our parents were able to accept our chosen careers without suffering a nervous breakdown in the process.

Come on, Nate. Don't forget, they placed themselves in mortal danger every time they ran a ski race.

True. But in comparison, you have to admit strapping ourselves into a race car or into the cockpit of a jet increases the danger by quantum leaps.

No longer smiling, Rick got out of the car to help Audra, but Pam had reached her first.

"Honey—you took so long I got worried about you." She opened the back door to retrieve the crutches for her cousin.

"Forgive me. I'm afraid I overslept."

The impassioned woman of a moment ago shot Rick a warning glance that forbid him to add one word of explanation.

Message received, he muttered to himself.

By this time Audra had swung her legs out, displaying amazing agility for someone wearing a full-length leg cast. With Pam's assistance she stood up and started walking toward the house on her crutches.

Pam put a detaining hand on Rick's arm. Her demeanor didn't resemble that of the radiant wife who'd introduced Rick and his father to her male cousins less than an hour ago. Some contentious family issue must have flared up during the time Rick had been gone.

"Thanks for picking her up. Did she seem all right to you?" Pam asked in an anxious voice.

Putting two and two together, Rick realized that if Pam had been at her cousin's bedside both at the hospital and here at the house, then she knew about the nightmares. Maybe she feared Audra had suffered another debilitating episode. Under the circumstances, Rick could well understand her concern.

"She's fine."

He didn't dare say anything else. It was important that Audra trust him.

They walked up the steps of the house together. "Is everything okay with you?" he asked her.

"I'm not sure. Better ask me after today is over, Rick," came her cryptic remark.

THE DINING ROOM was Audra's favorite place in the house. It had a huge eighteen-foot ceiling, an enormous fireplace and circular bay windows. In the past, with the addition of several round tables surrounding the main dining-room table, the room could hold forty-five Jarretts comfortably. But tragedy had struck, limiting their numbers.

Today the remaining fifteen family members were joined by Clint Hawkins and his son. Uncle David, whose thinning gray hair still showed traces of auburn, presided at the head.

Several of the other family members in the room had inherited the Jarrett trait of red hair. Audra had been forced to put up with a lot of teasing because of it. She didn't envy her cousins' children for what they'd have to deal with as they grew older.

Her uncle told Audra to sit at the opposite end of the table where she could rest her cast without any obstruction. Then he asked the boys—her male cousins now in their thirties—to get up and finish bringing in the rest of the food from the kitchen.

Audra didn't dare glance at Pam just then. The vexed expressions on the boys' faces would have caused both of them to break into laughter.

To Audra's relief, their uncle had placed Pam and Clint on his right, with Rick next to his father. Jim, Sherry and their two children sat on his left. Next to them came Greg and Diane and their two kids. Tom and Annette and their two offspring took up the rest of the places.

Being at opposite ends of the table meant Audra didn't have to look into a pair of intelligent gray eyes that had been privy to sights she didn't want anyone to see.

Trying to overcome the shock of finding Rick Hawkins standing over her when she'd awakened, screaming her head off, she concentrated on her food.

As far as Audra was concerned, Pam was the best cook in the Hill Country. She'd outdone herself with her country-fried chicken, giblet gravy, dumplings and a half-dozen side dishes that were her uncle's favorites.

Audra felt terrible for not contributing anything. The cast couldn't come off soon enough to suit her.

"This is a fine meal, Pam." Their seventy-two-year-old uncle appeared to be enjoying himself.

"Clint helped me. In fact, he made the dessert, a Hawkins-family recipe."

"Which one is that, Dad?" she heard Rick ask.

"Rocky road."

"I'll bet it's good," their uncle commented.

"My brother and I could never get enough of it, but then we're chocolate lovers."

So was Audra. She helped herself to the creamed potatoes with peas, waiting for the rest of the Jarrett side of the family to chime in. But the others just talked horses and ranch business among themselves, acting for all the world as if they were alone at the table.

According to Pam, none of the boys had ever shown the slightest interest in Clint or knew anything about him except that he'd come from Colorado. They'd never asked any questions. Their distrust of outsiders, plus their jealousy of Pam, had made communication impossible.

Pam, on the other hand, had welcomed their wives

into the family. She'd shown love to their children, and had done everything she could for them. Yet they ignored her new husband as if he didn't exist. Their unconscionable rudeness toward Clint and Rick infuriated Audra. This couldn't be allowed to go on.

She turned to Tom's thirteen-year-old son seated on her right. "Hey, Bobby? Have you thought of a subject for your technology report yet?"

He frowned. "I was going to show how phones have changed to become cell phones, but a lot of the kids are planning to do the same thing."

Good. He hadn't gotten started on it yet.

"Would you like an idea that's different? I can promise no one else in your class will have thought of it."

"What's that?"

"Skis and boots."

"Huh?"

"They've changed a lot since the days when someone tied his shoes to wooden slats with a couple of pieces of rope and used sticks for poles. I bet when Clint won his gold medal in the Olympics, his skis and boots were a lot different because of technology."

Bobby's head jerked toward the other end of the table. "*You* won a gold medal at the Olympics?" By now everyone else was staring at Pam's husband in surprise. It was about time the family opened their eyes and ears to the kind of man she'd married.

Clint flashed Audra a private smile. "It was a long time ago, but Audra's right. Since then, skis and boots have undergone tremendous changes to make them faster, lighter and safer.''

"What did you win the medal in?'' Michael wanted to know. He was Jim's eleven-year-old.

"The giant slalom.''

"Whoa.''

Delighted over the kids' reactions, Audra said, "He and his now-deceased wife owned and ran a ski business in Copper Mountain, Colorado.

"Fabulous skiers from all over the States and Europe flock there for the World Cup races. There probably isn't anything he doesn't know about the changes in ski technology.

"His wife won a silver medal at the same Olympics for the women's downhill, Bobby,'' Audra continued. "If I were you, I'd pump Clint for all he's worth. You're bound to get top marks with such an original report.''

She flicked her glance to Sherry. "Would you mind passing me the corn on the cob? It's so good, I've got to have another one.''

"Sure.'' Sherry picked up the bowl and handed it to Bobby, who gave it to Audra.

"Do you ski, too?'' Sherry directed her question to Rick. Jim's wife, like Annette and Diane, couldn't seem to take her eyes off Clint's son. And the boys didn't seem to like it.

Audra smiled to herself. The racetrack lover had blown into town. Watch out, guys. He's not only easy on the eyes, he's a breed apart from the rest of you.

"Every chance I get,'' came Rick's quiet reply.

"Rick won the Junior World Slalom Championship when he was a teenager," Pam volunteered.

"Cool!" This from several of the children.

Audra didn't know that. "Rick Hawkins is a man of many talents." All of them had to do with speed and danger.

At that comment, his gaze met hers head-on. She refused to look away. Pete had lost his life in a freak car accident. According to Pam, Clint figured it was only a matter of time until his son was seriously injured or killed on the track in a fiery crash. Audra didn't want to think about that happening.

Clint adored his boys. If anything ever happened to them he would never get over it. The pain would put a blight on Pam's marriage. And there'd been too much pain in the Jarrett family. Her cousin Pam didn't deserve any more.

Not only would it be a pointless tragedy, it would destroy Pam and Clint's newfound happiness. Audra wanted their joy to last forever.

She could always lock Rick up in a barn and keep the key. *There* was a tantalizing thought. But aside from hog-tying him, she was powerless to prevent something ghastly from happening.

Fastening her attention on Bobby once more, she said, "If you traced the Hawkins family's experiences testing out ski equipment, I have no doubts you'd tap into exactly what your teacher had in mind when she gave you the assignment."

Formula One race-car driving would have provided another fascinating topic for a technology report. It was a business so far removed from their insular world of horses and ranching, the boys would fall out of their chairs if they knew what Rick did for a living.

But now was not the time to enlighten them. This was Clint Hawkins's moment.

"Would you be willing to help me, Clint?" Bobby asked.

Pam's husband nodded. "There's nothing I'd like more. We can go in the living room after dinner and I'll give you some ideas to work on."

"There won't be time," Tom muttered.

But their uncle said, "Make the time!"

To Audra's delight, Clint went right on talking as if Tom hadn't said anything. "Do you have access to the Internet, Bobby?"

"Yeah."

"Then I'll supply you with some names of several ski manufacturers that explain their engineering innovations with graphics you can print out."

"Thanks!"

"I want to read that report when you're finished, young man."

"Sure, Uncle David."

"Don't clear the dishes yet," he warned Pam, who'd started to push herself away from the table. "I have something to say and want everyone to hear it."

Stillness spread throughout the room.

Those ominous words had the effect of a giant hand squeezing Audra's heart. If her instincts were right, the moment she'd been dreading for months had come. For her uncle to bring up private matters in front of Clint and his son proved how completely he'd accepted Pam's husband into the family.

No longer interested in her meal, Audra put down her fork.

"I'm not going to sugarcoat this. Our ranch has been losing money steadily ever since the tornado destroyed lives and livelihoods twenty-three years ago. It's left me with no option but to sell the property and the plane."

The muscles in Audra's stomach clenched.

"You all knew it was coming. That's why years ago I insisted all of you get college educations and make livings for yourselves while you helped me on the side with the ranching."

"You've already signed papers?" Tom asked.

"Let me finish." He glanced at each of them. "You don't have to wait for me to die to know what's coming to you. Everything's been sold except the hundred and twenty acres of fenced land with the bungalow I've left to Audra and you boys."

"A hundred and twenty acres," Tom blurted in anger.

Audra swallowed hard. She'd thought her uncle had already given Pam the bungalow.

Had he left her out of the will because she'd married Clint? Her cousin had entertained so many plans how she'd use her property. Audra couldn't bear it. That didn't sound like her fair-minded uncle. It had to mean he had less money than she'd thought.

Jim's face had gone as dark red as his hair. "You can't do anything with that small amount of land!"

Greg looked equally outraged.

"How much land did you want, Tom?" their uncle asked in his unflappable manner. "Did *you* have the money to buy it in order to help pay off our debts? Did any of you have the funds to save us?''

Tom ground his teeth. ''You know damn well we didn't!''

Audra flinched.

''Then be thankful you're being given anything at all, and I won't have you swearing in front of me or this family or our guest.''

Things were falling apart fast.

''My advice to you boys and Audra is to use the land and the bungalow for a place to come when you want a change from Austin. With fifty-two weeks in a year, that gives each of your families thirteen weeks to enjoy vacations, provided you can work out the arrangements without rancor.''

Rancor was the operative word all right. Audra took a shuddering breath.

''My Realtor has found me a condo at a retirement center in Austin. I plan to be moved out of here by the end of next week. Audra can live there with me until she decides what she wants to do.''

''Who's the new owner?'' Tom demanded. His surly tone wounded her.

''A wealthy businessman from Cleveland, Ohio, named Edwin Torney. It won't be long before he starts building a showplace out on the south thirty.

''You'll see workmen coming and going. They'll be using the road at the side of the bungalow for access. Another mailbox will be put up out by the road.''

Tom was livid. ''Why would he build anything when he's already stolen this house from us?''

"Nobody stole anything, Tom. That was going to be my next announcement." Their uncle looked around at each of them. "I've sold the house to Clint. He and Pam are going to live here."

One look at Pam, and Audra thought her cousin was going to collapse from shock. Apparently she hadn't known anything about the transaction. Clint put a loving arm around his wife.

Thank God, Audra's heart cried. *Bless you, Clint. Bless you, Uncle David.*

"Pam was always your favorite," Greg muttered. "Why don't you just admit you gave it to her!"

Their uncle rose to his feet. "Clint Hawkins sold his business back in Colorado. He was able to pay my asking price. With that money I've been able to pay off the loans stacking up at the bank.

"If any one of you could have done the same, the house would be yours. I gave you the opportunity long before he came into Pam's life. Let's all be thankful it'll continue to stay in the Jarrett family.

"But let me say this—if anyone deserved to have it given to them outright, it would be Pam. As a teenager she single-handedly took on the responsibilities of mother and sister to the rest of us at great cost to her own dreams.

"No one ever had a better friend, cook, housekeeper or ranching-accounts expert," his voice trembled. "No one was ever kinder or more loving and unselfish. I don't know what we would have done without her. Especially sweet little Audra, who was only five at the time and needed a woman's comfort."

Everyone looked in Audra's direction. Three pairs

of eyes glared at her, but it was Rick's solemn gaze that shook her. At this point she couldn't stay seated. After a struggle, she got to her feet.

With tears in her voice, she said, "No one could have been a better father to us than you, Uncle David. If you're willing to put up with me, I'd consider it a privilege to live with you in Austin."

He smiled and nodded to her.

"If you'll excuse me, I'm going to dish up that chocolate dessert."

Afraid she'd break down in front of everyone, Audra tucked her crutches under her arms and moved toward the door. Footsteps followed her into the kitchen.

When she turned around, she discovered Rick Hawkins in pursuit.

"Let me help you."

Before she could order him back to the table, he'd pulled the pan of rocky road from the fridge. Pam had already put the plates and forks on the counter.

Audra rummaged in the drawer for a spatula. With one crutch steadying her, she started cutting the dessert into squares. Darn if her hand wasn't trembling. Rick couldn't help but see. He stood too close. She felt suffocated by his nearness.

"Tell me about the tornado," he urged.

"You heard Uncle David."

"I was filled with dread by all he didn't say. Is it still too difficult to talk about?"

"No." She started putting the squares on plates.

"How many years ago did your uncle say it happened?"

"Twenty-three."

"That puts you at twenty-eight now."

Yup. Twenty-eight big ones and still single. No doubt the pit babes who swarm around you aren't a day over twenty-two.

"How come the tornado didn't destroy this house?"

Afraid he wouldn't go away until he had answers, she decided to tell him everything and be done with it.

"An F-5 tornado cut a mile-wide swath through the tiny community of Hillmont ten miles from here. It wiped out the town, whole ranches, trees, cars, trucks, houses, fencing, equipment, barns, horses, cattle and thirty members of our family assembled at a church where they'd gathered for a christening.

"I was just getting over the measles. Since Pam had already had them, she volunteered to baby-sit me and the boys who, according to Pam, balked at going to boring church.

"Uncle David had a bad cold that day so he stayed home with us. When the services were over, there was going to be a big party."

She sucked in her breath. "Everybody going to church left the ranch house. None of them ever came back."

Rick's expression darkened in horror and incredulity. She looked away, not wanting to see any more of his reaction.

"My parents and siblings were inside the church. So were Pam's parents and siblings, the boys' parents and siblings and Uncle David's wife, his married children and grandchildren.''

''Good heavens—''

''Uncle David is really our great-uncle. He was the oldest member of the family and the last surviving adult of the Jarrett clan. He took us all in and raised us.

''I know it broke his heart to have to make that announcement today. He's such a good man, and has bent over backward to be fair to each one of us. I don't think your father could possibly understand how grateful Uncle David must be that this house is going to stay in the family.''

A lump had lodged in her throat. ''T-there's an old saying that we suffer three deaths in this life,'' she stammered. ''First when we die, the second when we are laid to rest and the third when our name is never spoken again.''

Her gaze lifted to his once more. ''Your father has ensured that our ancestral home will stay in the Jarrett family for another generation anyway. I love Clint for loving Pam that much,'' she whispered.

Audra continued in a voice that disguised little of her anger. ''What I don't understand is how ungrateful the boys are. They're lucky he's been able to leave them any birthright at all. On top of taking care of us all their lives, he took out loans to pay for our college education—''

She broke off talking.

None of this was Rick's concern.

Embarrassed to have gone on and on, Audra finished dishing up the dessert. ''As long as you're here,

would you mind taking these to the dining room?''
She handed him two plates without looking up.

"I'll be back to help."

That's what she was afraid of. She didn't want to
spend another second in the company of Rick Hawkins, of all people.

Hopefully, he'd be gone by tomorrow. Audra had
no desire to get to know him any better. When you
got to know someone, you learned to care about them.

Who was she kidding? She already cared about
him. Until he'd rescued her from her nightmare, he'd
only been an attractive face in a series of wedding
photographs.

But a photograph only showed a face and body. It
didn't reveal the total person. Rick possessed layers
of desirable qualities that broke down the defenses
guarding her wary heart. When he'd followed her into
the kitchen to help her, to listen with compassion to
all she had to say, she realized he'd breached the outer
walls and was standing at the door of its inner cham-
ber.

CHAPTER THREE

THE IMPATIENT BLARE of a car horn coming from the front of the house couldn't be ignored. Rick's eyes sought his father's in a private message.

"It sounds like you've got to go, Bobby."

"Yeah. Dad wants to leave, but we're not finished yet."

"That's all right. Call the ranch house anytime and ask for me. I can help you over the phone."

"Thanks, Clint." Bobby took the paper he'd been writing on and handed Clint back his pen.

"You're welcome."

"You, too, Rick. See ya."

The young teen disappeared from the living room, leaving the two of them alone for the first time all day. Rick checked his watch. It was almost five o'clock.

He stared at his father. "You know the old saying, a picture is worth a thousand words?"

"You mean, after sitting through one meal with the Jarrett clan, you feel as if you've received a Ph.D. in family dysfunction?"

Rick folded his arms and sat back in the chair with his ankles crossed. "When I followed Audra into the kitchen to get the dessert, she told me about the tornado.'' His mind still reeled from everything he'd learned. "It's impossible to comprehend that kind of loss."

"I didn't know the details until Pam broke down on our honeymoon and told me. She keeps her pain well hidden. You have to bide your time with her."

Rick couldn't stay seated any longer. "The morning Nate and I drove you and Pam to the airport, I sensed a vulnerability about her. Only now am I beginning to understand why." He paused. "I'm glad you found each other."

His dad looked taken aback. "I'd hoped one day you might come to feel that way. I just didn't expect it to happen this soon."

"Being here has opened my eyes to a lot of things. It's too bad you've got enemies."

"Audra meant well, but I'm afraid her suggestion to Bobby fanned the flames."

"Dad, the mere fact that you exist, let alone married Pam and bought this house, has caused a major conflagration. I've never met such fractious personalities."

"It's time her cousins dealt with reality."

The edge in his tone prompted Rick to study his dad for a minute. "To think I used to wonder why Nate and I were attracted to careers with an element of danger…"

"Danger comes in many packages, son. Your kind kills instantly."

"I'll take my kind any day over three spiteful men who wished you on the other side of the universe today."

"I can handle it. Right now I want to spend some private time with you." He got to his feet. "Pam won't be expecting us until dark."

"Where are we going?"

"For a horseback ride."

"You've got to be kidding. I haven't been on a horse in years."

"It's like skiing. You never forget. Come on. We'll slip out the front door and walk around back to the barn."

Except for the absence of one car, it appeared everyone else was still inside the house, yet Rick couldn't hear voices. Its unique design of multiple rooms and an asymmetrical floor plan swallowed sounds.

Though the house was built in a wide-open space, there were some pecan and oak trees growing close to the barn to provide shade. Nearby he noticed a spring-fed pond.

They entered the barn and walked over to the first two stalls. "You take Pam's mare, Marshmallow. I'll ride the bay. His name is Prince."

"Is he David's horse?"

"No. Prince is Audra's pride and joy. He's been missing her and will welcome the exercise."

The mention of Audra prompted him to ask, "Was she engaged to the man who died?"

"No. From what Pam told me, Audra finally accepted a date with Pete when she didn't really want to."

"Why would she do that?"

"Perhaps to forget someone else."

There was no perhaps about it, or his father wouldn't have said it. For some strange reason, Rick wished he hadn't asked the question.

"Since the accident, she blames herself for relenting. Audra's convinced he wouldn't be dead if she'd just said no to him."

"Maybe that's why she's still having nightmares." Without preamble, Rick told his father about the encounter with Audra at the bungalow. "Her screams were bloodcurdling. They left me shaken."

His father nodded. "Both David and Pam are worried about her. She's pretty fragile."

"I've had buddies at the track who've been through the same trauma. It takes a long time to get over. Don't tell Pam or she'll tell Audra. I don't want to make an enemy out of her."

"I won't, but I *am* going to have a talk with Audra about moving back to the main ranch house tonight. She shouldn't be living out at the bungalow alone no matter how much she craves her independence."

"Agreed." When Rick thought about how easy it had been to climb in that back-bedroom window...

"I'll think of a good excuse to approach her. In the meantime, let's go in the tack room and get what we need."

Rick smiled as he helped his father bridle and saddle the animals like a pro. He could tell Clint was loving this new lifestyle. Wait until Rick got his brother on the phone and told him what was going on.

There had been so much that neither he nor Nate had understood when their father had first announced his engagement to Pam. That felt like a hundred years ago.

Once the stirrups were adjusted, Rick swung himself up and followed his father's lead along a well-worn path. They rode beyond the paddock to a field where the occasional line of trees appearing and disappearing among gently rolling hills denoted a winding creek.

His dad waited for Rick to join him. "It's the perfect time of evening to show you something I know you'll appreciate. Have you got your sea legs yet?"

Rick grinned. "I think so."

"Then let's go."

They set off through the wild grass, beneath bits of darkening blue sky and clouds. Though the temperature bordered on hot, Rick felt comfortable because the air was surprisingly arid.

"When I called you yesterday morning to touch base, it concerned me to learn you hadn't decided to sign those new racing contracts yet."

That makes two of us.

Obviously his dad had set their slow pace for a reason.

"What's holding you up? Between Trans T & T and Mayada, you've been offered an unprecedented amount of money. You'll have the same crew chief as before."

Rick's hand tightened on the reins. "I have no complaints."

His dad squinted at him. "I know you broke it off with Natalie when you left Arizona. Is she the reason you're hesitant to return?"

"Who's Natalie?" he teased to cover his anxiety.

"All right. I have the answer to that question at least." A troubled expression broke out on his father's face. "When your mother died, the fire went out of you. It's never come back, has it?"

Rick expelled a breath he didn't realize he'd been holding. "I can't deny that her death took its toll. But in all honesty, the thrill of competition hasn't been there for the last year."

"That must be a terrifying feeling."

"How did you know?"

"I've been putting myself in your place. You're at the top of your game with enough money invested right now to retire in luxury for the rest of your life, yet the excitement is gone and you're only coming up on thirty years of age."

His dad had nailed part of the problem, but not all. Rick didn't have a place to call his own anymore. Though Clint had told him and Nate they would always have a home with him, it wasn't the same thing. Rick needed a place where he belonged. It haunted him there was no longer a center of his universe.

"After you and mom met you did it right by making marriage and family your first priority."

Clint shook his head. "If she hadn't come along, I might have been where you are now, with several gold medals and the promise of more. Except that I'd be a single man of thirty who was in debt for the rest of his life."

"You were lucky."

His dad flashed him a shrewd look. "Have you thought of *trying* to find the right woman?"

"No. I don't believe in it." He frowned. "Either she shows up in the scheme of things like Mom did and like Laurel did for Nate, or she doesn't. If I have to work on meeting my intended, then I might as well stick to racing."

"Well—I'm glad we had this little talk."

"So am I. After breakfast tomorrow I'll head out for Phoenix and sign those contracts Neal's holding for me. I'm fortunate to have a job waiting for me I know how to do, right?" That's what Rick had to keep telling himself.

"A man needs work. If he knows how to be successful at it, that's a plus. Tell you what—I'll race you to that clump of blackjack oak in the distance."

Blackjack? Already he was an expert on Texas flora?

To Rick's surprise, his father took off at a gallop. He couldn't believe what a natural he was in the saddle. Just as if he was on a pair of skis. It was a pleasure to watch man and horse race toward the sunset.

After a moment Rick realized this was supposed to be a race. Already behind, he found that splashing through the creek not far ahead of him slowed him down even more. He had a devil of a time catching up to his father.

It wasn't long before he saw a sea of blue in the distance. "Is that a lake?" He'd reined in next to his dad. "I didn't see it on the map."

"I asked Pam the same question when she first brought me out here. Those are Texas bluebonnets. They grow wild here in the spring. You'll never see the likes of them in Colorado.

"If you'd come a few weeks later, you would have missed them. Though there's no fragrance, the sight is unmatched."

"It's spectacular!"

But Rick's thoughts were elsewhere. The word *bluebonnet* brought to mind the haunting lyrics of the country music sung by the fabulous female vocalist he'd heard on the radio last night.

I'm an uprooted bluebonnet,
I no longer have a home,
Do you hear me, windshield rancher?
Thanks to you I'm alone.
The light has now gone out,
I can't see in front of me,
There's no home to go back to,
Fear is my destiny.
The past is gone forever,
It walked out the door.
What once excited, excites no more.

In light of David Jarrett's announcement at lunch about the sale of his ranch, combined with certain tragic revelations from the lips of Audra Jarrett in the kitchen, those lyrics had just taken on even deeper personal meaning for Rick.

By tacit agreement he and his father rode to the edge of where the giant carpet of lavender blue began. Rick dismounted, then hunkered down to examine a bluebonnet. It was about a foot high with a tiny white top.

"The flowers on the stock are supposed to resemble a woman's bonnet."

He nodded at his dad's explanation, but for some odd reason the shape of the individual blossoms reminded Rick of Audra's curls. When she moved to Austin with her uncle, she'd be a displaced bluebonnet...

"Pam's from a great heritage. Her great-great-grandfather Thomas Jarrett came out here in 1897 from Middlesex, England. He built his holdings to six hundred thousand acres and erected the main ranch house. But in time there were problems, droughts, other tornadoes, wars.

"The land got carved up into smaller homesteads and sold off to extended family and nonfamily. Some of the ground was maintained for deer and wildlife to flourish, but even that had to go whenever there were hard times. Slowly but surely the land began to fall into other hands.

"Everything dwindled until there was only a thousand acres left, plus the bungalow and the ranch house. I'm sure that by giving Audra and her cousins those hundred and twenty acres of land in common, Pam's uncle is down to the bare bones, financially speaking."

"Audra's indebted to you for helping Pam keep the ranch house," Rick said.

"Audra's a sweetheart."

A wealth of emotion accompanied his father's words.

Resisting the urge to pick the bluebonnet he'd been studying, Rick mounted the mare once more and looked around. The sun had fallen below the horizon. It would be dark soon. He wondered if Audra dreaded the coming of night.

"We'd better get back." Clint's words broke into Rick's thoughts.

The horses knew they were going home and made a beeline in the direction of the ranch house. When they eventually came to the creek, Prince forded it first.

To Rick's surprise, Marshmallow balked. He didn't understand and urged her forward with a clicking sound. The next thing he knew, she neighed violently and reared back on her hind legs.

He glimpsed a snake wrapped around the mare's right foreleg, silhouetted against the sky. It had to be at least five feet long. The horse came down hard on the snake, screaming and stomping.

"Get Marshmallow out of here, son. Prince will finish it off!"

"I'm doing my best, but she's fighting me!"

He pulled on the reins, encouraging the horse to turn left. But she was just as determined to kill the viper as Prince was. Snorting hot air, she reared back and struck at the snake again and again.

Suddenly Rick felt the mare's hooves slip in the shallows. He jerked his feet from the stirrups to jump off, but he wasn't fast enough. They went down together with a huge splash.

The horse landed on her side on top of him. Pain ripped through his left arm and shot to his jaw. Bile rose in his throat.

Damn—he couldn't tell if he'd broken something

or been bitten. Some venom was so potent it worked immediately. All he knew was that the slightest move he made was excruciating.

He grabbed for the reins with his right hand. It was a struggle to get up and help the mare to her feet. The poor thing finally stood on all fours, shivering and snorting while water dripped off both of them. She seemed to be all right. It was a miracle.

On rubber legs Rick led her to dry ground where his father stood next to the bay, gentling him. The muscular snake lay inert in the grass. Prince pawed at it.

"Thank God that water moccasin didn't get a chance to sink its fangs into you."

"You may have spoken too soon, Dad." Rick was weaving on his feet. "I'm in pain from my arm to my cheek."

"Then you've broken something, because Prince pounded that snake to death before you fell in the water."

At this juncture Rick was weaving. His dad had to support him.

"Marshmallow has settled down. Let's get you up on her and we'll head back to the house. I'll call Pam for help."

Rick closed his eyes tightly. He would love to tell his father it wasn't necessary. However, this injury wasn't like any of the ones he'd received at the track over the years. He didn't know if he could climb onto the mare. Yet the thought of walking sounded equally untenable.

If the doctor were to ask what level of pain he was

in right now, he'd have to tell him there wasn't a number high enough.

AUDRA SAT in one of the living-room chairs with her cast propped on a footstool while her uncle David took charge of the family conference. The kids were in the small parlor off the kitchen watching TV. Greg and Jim and their wives had found places on the couch and love seat.

Pam kept looking at the grandfather clock.

Clint and his son had been gone longer than Audra would have expected, but she wanted to tell her cousin Pam not to worry. They were grown men who'd been taking care of themselves for years. Clint was probably giving it one last try to steer his son away from a profession that could wipe him out in seconds.

Too bad Tom, the angry mastermind of the three, had stormed off after dinner with his family, not waiting to find out what possessions their uncle was going to give him.

Uncle David might be one who was slow to make up his mind about something, but once he did, he moved like wildfire racing across a Texas prairie.

"To begin with, each of you will receive your own Jarrett-family memorabilia in the way of books, pictures and mementos. I've got them sorted in boxes with your names on them. They're in the study.

"Two of the five bedrooms upstairs contain furniture from the turn of the century. I'm giving those things, the baby grand piano in the living room and the dining-room table and chairs, which had been made expressly for the dining room, to Pam, to help get her bed-and-breakfast started.

"You boys can take everything from your old bedrooms, including the beds, tables, lamps and one piece of period furniture from the living room.

"I'm giving Tom the grandfather clock, Greg the rosewood writing desk and Jim the teacart, all of which were precious items your great-great-grandfather had shipped over from England.

"After the tornado changed our lives, I had the front parlor on the main floor converted into my bedroom. It has a couch and chairs. I plan to take everything from that room to furnish my new condo.

"As I said earlier, Audra can live with me as long as she wants. I'm giving her the old upright piano in the parlor and my wife's quilts. They include some she made and some her grandmother gave her. Audra has always admired them.

"When I die, my attorney will arrange for the condo to be sold and the proceeds divided among the four of you."

Audra loved him for giving her that security. She'd leave the piano with Pam until she had a place of her own one day. As for the quilts, she couldn't be more thrilled. They were exquisite. Priceless. She would have them mounted in special glass frames so Pam could display them throughout the ranch house.

Her uncle didn't know it yet, but she planned to live in Austin with him on a permanent basis. Pam had been waiting on him all these years. Now it was Audra's turn. She didn't want him to be alone.

Greg darted their uncle an angry glance. "You haven't said anything about the barn."

"It goes with the main house. If you boys want a barn, you can erect one behind the bungalow and keep horses there. Until that time you can board your horses at the Circle T. I've already spoken to Mervin, so he knows you're coming.

"You might want to think about dividing the property four ways and using it for collateral to build your own ranch houses and barns.

"While you've got your families here to help, you're welcome to start clearing things out tonight. Don't forget your saddles and camping gear in the barn. When Clint and Rick get back, I'm sure they'll be glad to lend you a hand with the heavy furniture."

Greg's gaze swerved to Jim's. "No thanks. We'll do it ourselves."

"My trailer's available when you want to load the horses."

"I'll stay in the bungalow until my cast comes off," Audra interjected. "Then I'll move to Austin with Uncle David. In the meantime, why don't you three get together and decide how you want to divide up your vacation times out there.

"My manager at the radio station will let me broadcast from the bungalow, so I'll be happy with whatever time period during the year you allot to me."

"We have to talk to Tom." Greg's voice was wooden.

"Of course. Just let me know."

Her uncle had done everything possible to be fair to the family he'd inherited, and this was how they repaid him. Audra reached for her crutches and got up from the chair, anxious to give him a hug and tell him how grateful she was.

While a subdued Diane and Sherry went over to examine the writing desk and teacart, Pam's cell phone went off. The next thing Audra heard caused her to come to a standstill in the center of the room.

"He sounds bad, Clint. I'll phone the hospital right now and send for a helicopter to meet you here."

Audra's heart gave a thud. "What's wrong with Rick?"

Pam had already started to call 9-1-1. "Marshmallow tangled with a water moccasin in the creek. She lost her footing and fell on top of him. My mare's all right, but Rick's in pain from his arm to his jaw."

A snicker from one of the boys coincided with Audra's quiet gasp. Her wrist went to her mouth in reaction to the news, causing a crutch to fall on the floor.

Sherry noticed and picked it up for her. Audra thanked her before crying out, "He wasn't bitten, was he, Pam? The venom's lethal."

If Rick died, her worst nightmare for her cousin would come true.

In the background she heard Jim whisper something to Greg about how stupid Clint was to be out there after dark.

"Silence!" their uncle demanded as Pam spoke to the police dispatcher. Once she'd explained the nature of the emergency, Audra heard her give precise instructions for the location of the ranch.

When their uncle rose to his feet, the boys left the

room with their wives. He waited with Audra until Pam ended the call. She lifted her head.

"The helicopter will be here as soon as it can. To ease your minds, Prince killed the snake before it could bite either of them, but Rick's in so much pain he can hardly stay on the horse."

"I had the same kind of accident years ago," their uncle said. "Sounds like a broken collarbone." Audra shuddered at the thought of it. "From which direction are they coming?"

"The bluebonnets."

"Let's go, Pam. We'll get in my truck and drive out to pick up Rick. Audra? You remain here and wait for the helicopter. Turn on the outside lights." They both hurried into the hall.

"I'll do it right now," Audra called after them. She found the boys in the foyer, huddled together. If she heard the slightest sound come out of their mouths, she was ready to knock them to kingdom come with her crutches.

Maybe they saw the murderous glint in her eye because for once they didn't bait her.

She moved to the front door as fast as her crutches would take her. There was a light switch to the side of it. She turned on the floods so the ranch house would stand out in the darkness.

When she moved to the roofed porch, the sound of the truck's engine had already grown faint.

She leaned against the post with her crutches and looked in the direction of Austin. Cirrus clouds obscured most of the sky. With barely a breeze to dishevel her curls, there was nothing threatening about the elements to prevent the helicopter from getting here without a problem.

Though Clint wouldn't have wished this painful accident on his son, Audra suspected there was a secret part of him that was glad Rick wouldn't be able to get behind the wheel of a race car for a while. So was Audra...

While she stood there, the sounds of the boys' demands over their children's protests jerked her from her contemplation. She turned her head in time to see Diane and both sets of kids march out the front door carrying various items from the upstairs bedrooms to their vehicles.

Sherry followed with framed pictures in hand. She stopped in front of Audra. "Did you know your uncle was going to do all this today?"

"I had no idea."

"Jim's so upset, I'm never going to hear the end of it."

Audra had it in her heart to feel sorry for her cousins' wives, who'd married young and more or less did what their chauvinistic husbands told them to do.

Annette had it the worst.

Tom's resentment over their uncle's control of the ranch was bad enough. But he was one of those men who didn't believe a woman should have any say in business. His wife didn't dare stand up to him for his rudeness to their uncle, or his cruelty to Pam.

"I think Uncle David's idea about dividing the property made a lot of sense," Audra murmured. "You and Jim could borrow on your portion of the land and build a house."

"That's not it. He can't believe Pam got the ranch house."

"Her husband bought it for her."

Sherry looked around. "Walk to the other end of the porch with me where the kids won't pick up on our conversation."

After Audra had complied, her cousin-in-law said, "I heard Jim and Greg talking in the hall. They think Uncle David's lying about the sale of the house because he wanted Pam to have it."

Anger consumed Audra. "Is that what you think, too?"

Sherry averted her eyes. "It does seem pretty amazing that she went to Josie Adams's wedding in Colorado and came back a little over a month later married to a man who was willing to spend that kind of money on her."

"They fell in love, Sherry."

"After such a short time?"

Audra cocked her head. "Seems to me that's what happened to you and Jim."

"But we didn't marry for almost a year."

"That's because you didn't have any money. Clint Hawkins is a fifty-three-year-old man who'd been running a successful ski-shop business long before he met Pam."

After a silence, "All I know is, this has caused trouble that's not going to go away."

"Do you know how you sound?" Audra was heartsick. "What you're saying is, it would have been all right if anyone else had bought the house except Clint."

Sherry lifted her head. "Look—I don't care about this place, but the boys care. It's part of their heritage. Jim's hurt. They all are. Pam could still turn the bungalow into a bed-and-breakfast the way she once planned."

Audra had to count to ten. "There's just one problem with that scenario. Contrary to what everyone expected, Uncle David didn't leave the bungalow to her after all. He had to sell the ranch house."

"Even so—"

"Even so *what?*" At this point Audra was livid. "What do you want Pam to do? Turn around and give the house back to the boys? How could she possibly do that when it's her husband's money invested?"

"I don't know. But there's been bad blood ever since she married Clint."

"I have news for you, Sherry. The boys have been angry since the day Uncle David asked her to help him make a family out of what the tornado chose not to destroy. Pam's been their scapegoat. But she has a worthy champion now, and all I can say is, watch out! Clint's the kind of man who'll make an awesome adversary if provoked. The boys will never prevail against him. You can tell them I said so."

"I'm not your enemy, Audra," she responded in a hurt voice.

Suddenly in the distance Audra could hear rotors whipping the air. She settled the crutches under her arms and started for the porch steps.

Looking back at Sherry, she said, "You're a fence-sitter, and you know what the scriptures say about that. You're either with me or against me."

CHAPTER FOUR

RELIEVED TO SEE the lights of West Austin Regional Hospital's AirMed helicopter, Audra negotiated the steps to greet the medical staff.

It hadn't been that long since Audra had been rushed to the hospital screaming for something, anything, to send her into oblivion. Rick Hawkins was a tough, powerful man both physically and mentally. If he couldn't make it back to the ranch without help, that meant he was in agony.

No sooner had the chopper landed when she saw the white truck approach with Pam at the wheel. Clint jumped down from the back. She had to assume her uncle followed with the horses.

Audra had thought Clint unflappable like Uncle David. But this was his precious flesh and blood who'd been hurt. His drawn, pale features revealed a parent frantic with concern.

''My son's been passing in and out on the floor of the truck.''

As the medical team worked to stabilize Rick and prepare him for flight, Audra realized that it hadn't been too long ago that Clint had lost his first wife in an avalanche.

From the look of anxiety on Pam's face, her cousin

was thinking the same thing. Audra hurried over to her. They clung to each other as they'd done so many times in their lives.

"Clint's given me the keys to Rick's car. He wants me to drive it to the hospital. That way when he's released, we'll be able to bring him back to the ranch in comfort.

"Will you take Rick's cell phone and call Nate? Then it won't be such a surprise when Clint tries to reach him."

"I'll do it as soon as you take off."

Within minutes Clint and Rick were on board and the helicopter rose into the air. Pam had packed a few items in a suitcase and climbed behind the wheel of the car, ready to drive off. It was all a blur to Audra, whose eyes had filled with tears.

Please, God—let Rick be all right. Let Clint be all right.

In the background she could hear Sherry and Diane urging their children to get in the cars. They were going home.

It couldn't be soon enough for Audra. With her back facing the parking area, she clicked on Rick's phone and searched the address book for Nate's number. After a moment someone picked up.

"Rick—" A female voice spoke up. "We were expecting you to say goodbye before you left for Arizona. We can't bear to think you've gone!"

The concern and warmth in the other woman's voice was wonderful to hear. It wiped out today's ugliness for a few minutes.

"Is this Laurel Hawkins?"

After a shocked silence, "Yes? Who's this?"

"I'm Audra Jarrett, Pam's cousin."

"Oh! I guess I don't understand. Is Rick with you?"

"Not at the moment. Laurel, is your husband there?"

"He is. I'll get him. Just a minute."

While Audra waited, she could see her uncle's silhouette as he came around to the front of the house. Now that he'd brought back the horses, there was one less person she had to worry about.

"Is this the redhead with the peg leg?" an appealing male voice spoke into the phone.

Audra laughed quietly in spite of her sober mission. Already she liked him. Naturally she did. Clint Hawkins was his father.

"Hello, Nate. I've heard so much about the hotshot, I feel that I know you."

It was his turn to chuckle. "Laurel and I have been wanting to meet you."

"Now that I've met Rick, I'm looking forward to meeting you, too."

"I didn't know he was going to the ranch first."

"I believe it was a last-minute decision. Your brother is the reason I'm calling. He's going to be all right, but he had an accident while he and your father were out riding horses this evening."

After a slight pause, "How bad is it?"

Such deep love in his voice reflected a lifetime of caring. The difference between the Hawkinses and certain members of the Jarrett household was like night and day.

"They tangled with a snake and Pam's horse fell on him."

"Good heavens."

"He's hurt from his arm to his jaw. Uncle David thinks he might have a broken collarbone. Right now he's on an AirMed helicopter with your father, headed for West Austin Regional Hospital. Pam has driven to the hospital in Rick's car, otherwise I'd put her on the phone."

"Rick's car?"

"Yes. The one he drove from Colorado. My cousin asked me to call so you'd be prepared when your dad contacts you."

There was a brief silence. "Thanks for calling, Audra. After we hang up I'll arrange for a flight to Austin tonight and come straight to the hospital. Let Dad know in case his cell phone can't reach me once I'm on board."

"I will. He'll be relieved when he hears you're on your way. You and your father will be all the medicine your brother needs to make a full recovery."

"Thank you. See you soon."

Her uncle could see she was juggling the phone with her crutches and took it from her after she'd clicked off.

"It seems Nate didn't know his brother had decided to come to Texas first. That seems odd, when we know how close they are."

"I'm sure there's a good explanation. The important thing is, he's flying down to be with his brother and father."

"You're right. They're lucky they have each other.

But then so am I, because I couldn't love you more if you were my own father.''

Her uncle's eyes moistened. ''That tornado took a lot away from the Jarrett clan. But I got you and Pam in return. The two sweetest girls in the Hill Country. I'm the lucky one.''

They both sniffed before he said, ''Let's go inside while we wait to hear the news about Rick. I want you to stay at the main house with me tonight.''

''I will.'' Audra adjusted her crutches and started moving toward the house with him. ''How's Marshmallow?''

''She made it back to the barn okay, but I'll call Doc Shriver to come out and take a look at her in the morning. What a shame for Rick's visit to end up like this.''

If her uncle had any idea Audra was thinking just the opposite, he'd be shocked. ''Tangling with a snake is no fun. I'm thankful neither he nor Clint was bitten.''

''That makes two of us.'' He opened the front door for her and they went inside the house to the living room. Her uncle looked around. ''All the excitement sure cleared this place out in a hurry.''

Audra heard the undercurrent of sadness in his voice. He wasn't talking about the furnishings that had already been carted off. After so many years of battling the boys, their mean-spiritedness had taken its toll on him.

There were no words to ease his heavy heart, or hers, in that regard. All she could do was rest one of her crutches against the wall in order to put a comforting arm around him.

Two hours later while she lay propped on the couch with a quilt and pillow, Rick's cell phone rang. Audra broke off talking with her uncle to answer it. Clint was calling.

"Clint?"

"It's Pam."

"Pam—" Her gaze darted to her uncle. "We've been waiting to hear from you. How's Rick?"

"Uncle David was right. Rick has a broken collarbone and bruised ribs. He also had a dislocated shoulder, but the doctor has already done the procedure to fix it."

Audra moaned before repeating the news to her uncle, who'd already suspected as much and only nodded his head.

"They've given him pain medication through his IV. He's asleep right now. The doctor was surprised he hadn't broken his arm, too."

"Knowing Rick, he'll probably think he can still drive," Audra said without thinking. "That is…when he wakes up."

"Clint said the same thing. The doctor answered with an incredulous laugh."

Audra smiled. "I presume that was a no."

"An emphatic one," Pam said. "If there aren't any complications, he'll be released from the hospital the day after tomorrow. For the next three weeks he's to do nothing but rest. Then he has to come back to the hospital for another X ray. At that point the doctor will decide what Rick can or can't do."

"That ought to be interesting." Again Audra related the latest to her uncle.

Pam chuckled. "It's a good thing his father's right here to make certain he minds."

"Do you think that's possible?" Audra teased.

"I guess we're going to find out."

She smiled again. "We shouldn't be this happy Rick's not going anywhere for a while."

When she happened to look at her uncle, she discovered he was smiling, too.

Chalk it up to one more person on the ranch who was glad Lucky Hawkins wouldn't be screaming around a racetrack anytime soon. Pam's happiness was of paramount importance to Uncle David, too.

Like trickle-down economics, what affected Clint affected Pam and everyone else in the Jarrett household. After talking with Nate Hawkins and his wife, Audra knew the same held true at their house.

"My husband hasn't been able to spend three whole weeks of undivided time with his son in years," Pam confided.

A new wife would be understandably possessive of her spouse's attention, but Pam wasn't like most people. She was such a giving person, it was no wonder Clint had fallen hard for her.

Audra cleared her throat. "Are you going to stay at the hospital with him?"

"Yes. They're bringing in a cot. Clint and I will take turns sleeping."

"That sounds good. I phoned Nate. He'll be arriving as soon as he can."

"Thanks for calling him. Clint will be thrilled to know his other son is on the way."

"Nate didn't know about his brother's visit here."

"Rick made a last-minute decision to buy a new car and drive down instead of fly. He probably didn't have time to tell his brother."

"Ah—that explains it."

"Before we hang up, how's Uncle David? Today must have drained him."

Audra couldn't talk freely with him sitting in the wingback chair next to her. "Why don't you ask him yourself? He's right here. I'll talk to you later. Give Clint my love."

"Will do."

"Hold on."

She handed the phone to her uncle. Rick's accident was the very thing needed to fill her uncle's mind with other thoughts besides today's painful experience with the boys.

Audra lay back against the pillow with a sigh and closed her eyes. Today had been a day like no other.

The racetrack lover whizzed into town all right. Reliable sources indicate he's going to be making a longer pit stop than usual.

IT WAS FIVE IN THE MORNING when Rick saw his brother walk into his hospital room. The nurse had just injected more medicine in his IV. He was feeling no pain at the moment. Nate looked good to him. "Who told you to show up?"

His dark-blond brother pulled a chair next to the bed and sat down. Despite the concern in his blue eyes, Rick noticed he was smiling as if entertaining a private joke.

"What goes around comes around. Now you know how I felt when I got off the plane from Philadelphia and discovered you'd brought Dad along to make me realize Laurel truly did love me. Thank God you did," he added.

"Marriage agrees with you. Where's that beautiful wife of yours?"

"Home in Colorado Springs with the sweetest little baby girl in the world. They're both waiting for a status report on you."

"I've been hurt worse."

"I don't remember when," Nate challenged. "While the nurse was taking care of you, I've been outside the door talking to Dad and Pam. He tells me you're going to be laid up for a month or so."

"That's what *he* thinks," Rick muttered. "This sling feels like a straitjacket! I might be able to stand it for a couple of days, but no longer. He should never have gotten you up in the middle of the night to fly down here."

"Though Dad's feeling all kinds of guilt for taking you horseback riding, he wasn't the one who called me."

"Then it must have been David," Rick muttered. "He had to bring in the horses while Pam drove me and Dad in the truck. What a hell of a way for this day to end."

"Accidents happen."

"You should have seen our father out there, Nate. He was so excited to take me riding. I swear you would've thought he'd ridden horses all his life. We saw bluebonnets. Thousands of them. Just like her curls…''

"Whose curls?"

The drug made Rick's body feel disjointed, as if he was floating. ''This snake spooked Marshmallow…she fell on me… Damn if it didn't hurt. I'm sure David's been on the phone to the vet by now, too.''

''Rick—'' Nate leaned forward with his hands clasped between his knees. ''It was Pam's cousin who phoned me.''

''Which one? She has three of them. They hate Dad.''

''Why would they hate him?''

''It's a long story. There was this tornado. So many died. Audra was only five…''

''Audra's the one who phoned us.''

''Audra?''

Rick tried to sit up, but if he tried to move, he fell back dizzy against the pillow.

''I asked her if she was the redhead with the peg leg.'' Nate's voice sounded far away. ''Why does her phoning me surprise you?''

''Audra and I—we didn't get off to the best start. Doesn't know how she feels about me…yet.''

''I see.''

''We…dance around each other.''

''I'd say her phone call showed major concern.''

''Pam—it had to be Pam who told her to contact you.''

Nate cocked his head. "How old did you say she was?"

"I didn't," he said. "Twenty-eight."

"Where did I get the idea she was Pam's age?"

"Don't know. Thought the same thing."

"Tell me about her."

A dozen images filled Rick's mind at once. Particularly the one where he'd been driving her to the main ranch house.

"That's hard to do. When I asked her about the man who'd died in the accident—you know—the one that broke her leg?—she told me even if my father married her cousin, it didn't make us related. Or entitle me to information that was none of my business."

"Really."

"Do you know what she reminds me of?" Rick was so high, he was blabbing his innermost thoughts.

"I don't have a clue."

"One of those bottle rockets we used to light on the Fourth of July. The kind that shot sparks in every direction the second you set flame to the fuse. And while you were still nursing your burned fingers, it had already reached altitude. Remember how we had to run like hell for cover because either it would find us during its descent or start a forest fire?"

"What do you suppose it was about you that set her off?"

Rick was trying to stay awake. "Since the crash... horrific nightmares. Our introduction came during one of them."

"You were in her bedroom?"

Rick couldn't open his eyes. "Not at first... When I broke in her window...she was lying there on the bed. Her leg...it was in a long cast and—"

"And *what?*"

"She was screaming. This knockout redhead was screaming. I had to wake her up—had to—couldn't stand to hear the pain. Her eyes...Mom's color."

RICK HAD PASSED OUT.

Nate sat there for a full ten minutes staring at his brother. The last thing he expected to hear after flying down to Austin were the ramblings of a man who couldn't seem to talk about anything but some gorgeous, redheaded female.

Not just any female.

He bowed his head. He'd never seen Rick like this in his life. It had nothing to do with his drugged state.

Something strange was going on here. Something Nate couldn't ever remember feeling around his brother before. He needed to talk to Laurel about it.

Without making any noise, he got up from the chair and moved it aside. He'd told his father and Pam he would join them for breakfast in the hospital cafeteria after his visit with Rick. But first he had a phone call to make.

He left the room and took one of the central elevators to the main floor. As soon as he reached the driveway in front of the hospital, he pulled out his cell phone and called home.

"Nate—I've been waiting for your call, darling." He could hear the longing in his wife's voice.

Last night was the first time they hadn't slept together since their wedding. He missed her more than he'd thought possible.

"Are you and Becky all right?"

"We are now that I know you arrived safely. How's your brother?"

My brother.

"That's a good question."

"Is he worse than you were told?" she cried in alarm.

"No, sweetheart. Not in the way you mean. He has a broken collarbone, bruised ribs and a dislocated shoulder. According to Dad, the doctor said he'll be fine in a month if he takes it easy."

"But there's something else wrong. Did Trans T & T decide not to sponsor him after all?"

"No. What I'm talking about has nothing to do with business. Are you ready for this?" He gripped his cell phone tighter. "It seems Ms. Audra Jarrett has happened to Rick."

"Not the cousin with the broken leg—"

"The very one."

After a long pause, "But he just got there—"

"If you remember, it took all of five minutes of my being around you to transform my world forever. I'm afraid that's the way of the Hawkins men, starting with my father."

"Have you met her?"

"Not yet."

"When will Rick be released from the hospital?"

"Tomorrow, barring complications. Right now he's sleeping off the medication they gave him a little while ago."

"He must be in terrible pain."

"To be honest, I think pain from the accident is the last thing my brother's feeling."

"I wonder what she's like."

"In Rick's words, she's a knockout redhead with blue eyes like our mother's."

"He adored your mom. This sounds serious."

"That's what I'm thinking."

"Do you have any way of knowing if she'll be visiting him today, so you can meet her?"

"I'm going to eat breakfast with Dad and Pam in a few minutes. If her cousin has any intention of coming to the hospital, I'll find out. But my intuition tells me she won't be making a visit."

"Why do you say that?"

"After listening to Rick's mutterings, I've gathered they're like two enemy aircraft circling each other trying to decide how and when they're going to engage." In the next breath he related the analogy of the bottle rocket.

His wife chuckled. He loved it. He loved her.

"Do you think your father suspects anything?"

"Very little escapes Dad. It'll be fascinating to find out."

"Even if Audra doesn't show up, you'll be able to meet her tomorrow when you help him take Rick back to the ranch."

"I'm not staying away from you another night," Nate declared. "Now that I know my brother is suffering from something else a lot worse than a broken collarbone, I'll be taking the next transport out of here. Expect me home late this afternoon."

"I can't wait!"

"That makes two of us. Give Becky a dozen kisses. Tell her they're from her daddy."

"I already have. She's tucked right here next to me."

"Plan to be tucked in early tonight, Mrs. Hawkins."

"Promise?"

"Better catch up on your beauty sleep now. I'm giving you fair warning."

"I love you, Nate. Hurry home to me."

He rang off and headed for the hospital cafeteria, eager to find out if his father had picked up on any romantic feelings between Rick and Audra.

"Nate?" his father called to him as he walked through the swinging doors.

"I'll be right with you." Now that he knew his brother was going to be fine, Nate found he was hungry. He picked up a tray and ordered ham and eggs.

After paying the cashier, he joined his father at a table over against the wall. "Where's Pam?"

He drained the rest of his coffee. "She went to the gift shop to find Rick some sports magazines."

"As long as she's not here, there's something vital I wanted to talk to you about in private."

His father's mouth lifted at one corner. "This wouldn't have to do with Audra, would it?"

A grunt escaped. "Rick was so out of it he was blabbing right and left," he said, making inroads on his food.

"Pam's little cousin has made an impact."

Their eyes met with that perfect understanding refined over a lifetime of communication between father and son.

"Has Audra been similarly affected?"

His dad pursed his lips. "She's a deep one, difficult to read."

"Rick never could resist a challenge."

Now it was his father who made the odd sound in his throat. "I can guarantee Audra isn't like any woman Rick has ever met, or will meet."

Nate's eyebrows lifted. "That's the best news I've heard in ten years."

"Maybe."

"How come?"

"Let me tell you a story about the family I married into so you'll have a better understanding of Audra's complicated psyche."

By the time his father had finished explaining about the tragedy that had struck the Jarrett clan, including the painful years of fallout, Nate's excitement had been replaced by gut-wrenching incredulity.

"I'm afraid that's only the tip of the iceberg where Audra's concerned. She was in love with someone several years ago. Obviously it didn't work out. After a long period, she started dating again. The man she was out on a date with got killed.

"They were trapped in his car for what must have been an eternity to her. Pam believes Audra's nightmares not only have to do with the crash, but the trauma brought on by a lifetime of dealing with her hostile cousins, a broken heart and now the sale of the ranch."

Nate shook his head. "Does Rick know all this?"

"He sat through a family dinner where David broke the news about the new owner of the property, who'll be flying in next week. When he announced that I'd bought the ranch house, everything fell apart and pretty well gave Rick the whole picture. But he'd be in the dark about the man who hurt Audra."

There was too much to absorb at once. "Dad, Rick said Audra's cousins hate you. Was that an exaggeration?"

His father pondered the question. "I guess time will tell."

"I don't like the sound of that."

"To give you an idea of how bad things have been, at Pam's urging David didn't come to our wedding. She said it would inflame the boys too much. Audra wanted to be Pam's maid of honor, but Pam begged her to stay with David, who needed her a lot more."

"Good grief. So that was why there was no one there to give Pam away. Rick and I couldn't understand why her entire family would absent themselves. Have you told Rick?"

"Not yet. He was in such a morose state when I called him, I asked him to come to Texas on his way to Phoenix. To my surprise he took me up on it. After he arrived, I decided the best thing to do was just listen to anything he had to say."

That's what Nate had done this morning. He'd listened to Rick.

"Your brother's hurting," his dad whispered. "Frankly, I'm worried about him."

"Once you were worried about me," Nate quipped in an attempt to lighten his father's mood.

"Once?"

A smile broke out on Nate's face. "You know what I mean."

"I do. But this is Rick we're talking about. He's approaching thirty and world-weary already. That's too young an age to have seen it all, done it all."

"Not all. The best part is yet to come, Dad. Take it from the newest bridegroom in the family."

His father squeezed his arm. "I'm glad you're here. How long can you stay?"

"I'll go upstairs with you and Pam to visit Rick for a little while, then I'm flying home. But I'll be back next week with Laurel and Becky. We'll vacation for a few days. By then Rick won't be on heavy painkillers."

"That's a good idea. Why don't you see if Brent and Julie would like to come. We've got plenty of rooms for everyone."

"I admit Brent's good for Rick. They've gotten close. Unfortunately, it would mean taking the kids out of school again."

"Maybe they could find a sitter."

"I'll talk it over with Laurel tonight and let you know."

"Good. I'm feeling better already. Let's go see Rick."

Nate caught his father's arm. "I'm sure Pam's with him. She left us alone on purpose. Your wife's too accommodating. I'm beginning to understand why you fell in love with her."

His gray eyes glistened over. "Are you telling me my marriage doesn't hurt you as much anymore?"

''If you want to know the truth, I'm happy for you.''

Last March he couldn't have imagined himself saying that to his father, let alone meaning it.

After Nate's mother had died in an avalanche, he'd resigned his commission in the air force to help his grieving father run his ski business. What he hadn't counted on was the advent of Pam Jarrett in Clint's life, or his dad's decision to marry again so soon and move to Texas.

The shocking turn of events had come as a blow to both brothers. However, by that time Laurel and little Becky, the daughter of Laurel's first husband, Scott, had come into Nate's life. Scott, who'd died in a jet-plane crash, had been Nate's best friend in the air force.

Nate's chance meeting with Laurel months later had resulted in marriage, something that had shocked Scott's parents. The whole experience of dealing with Laurel's in-laws had opened Nate's eyes. He'd understood their shock and grief over learning that their daughter-in-law was in love again soon after Scott's death.

It had made him more understanding of his father's deep feelings for Pam, of his desire to be married. After getting to know her, Nate realized what a wonderful person Pam was.

As for Nate, he now had a home in Colorado Springs with a wife and baby he adored. Both men had found joy, but not Rick.

His poor brother, who'd also given up racing to help his father, had gone into a decline. The Hawkins home as Rick had always known it was gone. He found himself alone and deserted, physically and emotionally. Having lost his bearings, he didn't know where or how to recover.

But maybe all that was about to change now that he'd met Audra....

CHAPTER FIVE

THE MIDDLE-AGED night nurse breezed into the hospital room.

"Is your pain worse, Mr. Hawkins?"

"No," Rick muttered.

"Can't sleep now that your family's gone home for the night?"

Rick had told his dad and Pam to get a motel. They'd looked exhausted. He'd hoped Nate could stick around longer, but he understood his brother had to get back to work. And back to Laurel and the baby, of course.

Now depression was setting in again.

He prayed for sleep to come. Those lost hours were the only time he found release from his inner turmoil.

His thoughts flew to Audra. What irony that she was probably lying in her bed right now praying *not* to go to sleep. When her eyes closed, the nightmares began. Which was worse?

He glanced at the nurse. "Does anyone around here ever manage to rest?"

Despite his comment, her pleasant smile remained in place. "According to the computer, you did a fairly good facsimile of sleeping earlier today. How can I help you? Are you thirsty? I've got juice in the fridge.''

''No, thank you. It's Friday night, right?''

She glanced at her watch. ''Literally speaking, this is Saturday and it's 2:00 a.m.''

''Maybe you can help me find the radio station I was listening to the other night about this same time. The broadcast came out of Austin. There was a female disc jockey who played a mix of country and classical recordings.''

''I know which one you mean. The program airs Monday, Wednesday and Friday nights. You're in luck. Everybody who's awake after midnight listens to it.''

The nurse, fiddling with the knobs of a radio beside Rick's bed, found the station right away. ''It's 580 on the AM dial. There you go.'' She put the radio near his right hand so he could adjust the volume himself.

''Thank you.''

''You're welcome. Press the button if you need anything else.''

Strains of a Rachmaninoff piano concerto came through. Rick closed his eyes. He recognized Ashkenazy as the pianist. In Rick's mind he was the best interpreter of the famous Russian composer's works.

Rick's mother had preferred Horowitz's recordings. They'd both had their favorite artists and composers. Half the fun of listening to music with his mother had been arguing with her. She'd thought Mahler's compositions went on too long. He found Prokofiev jarring. They'd both agreed Grieg's *First Piano Concerto* was the perfect piece of music.

"Don't you love the way the Rachmaninoff Third ends?" the deejay said.

Her voice. It had a melodic quality. He'd heard it before, on the radio but somewhere else, too.

"After it's over, I feel alive, ready to burst from the intense buildup."

Rick felt the same way.

"You've just heard Vladimir Ashkenazy at the piano. Another night I'll play the Horowitz recording, which is very different. In my opinion, Horowitz was the greatest pianist who ever lived. It's criminal that because of old technology his recordings will never do justice to his genius."

Who would have thought a Swede like his mom, and a Texan like the deejay, would have so many opinions in common?

"For those of you who've just tuned in, this segment of the program has been devoted to the piano concerto. Our concluding work is Beethoven's Fourth with Claudio Arrau. Lie back and enjoy. After the station break, we'll do a little country."

Beethoven was another of Rick's favorite composers, but he'd listened mostly to his symphonies. This concerto revealed the composer's passion. Rick found himself concentrating on the music. He'd have to buy a CD of the piece.

As soon as the commercials were over, he heard her say, "Welcome to the last segment of tonight's show. I'll be taking requests.

"To start things off, this next song is dedicated to

a guy from out of town who's not doing too well since a horse named Marshmallow fell on top of him. Wherever you are, Rick, let's hope you'll be feeling better soon.''

Rick heard his name mentioned in connection with Pam's mare and almost fell out of his hospital bed.

''It's called 'Racetrack Lover.'''

What?

Suddenly he was hearing the same great female vocalist he'd heard the other night. The song had that wonderful country sound with the terrific guitar backup.

Hey cowboy, can you hear me?
Better hold your sweetheart tight.
There's an exciting new man.
Coming into town tonight.
He's lucky on the track and lucky with the women,
He'll mess with your gal,
Consider that a given.
Tall, dark and sexy,
Handsome as sin,
He's the racetrack lover,
Who's about to drive in.
If you don't want a broken heart before daylight,
Keep your gal out of sight and locked up tight.
Better put her in the barn,
And throw away the key,
D-o-o-o-n't let him get near her,
Or believe you me,
He'll take her for a ride,

And rob you blind,
Before he spins his wheels,
And leaves her behind.
He's a charmer,
He's a talker,
He's a no-strings guy,
He's the racetrack lover in town on the fly.
Hey cowboy, can you hear me?
Better hold your sweetheart tight,
There's an exciting new man coming into town
tonight.

Good heavens. It was Audra.

A surge of adrenaline shot through his veins faster
than the painkiller administered through the IV they'd
taken out of him before dinner.

She was a disc jockey who also composed *and* performed!

Was that a live band backing her up?

With her broken leg, he thought she'd taken time
off from work and never left the ranch. Now it turned
out she had her own radio program? That meant she
made the trip to Austin and back in the dead of night
three times a week.

Who drove her while she was in a full-leg cast?
Her uncle? A friend?

If so, was the person female or male?

When Rick had been flown to the hospital last
night, he'd imagined her all alone in that isolated bungalow terrified to fall asleep. Instead, she'd been busy
somewhere writing a song about him.

Racetrack Lover.

He frowned at her perception of him.

Unless by some stretch of the imagination she had an uncommon interest in one of the drivers from the Formula One racing circuit who had a bad-boy reputation with the pit babes, he couldn't understand why she thought he went around breaking hearts.

Riddled with questions only she could answer, he memorized the request-line number she repeated while he rang for the nurse. An old Johnny Cash song played through to the end before help arrived.

"Mr. Hawkins?"

Finally! "I'm sorry to bother you, but could you put the phone in my hands. I can't reach it." His cell phone was probably lying in the back of Pam's truck.

"Sure."

"Thank you."

She did as he asked. "Remember to dial nine for an outside line. I'll be back to take your vitals after you're through talking."

He nodded, already having pushed the button before he forgot the radio station's call-in number.

The line was busy.

For the next fifteen minutes he kept pressing the redial button. By the time it rang through, there was a recording that said no more requests were being taken.

He muttered a curse.

"It's that time again, ladies and gentlemen. We're coming up on three in the morning. I'll be taking your requests again Monday at midnight on KHLB, the Hill Country station out of Austin at 580 on the AM dial. Thank you for listening to the *Red Jarrett Show* where I aim to bring you a little bit of the best of everything.''

The *Red Jarrett Show.*

He liked the sound of it. She'd probably been called Red growing up. He bet the nickname had pushed her buttons more than once. At twenty-eight she'd evidently passed beyond the point where it rankled.

The woman had talent. Tremendous talent.

Her commentary was as scintillating as her performance.

Who's taking you home tonight, Audra? For sure it's not the Racetrack Lover.

That man won't be driving his brand-new M3, let alone any car, for a while.

The overhead light went on. "Sorry, Mr. Hawkins. Once I'm through here, you won't be bothered again until the morning nurse comes on duty at seven. I understand you're going to be discharged at noon. She'll be the one to explain the doctor's orders before you go home.''

Home?

He didn't have one.

Neither did Audra.

The Jarrett ranch house now belonged to his father and Pam.

Except for a hundred and twenty acres and a bungalow, the main portion of the Jarrett Ranch now belonged to some millionaire businessman from Cleveland, Ohio, named Edwin Torney.

Like tremors that continued to shake the ground after a major earthquake, the tragic words from the first song he'd heard Audra sing kept running through his head. ''Windshield Rancher?'' The poignancy of those words had magnified a thousand times after what he'd learned in the last forty-eight hours.

''UNCLE DAVID?''

''Audra? What are you doing calling me? You're supposed to be sleeping in after your show. How come you're awake? It's only nine-thirty.''

She knew he worried about her recurring nightmares as much as Pam did. ''Since I went off the air I've been busy cleaning.''

A lot of cleaning, topped off by a nightmarish phone call from Tom had made her angrier than she'd ever been in her life.

''Cleaning? Now, Audra—''

''Have you talked to Pam and Clint?'' she broke in. ''Are they bringing Rick home today?''

''I just spoke to Pam. They'll be on their way soon.''

''Good.''

''If you need something from town, call Clint on his cell phone.''

''I'm fine. It's you I have to talk to. It's important. Could you come over to the bungalow now?''

''What's wrong, honey? No—don't answer that. I'll be right there.''

''Thank you. The front door's open.''

She'd been standing in the kitchen to make the call. By the time she'd pulled the cherry-pecan muffins from the oven, she glimpsed her uncle's blue half-ton pickup through the window.

"Audra?" he called out a minute later.

"I'm in the kitchen!"

"It smells good in here," he said as he entered from the living room.

"Sit down and have breakfast with me."

He took a seat at the drop-leaf table next to the window. His concerned eyes smiled at her in admiration. "That broken leg hasn't kept you down one bit."

"I can do everything but drive." She put a platter of bacon and eggs on the table, then sat down across from him, leaning her crutches against the wall.

No doubt he'd fixed himself hot cereal earlier that morning, but her uncle didn't let it prevent him from eating again.

"These muffins are worth a king's ransom."

She chuckled. "You always say that about everything Pam or I cook."

"Because it's true."

Audra finished munching on a piece of bacon. "Don't give me any credit. I learned it all from her. In fact, she's the person I want to talk to you about."

"Go ahead, honey."

"Uncle David, when you were defending Pam to the boys at dinner the other day, it was as if every word you said had been pulled straight out of my heart. No one deserves happiness more than she does."

"That's a fact."

"Now that she and Clint have found each other, I believe they're headed for a wonderful future. But it could get ruined if they're not left alone to settle into their marriage without trouble hemming them in on all sides.''

While she'd been talking, he swallowed the last of his coffee. ''Have the boys been badgering you girls without my knowledge?''

Nothing got past her uncle.

''Not until this morning when I had a call from Tom. He said he'll be dropping by the main house later today to get his things moved out. He also informed me that the boys had held a meeting.

''It was decided that I have to vacate the bungalow this weekend. They're planning to take over the place on Sunday evening and use it for their headquarters while they build a new barn out back.''

Her uncle's lip's tightened.

''There's more. They've hired an attorney to get a court order prohibiting any guests staying at Pam's bed-and-breakfast to ride beyond the creek, since the property on the other side is theirs.''

''He said that, did he?''

No doubt her uncle was imagining the same thing she was. That this was only the beginning of the harassment in store for Pam and Clint.

Her uncle's anger was intimidating because he rarely raised his voice. She admired that quality in him. It was one she'd been trying to emulate without much success. Since they both had red hair, she couldn't use that as her excuse.

''I have a plan that could solve a few problems for the time being, provided you help me.''

A pained expression crept over his face. ''You and Pam have always had to figure out how to cope with your cousins to keep the peace. When is it ever going to end?''

She put a hand on his arm. ''Please don't be worried on our account. You're the one who's carried the load all these years. But circumstances have changed around here. As far as I'm concerned, the boys have just declared war on Pam and Clint. I'm prepared to put up a fight if you are.''

He patted her hand before letting it go. ''What's your battle plan?''

''We'll need Rick for this to work, so I'm thinking it's providential that his accident happened on Jarrett property.''

''Go on.''

''What I'm proposing is that you and he move in here while he convalesces. We've got three bedrooms. I'll take care of him while you keep him company. I know what he needs after being in the hospital. We'll all get along fine.''

She smiled. ''Can you imagine the look on Tom's face when he and the boys show up here on Sunday night and discover you and Rick in residence? I own a quarter of the place. As long as I still have this cast on, I have squatter's rights.

''They don't have a clue how tough Rick is, but as you and I both know, he's a big boy who can take care of himself. Between you and Clint's son, they won't be able to run me out of here until I'm ready to leave.

''And here's the beautiful part. While they're forced to cool their heels, Pam and Clint will have some time alone to get their bed-and-breakfast going.

Those two have got to be given their privacy. When they want a little company, they can mosey on over here for an hour.''

Her uncle's eyes lit up. ''It's an inspired plan.''

''I'm glad you agree. Now your job will be to convince Pam and Clint that it's what you think is for the best for everyone. They won't say no to you. They love and respect you too much.

''Rick's so independent I think he'll be relieved his dad's new wife won't have to wait on him around the clock.''

With a nod, her uncle pushed himself away from the table and got to his feet. ''Thank you for the delicious breakfast.'' He leaned over to kiss her cheek. ''Your concern for other people's happiness at a cost to your own is one of your crowning virtues, honey.''

He put a hand on her shoulder. ''Don't get up. Finish your food. I'll go back to the house and wait for them. I've got a few things to do before our patient arrives.

''When it's all settled and they're on their way over here, I'll give you a ring. Since Tom's coming for his things, don't expect me until late tonight.''

''I'm glad Clint will be there with you.''

''It ought to be an enlightening experience for the boys to find themselves up against the Hawkins men,'' her uncle mused aloud.

Enlightening was hardly the word.

Shame on you, Audra Jarrett, for your uncharitable thoughts.

''WE'RE ALMOST THERE. How are you holding up?''

''I'm fine, Dad,'' Rick lied. It was time for another pain pill.

Unfortunately, there was no medication he could give his anxious father, who continued to cast him sideward glances. Rick didn't think he could deal with the situation much longer.

Guilt plagued his dad. Though it was ridiculous for him to feel responsible for the horseback-riding accident, Rick understood.

In Clint's eyes his son wasn't an ordinary person. He was a race-car driver who needed to be in top physical and mental condition. Those contracts waiting to be signed in Arizona were going to have to sit there for a while longer.

But Rick knew the accident didn't comprise all his father's guilt. There was another component.

A much bigger one.

The one that had driven Rick to retire early from racing.

The one resulting in a depression Rick hadn't been able to throw off or hide from his father.

If Rick knew it wouldn't devastate his dad, he'd ask his buddy Chip to fly down from Colorado and drive him to Phoenix. The guy was having marital problems and needed to talk. They could both vent.

Once there, Rick would check into a hotel and take advantage of the room service until he felt well enough to get around.

To stay with Nate or Brent while he recuperated was out of the question. Their wives, one who was pregnant, the other who'd just had a baby, weren't in any condition to wait on him.

Everything came back to Pam, the giver. She'd insisted he sit in front so he'd have plenty of legroom. She would be doing the honors in the nursing department.

It wasn't fair to her or his father. Hell, it wasn't fair to their marriage. Since she'd been a teenager Pam had been waiting on people, three of whom were boorish ingrates.

More recently she'd had to cut her honeymoon short to be at Audra's bedside. Pam deserved the luxury of being a wife in her own home without having to nurse him, too.

Rick would give it three days at the most, enough to help his father get over the worst of his guilt. Then he'd phone Chip for help.

"There's Uncle David," Pam exclaimed. "I wonder how long he's been waiting on the front porch. I hope there's nothing wrong."

The older man walked down the steps toward the car. Rick lowered his window as David drew up to his side.

He studied Rick for a moment. "Thought I'd catch you before you drove in and tried to get out of the car when you're hurting so much. You look a lot better than you did when they lifted you in the helicopter."

"Sorry to have ruined the day for everyone."

"That's foolish talk, Rick. I'm not going to ask how you feel because I already know. Years ago I broke my collarbone during a cattle drive. The worst part is being patient while you wait for it to get better."

"You're right," Rick murmured. Pam's uncle was a good man. "I'm already going crazy."

"How would you like a job to keep you sharp while that bone heals?"

David Jarrett didn't ask idle questions. Rick's curiosity was piqued.

"What do you have in mind?"

His expression sobered. "Stay at the bungalow with my little Audra while you're recovering. Let her wait on you. She's well enough to be going crazy herself while she's cooped up out there. Though she would never admit it, she needs company and protection until that cast comes off."

Rick had thought the same thing from the moment he'd invaded her bedroom without invitation. In fact, he'd gone so far as to be angry that no one was there to help her get through those nightmares.

"There's nothing I'd like better," he said in all honesty. "But what makes you think she'd welcome me?"

"I was her guest for breakfast this morning. She'd had a phone call from Tom. It shook her up, and she asked me if I'd sleep there until her cast comes off."

In Rick's opinion Tom was a dangerous man.

"What did he say to her?" Pam sounded alarmed.

"He and the boys want her out of there this weekend so they can have a place to live while they build a barn."

Those bastards!

"The problem is, I'd promised my best friend Harry that after I'd sold the property, I would stay at the Cattlemen's Club until next weekend when the condo's ready.

"What I hadn't counted on was the boys being this bitter. They're already ganging up on Audra, and that's something I won't tolerate."

"Please don't change your plans, Uncle David," Pam pleaded with him. "I know how much you've looked forward to spending time with Harry. Go and enjoy yourself with him and your other friends. Clint and I wi—"

"David asked me to stay with her. That's exactly what I'm going to do," Rick broke in before Pam could say anything else.

The older man looked relieved. Whatever love Audra didn't get from her cousins, her uncle made up.

"Thank you, son. Just between you and me, she's been looking for a way to pay your father back. He was so understanding about Pam having to cut short their honeymoon to be with her at the hospital and after, she's felt guilty ever since. She'll see this as a way to even the score."

Sounds of protest came from the other two in the car. Rick, on the other hand, understood that kind of guilt very well. Things couldn't be working out better for him.

"I need to do a little fence-mending of my own, David. Audra and I didn't get off to the best start. I'm afraid I broke into the bungalow during one of her nightmares. I thought she was being attacked."

"Clint told me." David cleared his throat. "I have to confess, I'd sleep a lot better if I knew she wasn't alone at night. If those terrible dreams haven't stopped by the time she's living in Austin, I'm going to take her for professional help,'' he declared.

''I had a buddy at the track who became trapped in his race car. He suffered the same kind of problem. He moved to his parents' for a while and the nightmares finally went away. She shouldn't be alone.

''Dad? Why don't we drive to the bungalow right now. I'm starting to feel tired and the pain pill is wearing off. You can bring my other things over later when it's convenient.''

His father nodded. ''Since you've just left the hospital, that would be for the best. Once you're settled, you shouldn't have to move again.''

David eyed Rick. ''I'll tell Audra you're coming instead of me. One thing's for certain. Cast or no cast, she'll make you the best nurse in the Hill Country.''

Even for the Racetrack Lover?

There was an unmistakable tremor in David's voice before he stepped away from the car.

By the time they'd covered the three miles to the bungalow in silence, Rick discovered that despite his pain, his black mood had improved. In a few minutes he would come face-to-face with Red Jarrett in the flesh.

They'd met before, but now he was in possession of certain facts that made her even more fascinating to him.

For one thing, he wouldn't have to wait until Monday night to call in on the radio request line to talk to her. Instead of staying with his dad and Pam for the next three days, he'd be living with Audra for an indefinite period. He'd get answers to certain questions he'd been wanting to ask her.

For another, it would give his dad and Pam time to be alone for a change.

His thoughts went back to his first skirmish with Audra.

Let's agree to stay out of each other's way. It shouldn't be too difficult. Inside of twelve hours, boredom will consume you. By nightfall, we'll be breathing the dust from your tires when you peal out of here for heaven knows what race with death you have scheduled next.

Her prophecy had been way off.

Inside of twelve hours, a helicopter had borne him away. Two days later, he was back at the ranch with no schedule in mind, no imminent race with death and no sign of boredom.

While his father steadied him up the porch steps, Pam opened the front door of the bungalow.

This time Rick heard no bloodcurdling screams, only the musical quality in Audra's voice after Pam announced their arrival.

"Come on back, Rick. Your bed's waiting for you! Uncle David told me you're willing to let me take care of you. You're a brave man. I promise that if I whack anyone with my crutches, it won't be you."

His dad turned to him with a puzzled look. "What did she mean?"

Rick would have grinned if it didn't hurt to smile. The pain from his broken collarbone radiated all the way to his mouth. "It's one of Audra's dark jokes."

''You understood it?''

''Yes.''

This side trip to Texas was getting more exciting by the second.

CHAPTER SIX

"HERE ARE the doctor's orders."

Audra took the sheet from Pam, aware of Clint's and Rick's voices filtering down the hall to the kitchen.

"He can take painkillers every four hours, and he's supposed to be propped up when he's in bed."

"I've been there and done that with my leg. What he needs is rest." Audra put the paper down on the counter, trying hard not to smile too gleefully at her cousin.

Pam didn't know it yet, but by tonight she would be alone with her husband in that wonderful old ranch house they now owned. Uncle David had pulled through, big-time.

"Clint's second born is safe with me. So get out of here and go home. Lock yourselves in your bedroom and give his daddy some of your TLC. Who knows? Maybe Rick won't always be the baby of the Hawkins family."

"Audra—" Pam blushed a lovely shade of pink for a brunette.

"That little room upstairs you've used for sewing would make a perfect nursery."

"Maybe, but it's not fair to be the child of older parents."

"Tell that to Harry Moore's son or Blanche Kendall's daughter. Both their mothers were older than you when they conceived. You've barely turned forty. You're young yet!"

"At my age the eggs aren't al—"

"Don't think about that," Audra cut her off.

"But by the time we had a child in college, Clint would be Uncle David's age."

"Is Clint against the idea?"

She shook her head. "No, but he wants me to be very sure because he knows if anything happened to him, I'd have to raise the child by myself. Let's face it, Audra. I'm not twenty-two anymore and haven't been for a long time. Can you see me getting down to make mud pies with my toddler?"

"Why not?" Audra challenged. "Any limitations you place on yourself are in your mind. If Clint weren't young at heart, he wouldn't have married you. I'd say the child that gets you two for parents will be the luckiest person alive.

"Between your two gene pools you might raise another Olympic gold medalist or state rodeo champion. Wouldn't it be fun to find out?" When Pam averted her brown eyes, Audra said, "Well, wouldn't it?"

She didn't hear her cousin's answer because Clint walked into the kitchen. His serious gaze sought Audra's. "He's taken his pill and will probably fall asleep soon."

"He's not in the hospital with nurses keeping him

awake taking his vital signs all night, so there's no probably about it."

Clint's mouth widened in a smile that reminded her of Rick's before his accident. "Thanks for looking after him, Audra."

"My pleasure. Now that you've said it, you don't have to say it again. I've been telling your wife to go home and take you with her."

Who knew when Tom and the boys would show up at the main house to get their things? Audra didn't want her uncle to be alone to face them. He needed the emotional support he'd derive from Pam and Clint.

"We're leaving." He gave her a kiss on the cheek.

After they'd closed the front door, she looked out the kitchen window to watch them drive away.

Life had to get better for them. It just had to!

As for Audra, knowing Rick was in the house made it a good day. Bring on the boys. Let them try to cause trouble. She wasn't going to roll over and die to keep the peace. Not this time.

Reaching for her other crutch, she moved down the hall to the master bedroom and bathroom she'd readied for Rick. It was time to check on him.

His dad had helped him get into bed. Dressed in navy sweats and nothing else, his appealing physique was quite a sight. She guessed it was warm enough to sleep without covers.

The quilted spread at the foot of the queen-size bed was a small Waverly Print of cranberry and pink on white. There were accent pillows in those shades. The curtains were made of the same print.

Over the last few years Pam had used some of the money she'd made doing accounts for other ranchers to give all the rooms in the house a much-needed face-lift.

In anticipation of opening a bed-and-breakfast one day, the living room contained a couch and love seat in earth tones. She'd hung framed photographs of the ranch as it had appeared in former times. Beautifully matted in café au lait, they provided splashes of warm color.

She'd had off-white carpet laid throughout the house in order to lighten and modernize the interior. The bedroom Audra had been using was decorated in a blue-and-white French toile, which covered the queen-size bed and the windows. A huge photograph of bluebonnets in bloom hung on one wall. Pam had given it to Audra for her last birthday.

The third bedroom, where Audra kept her instruments and soundboard, contained two twin beds with quilted spreads in a cheerful yellow-and-white plaid shot with gold and brown. The curtains and lamp shade were made of the same material.

Improvements still needed to be made to the kitchen and bathrooms, yet on the whole the house had loads of charm thanks to Pam's decorating flair.

Audra had to admit no background design or furnishings could draw her interest like the patient before her, a live male whose black body hair stood out against the white tape and sling holding his left arm in place.

She didn't need a crystal ball to divine how many hearts he'd broken without knowing it.

"Hi."

To her surprise he was awake.

"Hi, yourself," she said from the doorway. "Welcome to the halfway house. Together we make one person."

Audra was treated to a lazy smile. "Thanks. I came through the front door this time."

"I noticed. Thank *you*."

He eyed her through veiled black lashes. "So what do you think of the Racetrack Lover now?"

Rick had heard her show?

Audra was thankful for the crutches holding her up. "I'm thinking there's got to be some woman out there who's wondering why this pit stop is taking so long."

"If there were a woman out there, I wouldn't be here."

That was what Boris had said. Like every foolish woman in love, she'd believed him.

"Uncle David says it's good to break a bone once in your life. While it heals, the waiting process builds character."

"Do you believe everything he tells you?"

"Why do you think I've been living out here where I can't offend anybody?"

She wished he didn't have such an appealing chuckle.

"Sorry you got coerced into this, Rick, but I took you at your word when you told me your dad and Pam's happiness was of the utmost importance to you."

He rubbed one toe against the other. "Nobody had to twist my arm, Audra. The only reason I didn't phone my friend Chip to come and get me was because of Dad. He wanted to make up for the guilt he's been feeling. I had to let him and decided to stay with him for a few days when it was the last thing I wanted to do.

"Being invited to stay here has saved me from feeling like a total burden to them. I'm indebted to you."

"I'm glad you're okay with it." Audra cocked her head. "Clint's guilt is understandable. After losing your mother in a freak accident, the idea that you could have been killed because he took you horseback riding filled him with terror."

"His guilt goes deeper than that."

"You mean because you retired from racing to help him, and then found out he didn't need any help?"

His gaze held hers. "Does Pam tell you everything?"

"Probably as much as your dad tells you."

His lips twitched. "I guess we don't have any secrets left."

She rested her chin on top of one of her crutches. "Nope. That's why I figured we'd get along here while the two lovebirds try to make a nest."

"*Try* being the operative word," he muttered. "Correct me if I'm wrong, but Tom seems capable of violence. Is he?"

"If you're asking if he's ever struck me, the answer is no. I don't believe he's ever hit anyone."

"Not that you know of anyway," he persisted.

"No. Losing his parents made him angry. He's been in that state ever since, and gets the other two stirred up. It's a situation that's gone on as long as I can remember.''

Rick grimaced. "It's gotten worse. We both know your cousins won't divide the time fairly so you'll be able to enjoy this house in the future.''

"I didn't ever say that.''

"Yes, you did.'' Her head reared in reaction. "I heard you singing that 'Windshield Rancher' song on my way to the ranch.''

The knowledge that he'd listened to her radio broadcast Wednesday night stunned her.

"Did your father tell you I did a show over the air?''

"He only said you worked in radio. I found your program quite by accident. The song you sang was so sad, I felt it in my gut.''

Oddly enough, it was his voice just now that sounded haunted.

"You said it all, Audra. You realized your uncle had to sell, and when he did, you knew the boys would make it impossible for you to share in anything left to you. Admit you're frightened of them.''

Rick Hawkins knew too much.

"Not for me. I want them to leave Pam and Clint alone.''

His features hardened. "My father won't let them hurt her.''

"But don't you see?'' she cried out. "He shouldn't have to do anything! They ought to be able to live out their lives free of trouble from three stupid men who've been given everything and don't have the good sense to see it.''

''They need professional help.''

''Uncle David blames himself for not getting them therapy after the tornado struck. Like most people, he kept hoping things would get better. Now it's too late.''

''If they were troubled before the tragedy, therapy might not have helped them,'' he theorized.

''He and Pam have talked about it with me so many times. No matter how difficult the boys were as children, the trauma of losing their families was probably too much for them. We've all hoped marriage and children would have a softening effect on them.''

''Their wives didn't have much to say at dinner.''

''You're being diplomatic. Let's be honest. They didn't have anything to say. Sherry asked you a question and caught a glare from Jim. Later that evening she said some disturbing things to me.''

''Like what?''

Without preamble, Audra told him the gist of their conversation on the porch while she was waiting for the helicopter to arrive.

When she'd finished, Rick said, ''If Dad's attorney showed your cousins the legal documents proving he bought the ranch house at fair market value, it would only inflame them. They're going to believe what they want to believe.''

''I know, and their wives have to go along with them if they want peace. It's a difficult situation made worse because there are children involved. I love the kids.

''The thing is, I have every faith in Clint and Uncle

David, but the boys' resentment is so much deeper now that the property's been sold."

"It's not deeper, it's white-hot since my father bought the main house," Rick declared. "Three angry men out of control might do some real damage. If they start to harass you or Pam, there are ways to stop them."

"I know. I'm just praying it doesn't come to that. Right now you're the person I'm most worried about. Are you hungry or thirsty?"

"Not yet."

"Tell you what. Try to sleep. I'll bring you a tray in an hour. It'll be the kind of food that appealed to me after I got home from the hospital."

"Sounds good."

"Your cell phone's in the drawer of your night-stand. Pam gave it to me to call your brother. Would you like me to put it by your right hand?"

"No, thank you. How about playing your guitar for me?"

"Why don't we wait until tonight. I'll put on a little show for you after Uncle David gets here. He loves music. We'll do it in the other bedroom where I broadcast. You can lie on the twin bed. If you fall asleep, I'll leave you there until morning."

She'd started to turn around with her crutches when he called to her.

"What is it?"

"Your uncle won't be coming."

Her eyebrows knit together. "Your father told you that?"

"No. David did."

''I don't understand.''

''Maybe you'd better call him.''

''I will. Tom said he was going over there today to clear out his things. If Uncle David has decided not to come tonight, Tom's the reason. I'll be in the living room if you need me. Just shout. I'll hear you.''

As soon as she'd made her way through the house to the couch, she sat down to rest her leg and pulled her cell phone from her skirt pocket. It indicated ten after five. The day had flown by without her being aware of it.

Much as she hated to disturb Pam and Clint, she needed to find out if there'd been some kind of confrontation with Tom.

''Pam?''

''Hi! How's the patient?''

''He's fine. What I want to know is, did Tom show up?''

''Yes. He came in Greg's truck because it's bigger. They took everything in one load, including the grandfather clock. Now they've gone.''

''Were there any problems?''

''They didn't talk to me or Clint. Before they walked out the door, they told Uncle David they'd be using his trailer to move the horses from the barn to the Circle T tomorrow.''

''I'm glad there wasn't trouble.'' Maybe everything was going to be all right. ''Is Uncle David handy?''

''No. After the boys left, he drove to Austin.''

''How come?''

''Honey—you know why.''

''I do?''

"He's going to spend the week at the Cattlemen's Club with Harry."

Audra gripped her cell phone tighter. "When did he decide to do that?"

"I don't know, but I thought *you* knew. I assumed he'd told you about it at breakfast."

"He didn't say a word."

That meant she was going to be alone with Rick. What was her uncle doing?

"Do you think there was some emergency with Harry?"

"No, otherwise he would have told us. At least I think he would have."

"Pam, I've got to phone him and find out what's going on."

"Call me back."

"I will."

With a hand that had started to tremble, she punched in her uncle's cell phone number and waited. After five rings he picked up.

"Audra?"

"Uncle David—what's this about you staying at the Cattlemen's Club with Harry? I called the ranch house to talk to you, and Pam told me you'd left for Austin."

"That's right. As soon as Tom and Greg drove off, I packed a suitcase and cleared out. After all, I'm as anxious as you for Pam and Clint to have their home to themselves."

"But I'm at the bungalow alone with Rick!"

"I thought he made you feel protected."

"He does, but that's not the point."

"Honey, if you're uncomfortable, I'll pack up and come home right now."

"No! Please don't do that! I just don't understand why you didn't tell me this morning."

"Well, Harry's been after me to come stay with him at the club. I hadn't quite made up my mind until after I'd told Rick you were planning to take care of him and he agreed.

"I got to thinking about the situation and realized you'd end up waiting on both of us. I didn't like that idea, so I decided to join Harry. I would have phoned you from Austin tonight."

Her thoughts were reeling.

At first she'd thought her uncle was up to a little matchmaking, but now she wasn't so sure.

Harry Moore was her uncle's best friend. He'd been living at their club since his wife died last year. Maybe her uncle had wanted to live there for a long time but hadn't felt he could leave Audra without protection. If that was true…

On the heels of that thought came another one.

"Uncle David, did you buy the condo for *my* sake?" she cried. "Because if you did, and you'd prefer to live at the club around your friends, your sacrifice would kill me! I can find my own apartment and be perfectly happy."

"I know that, honey. The truth is, I don't want to live with a bunch of old men."

She weighed his comment. "Honest?"

"The Realtor pointed out there were quite a few single women and widows who own condos in the complex. The place has a social center with organized activities. I'm looking forward to the experience. If I find I don't like condo living, I might consider moving to the club.''

Audra stared into space. Was he telling her the truth?

Her uncle had given up some of the best years of his life to raise his orphan family. If Pam could meet Clint, maybe there was a wonderful woman out there for her uncle. The mere possibility filled her with excitement.

That settled it.

When the cast came off, Audra had every intention of finding her own place to live because it appeared someone else in the Jarrett family was going to need *his* space, too.

''Enjoy yourself, Uncle David. Forget everything and have a great time!''

''I intend to. How's it going with Rick?''

''I haven't had to lift a finger. So far he's been lying on the bed resting. In a few minutes I'll start his dinner.''

''I can remember when I was laid up. My friends used to come and see me after work. We played poker every night. It helped relieve the boredom.''

''Are you talking spit in the ocean?''

''Or five card stud. Give Rick a break and let him win a few hands to keep things friendly.''

She smiled. ''That might be kind of fun. Is that what you're going to do tonight? Play cards?''

''Harry's getting us up a game with some of the other fellows as we speak.''

Her uncle sounded happy. ''Then I'll let you go.''

"Honey? I'm only as far away as the telephone if you need me."

"I was just going to say the same thing to you." She hung up the phone in a daze.

"IF IT'S ALL RIGHT WITH YOU, I'd rather be an audience to your show than play cards tonight."

Audra's well-shaped head with those bouncy dark red curls jerked around in Rick's direction. He'd caught her off guard. Her gorgeous blue eyes were filled with so many emotions, it would take hours to sort them all out.

"I didn't mean to eavesdrop. After I got up to use the rest room, I found my own company depressing and decided to come find you."

She stared at him across the expanse of the living room. "Considering what a physically active man you are, it must be horrible for you right now. Like you're in a straitjacket."

"It's exactly like that, but then you're the one person who would know all about it."

"The difference is, I can still earn my living."

"Another month without work isn't going to put me out on the streets."

"I'm sure that's true. A sports celebrity of your fame has probably invested enough to keep you financially set whether you ever did another day's work in your life or not."

She reached for her crutches and got to her feet. "But everyone still needs a reason to get up in the morning. I'm sorry you had to encounter that snake."

"It was worth it to see the bluebonnets."

Her mouth broke into a smile that reminded him of a rosebud opening to the sun. "They *are* beautiful."

"Yes" was all he could say because his eyes were filled by the beauty he was taking in right now.

"Would you like an omelette or a hearty soup for dinner?" she called over her shoulder on her way to the kitchen.

He followed. "Eggs sound good."

"Go back to bed and let me wait on you."

"I'd rather eat at the kitchen table. It's easier."

"Then I'll hurry."

He marveled at her ability to function with those crutches. In a few minutes she'd placed a fabulous-looking omelette in front of him. It was filled with ham, green peppers and onions, just the way he liked it.

"Coffee, tea, water or a soda?"

"Do you have cola?"

She nodded and pulled one from the fridge. "I sense an addiction."

He chuckled. "Guilty as charged. It comes from years of reaching for one from the vending machine at the track."

After she'd popped the opening, she set it by his plate. Before she sat down with her own omelette, she buttered a couple of muffins and put them on a plate with a dish of applesauce, which she placed near him.

He hadn't thought he was hungry until he started eating. Suddenly food tasted so good he found himself devouring everything in sight.

"These muffins are fantastic. Where do you buy applesauce like this? It's so sweet you think you're eating candy."

Her eyes lit up. "You're enjoying the apples from the ranch. Pam and I do a lot of canning in the fall."

"If this is the way things are going to be while I'm here, the mechanics will have to stuff me into my race car with a crowbar."

"That would be quite a sight all right. I can see the headlines now. Racetrack Lover Raids Honey Pot Once Too Often."

Laughter burst out of him.

"Come to think of it, Dad better watch out, or that lean physique he's so proud of isn't going to be lean much longer."

She shook her head. "Two plump Hawkins men? I can't picture it."

"I don't know. Pam's been teaching him how to cook Tex-Mex. I've been treated to one of his meals. He could be in big trouble, no pun intended."

Her smile turned wistful. "My cousin adores him."

"If he wasn't crazy about her, he wouldn't have married her."

Audra put down her fork. "I have a strong hunch my uncle would like to get married again, but I've been so blinded by the situation around here, I didn't realize it until I spoke to him on the phone before dinner."

"What did he say?"

In a few minutes she'd told him the essence of her conversation with David.

"I thought you looked dazed when you finished talking to him."

"*Dazed* doesn't quite cover it, but it will do for want of a better word."

"That's the way I felt when I decided to surprise my grieving father and found him in the kitchen embracing Pam like he'd once embraced my mother."

"*That* was the first you knew about them?"

"Yes."

She looked horrified. "Does Pam know?"

"No, thank God. I tiptoed back outside the house, came in again, shut the front door hard so they could hear it, then called out to him."

Audra's eyes glistened. "Pam would die if she knew."

"So would Dad."

"The day after she met your father, she called me. 'Audra?' she said. 'I met the most wonderful man yesterday morning. We spent all day and evening together. I'm in love with him. He thinks he's in love with me and has begged me to stay so we can get to know each other. I don't know what to do. He just lost his wife and he's got these two amazing sons who worshiped their mother and would never understand in a million years!'"

Rick leveled his gaze on the desirable, vulnerable woman seated across from him. "Pam was right..." His voice trailed off. "Fortunately, it didn't take a million years to come to terms with the fact that our father had met a woman who made him want to embrace life again. Knowing the history between her and the boys, I'm beginning to understand how tough it was for her to have to walk on eggshells around me and Nate, too.''

"It *was* tough,'' Audra confirmed. "But Pam was willing to walk through fire for your father.''

"Now it's Dad's turn,'' he whispered.

"Rick—'' Her haunted eyes searched his. "Does their marriage still bother you?''

"No.'' It felt good to say it and mean it. "What about you?''

"What do you mean?''

"How long did you grieve over losing your best friend to my father?''

She took her time. "I can't answer that question. It's all mixed up with my grief over my uncle, who's sacrificed his adult life for all of us at great cost to his own.''

"Aren't you forgetting something?'' Rick drawled. "He'd already been married and had children before tragedy struck. If he had it to do over again, I have no doubts he'd have made the same choice. He's an extraordinary man.''

"I know. He deserves all the happiness in the world now.''

Rick frowned. Her uncle's decision to stay in Austin had thrown her in ways he suspected David wasn't aware of.

"Audra, maybe it would be better if we both moved back to the main house. I'll phone Dad right now.''

"No!'' she cried. "You can't! It would ruin everything for Pam and Clint. If Uncle David found out, he'd come right back. He believes I'm all right as long as you're here with me. I wouldn't take that away from him for anything."

Meaning what?

"Are you uncomfortable to be alone with me?"

"Of course not," she said too fast. "I didn't mean that the way it came out."

"Then what *did* you mean?"

"Nothing!"

A redhead couldn't lie without it showing. Her cheeks filled with color before she got up from the chair and reached for her crutches.

Interesting.

"I'm going to bring you a pain pill. After you take it, I'll do a little singing for you until you're ready for bed."

CHAPTER SEVEN

NATE TOOK his cell phone from the dresser. "Sweetheart?" He leaned down to kiss Laurel. "While you nurse Becky, I'm going to try and reach Rick again for an update before we go to bed."

She kissed him back with equal hunger. "Give him my love."

It felt as if they were on an eternal honeymoon. He never wanted it to end.

After leaving a peck on Becky's soft cheek, Nate padded out of their room to the guest bedroom, where he could talk without disturbing the baby.

Sinking onto the side of the bed, he phoned his brother. To his chagrin, Rick's cell was still turned off. Nate didn't like bothering his father or Pam, but he had to know Rick was all right.

It wasn't quite ten o'clock Texas time. He imagined they were still up. After several rings his father answered.

"Dad?"

"Nate—I was about to call you."

He frowned. "Has Rick had a setback of some kind?"

"Anything but."

"That's good to know." Nate felt his body relax.

"I've tried to get him several times today, but he's turned off his phone. Do you think he's asleep right now?"

"I doubt it."

"Then he needs heavier painkillers."

"No, he doesn't. He's got everything he wants right where he is."

Nate blinked. "That sounded cryptic. Wait—you're talking about Audra."

"I'm glad to see marriage to Laurel hasn't dulled your wits completely. How is the love of your life, by the way?"

He grinned. "Wonderful."

"And my little granddaughter?"

"Thriving and hungry at the moment."

"That's what I like to hear."

"I guess I'll have to wait until tomorrow to touch base with Rick."

"When he's ready to talk, he'll call you."

"Dad, you're sounding mysterious again."

"Maybe it's because I'm as in the dark as you are."

"What do you mean?"

"When we brought Rick home from the hospital today, Pam's uncle walked up to the car. It seems Audra suggested that Rick live at the bungalow with her to recuperate so Pam and I could be alone."

"You're kidding! Rick says she's still in a cast."

"That's right. To make this tale even more intriguing, Audra thought her uncle would be staying with them, too. Instead, he made a last-minute decision to check himself into the Cattlemen's Club in Austin.

"His old rancher friend Harry Moore has been living there. Apparently he's been urging David to join him until David's retirement condo is ready for occupation."

Nate sat forward. "So Rick's out at the bungalow now?"

"Yes."

"Knowing my brother, he wouldn't put himself in a situation like this unless it was exactly what he wanted."

"Oh, he wanted it all right. I never saw anyone so eager to take a near stranger up on her offer. If I weren't delighted at the turn of events, my feelings would be hurt to think he didn't give his old dad a second thought."

At this point Nate started to get excited. "I haven't met Audra, but something tells me she wouldn't have extended the invitation if she's still dying of a broken heart. What does Pam think?"

"She's not saying yet. That's her way."

"Under the circumstances, I don't imagine he'd like the family descending en masse for a while."

"I'm with you. Let's not try to fix something that isn't broken."

Nate burst into laughter. "What an irony, when she's in a leg cast and his arm and shoulder are taped and trussed."

His father chuckled. "They make quite a pair."

"Wouldn't it be something if that was really true," Nate murmured on a more sober note.

"If she should turn out to be the one, I'll have to remind him of something he said to me on our ride."

"What was that?"

"I asked him if he'd ever really tried to find the right woman. He said no. If she didn't come along in the scheme of things like your mother or Laurel, then he'd just as soon stick to racing."

"I can relate." Nate let out a troubled sigh. "If Audra only knew it, Rick's every bit as fragile as she is."

"No matter what happens, I'm glad he's out there."

Nate picked up on a different nuance in his father's voice. "What's going on?"

"At dinner the other day she told her cousins she'd like to stay in the bungalow until her cast comes off. Now they've given her an ultimatum. They want her out by tomorrow evening."

As his father explained the details, Nate's mouth thinned in anger. "Rick will put a stop to that."

"I'm sure he will."

"Dad, if you need reinforcements, I'll be there."

"I know that, but these are early days. You've got a job to do training pilots. Once the boys cool off, everything's going to be fine."

By now Nate was on his feet. "What if you're wrong and it doesn't get better?"

The whole situation was surreal. Like one of those range wars in an old western, where the good guys had to round up a posse to chase after the bad guys.

"Then I'll deal with it."

"I don't know."

"According to Pam, this is nothing new."

"Yes, it is. You bought the family home. You're a live target, Dad. One angry man can cause trouble. Three angry men can start a revolution."

"They can try…"

When Nate was a boy, the steel in his father's voice as he delivered a righteous rebuke could shape him up in a hurry. It still could. Hopefully it would put the fear in Pam's cousins.

"Promise you'll call me tomorrow and keep me posted on everything?"

"Of course."

"If I don't hear from you, Laurel and I will be flying down to find out why. Good night."

He clicked off and felt a pair of arms slide around him from behind. "What's wrong, darling?"

He turned to the woman who'd transformed his life. "I'm afraid all hell's about to break loose on the Jarrett Ranch."

WHILE AUDRA had been playing her guitar for Rick in the semidarkness, the pain pill seemed to have done its job. He lay on the twin bed with his eyes closed. When she listened to his breathing, it sounded as if he'd finally passed out.

But like a baby you thought had gone to sleep but cries to be held again the second you walk away, she decided not to chance it.

"I'll play one more song. Then it's time to sleep." She turned on her backup tape and picked up her guitar. "This one's called 'You Should Have Asked Your Mama.'"

You should have asked your mama,
Before he played you for a fool.
She would have told you, darlin'?
In the end they're always cruel.
Never trust a man,
Who looks deep into your eyes.
He's setting you up,
To believe all his fancy lies.
Always walk away,
From his devil-may-care smile.
Cut a swath around him,
That's at least a country mile.
Don't try to find him,
Where he says he's going to be,
'Cuz tonight he's somewhere else,
You just wait and see.
He doesn't love you, doesn't want you, doesn't
need you desperately.
It's a story, it's a myth,
One you made up in your heart.
It's a painful fabrication,
Of which he has no part.
You're forgotten, you're a joke,
You're a fire without the smoke.
Are you starting to understand?
You can't clap without a hand.
You should have asked your mama,
Before he played you for a fool.
She would have told you, darlin'?
In the end they're always cruel.

Carefully lowering her guitar to the other twin bed,
she shut everything down, then slid off the stool and

reached for her crutches. Halfway out the door she heard, ''Who hurt you that badly, Audra?''

She kept on walking to her bedroom. She didn't want to talk about Boris. He hadn't mattered to her for a long time.

After getting ready for bed, she lay down on top of the sheet in her black-and-white prison-striped, oversize nightshirt.

Before she'd started singing for Rick, she'd placed ice water and a couple of pain pills on the nightstand near his right hand. Though she doubted he'd need anything else, she left her door open to listen for him.

As she lay there, her mind played over the day's events for what seemed like hours. She couldn't shake off the feeling that when Rick had first seen Pam and Clint together, his pain had gone marrow deep.

Audra's mother and father were a vague memory. She had no idea what it would feel like to see her father kissing another woman. But the look in Rick's eyes, the tremor in his voice, all had given her a strong idea of what that experience would be like. The sense of betrayal had to have been of staggering proportions.

That was what Pam had tried to tell Audra. No wonder her cousin had been so frightened to get involved with Clint. But Audra had been too excited for her cousin. She hadn't understood.

What Clint's sons had gone through was far worse than Boris's betrayal of Audra. She'd only known him for a season. She hadn't loved him her whole life the way Rick and his brother had loved their parents.

Audra had written that song after coming home

from Europe. At the time, she'd believed she was hurting more than any other woman alive. With hindsight, she could see that Boris had needed to be admired by women who made him their whole world.

Audra had represented competition. He couldn't stand anyone making a fuss over her when he was around. She understood that now. In light of today's revelations, it seemed so trivial.

Her uncle's pain. Could anything have been worse than that? To lose his entire family...

What about Clint's pain? To learn that his beloved wife had died in an avalanche, when it was the snow that had brought them together?

How did Laurel Hawkins ever get over losing her first husband, whose jet malfunctioned and crashed? She'd been carrying his child...

Tonight Audra felt as if she'd received a university education in the study of bereavement. Exhausted under the weight of it, her eyes closed. The next time she was aware of her surroundings, she heard a banging sound followed by a man's groan coming from the hall.

Rick.

Her heart started to run away with her. "Rick," she cried out. "I'm coming!"

She grabbed for one crutch and got up from the bed. As soon as she reached the hall, she turned on the light.

"Audra?" With his free hand against the wall, he stood there weaving in place. "I'm sorry to have wakened you. I thought I was still in the master bedroom.

When I got up to use the bathroom, I couldn't find it.''

"I shouldn't have let you fall asleep in there. You're on heavy pain medication. No wonder you became disoriented." She took the few steps necessary to reach him and grasped his hand. "Come on."

When she'd first seen Rick Hawkins looming over her bed after her nightmare, she couldn't have imagined the day coming when she would be leading him around like a helpless child. He must have taken both pills at once to produce this unsteady state.

She turned on his bedroom light, then the bathroom switch.

He went inside and shut the door.

Audra puffed his pillows while she waited. He finally emerged. Ignoring her proffered hand, he made it to the bed on his own power and stretched out with a deep sigh.

The room was cooler now. She pulled the covers over his sling to his shoulders. "I'll bring you some ice water."

"I don't want any. Stay and talk to me."

"You need to go back to sleep. It's the middle of the night."

"No, it isn't. The clock on the bedside table says ten after seven."

Audra couldn't believe it was morning already.

"Sit next to me. There's room."

She'd offered her services as his nurse. If he needed company, she had no choice but to give it to him. Resting her crutches against the bed, she sank onto the edge, extending her leg.

When she turned to look at him, she was met by the full brunt of his male appraisal. Her whole body began to tremble.

"For a second in the hall when the light went on, I thought I was looking at a giant bumblebee."

A chuckle escaped her. "You poor thing."

His warm gray eyes smiled at her. "Where did you get that?"

"Pam made it for me. It's one of her more colorful masterpieces. Don't tell your father, but I think she's making pajamas for him out of the same material for his next birthday."

Laughter burst out of Rick. "I want a pair, too."

"I'll see what I can arrange. If she's got enough material, she can do up a pair for your brother as well. You're both the same size."

"Our mother used to dress us like twins when we were little. How did you know that about Nate?"

Heat stormed her cheeks. "Pam's marriage photos."

"You should have been there," he said in a low voice. "You and your uncle."

The mention of the wedding seemed to chase their lighthearted rapport away.

She bowed her head. "Pam didn't want anyone around in case your father woke up the next day and regretted what he'd done."

His hand covered hers and remained in place. It was a strong masculine hand whose touch sent a current of electricity through her system.

"What he felt for her was so intense, he had to act

on his feelings even though he knew it might hurt Nate and me for a time.''

''I've been thinking about it all night, how painful that experience was for you.''

''Are you saying you never went to sleep?''

At the question, her head lifted.

''Is that the reason I didn't hear you having one of your nightmares? Or was I too drugged to be aware of anything?''

She gazed at him in shock. ''I *did* sleep, but I didn't have a nightmare.''

''Have you suffered nightmares every night since the accident?''

''No. Sometimes I don't dream.''

''Well, let's be thankful last night was one of those times.'' His fingers squeezed hers gently before letting them go.

''I had a racing buddy who kept dreaming about an accident he'd been in. The dreams stopped after he went home to his family and stayed with them for a while. If having another body around here has relieved your subconscious for one night, then I'm glad I'm here.''

''I am, too,'' she said honestly. ''You're more open than your father. He and Pam are so alike in the way they hold everything inside. You have to wait and wait until they're ready to disclose what they're thinking and feeling. They won't be pushed.''

''You've just touched on the one area that has driven me and Nate crazy over the years.''

''You weren't alone. I've always had to bide my time with Pam. There've been moments when I thought I'd go mad. Talking with you has helped me understand their relationship much better than before.''

His eyes narrowed on her features. ''I had very little understanding of much of anything until I came here. Knowing what I know now, nothing could have made me miss this trip.''

She darted him a teasing glance. ''That's your painkillers talking. When they've worn off, you'll be singing a different tune.''

A moment of quiet followed her comment.

''Last night you brushed it off, so I'm going to tell you again. Like my mother, I've been a music lover all my life. I know talent when I hear it. There's no question you've got one of the greatest voices I've ever heard. You're very versatile.

''One minute, you're an angel playing her harp, singing heavenly music in a cathedral. In the next, you're a crooner right out of Nashville, with words pouring straight from your heart. The nurse at the hospital told me everyone listens to your show, and no wonder. I want to hear how it all began. Don't leave anything out.''

No no no, Audra. Don't be flattered by his compliments. Don't answer his questions. This is how it all got started before. Don't get sucked in. He knows how to play you because he's bored and missing his latest woman.

Of course he had a woman out there somewhere. But he'd gotten sidetracked here visiting his father. Naturally he had to get better first before he returned to her and the life he'd been living for over a decade.

Audra felt for her crutch and got to her feet. "It's not a topic for seven-thirty in the morning. Maybe later when we've both had more sleep. I'm going to bring you fresh ice water and your pills. What else would you like before I go back to bed?"

"How about handing me my phone?"

"That's easy."

She opened the drawer and put it in his hand.

Yup. The Racetrack Lover was definitely coming back to life. What kind of woman captured the attention of a man like Rick Hawkins for longer than a day, or a week, or even a few months?

"Thank you, Audra."

She avoided looking in his eyes. "You're welcome. I'll be right back."

"Do you have any peanut butter?"

She paused midstride. "I think so. Do you like jam or honey on your sandwich?"

"Honey, of course."

"Of course." She chuckled.

"Make that two sandwiches and a glass of milk."

After a couple of trips, she'd brought him everything he needed and told him to call out to her the next time he wanted anything else.

"That works both ways," he murmured.

"I'm taking care of *you,* remember?"

He'd already devoured one sandwich. "I haven't forgotten anything. Not even the fact that your cousins will be showing up sometime today."

THEY CAME at three in the afternoon.

Audra had run a bath for him. Low enough not to

reach his sling. Warm enough to make him feel human again. The aroma of a roast cooking in the oven had him salivating.

He'd just dried off and pulled on a clean pair of gray sweats when he heard the sound of trucks rolling in at the side of the house. Doors slammed.

This was something Rick would have to play by ear. He wouldn't interfere unless he was forced to. On the way out of the bedroom he reached for his cell phone.

"It looks like you've got company," he said when he met Audra in the hallway. She'd just come out of her room on both crutches, dressed in a white top and flowered skirt.

Her curls were still damp from her shower. He detected the scent of peaches. Could there be a sweeter smell from a sweeter woman?

Rick followed her to the living room. He could hear the sound of someone jostling the handle of the front door. No one had bothered to knock.

He sent her a questioning glance. "Do they have a key?"

"No. After Pam finished decorating out here, she had the locks changed."

"Then the boys have assumed you've done their bidding. Let's find out how far they're willing to go to get in. Why don't we sit down on the couch."

She obliged by finding a place at one end of the couch. Fortunately it was the good end because it allowed him to sit next to her and slide his right arm behind her.

Her body stiffened. "What are you doing?"

He smiled to himself. "Getting comfortable."

"Doesn't that hurt your collarbone?" If he wasn't mistaken, there was a tremor in her voice.

Rick had forgotten all about his pain. In truth, it wasn't as severe today. "I'm feeling fine."

More sounds ensued. One of the men was picking at the lock.

Right now Audra reminded him of Marshmallow, who'd continued to shiver and tremble after her nasty fall in the creek. Rick kneaded her shoulder to gentle her. The skin felt warm and alive beneath the cotton fabric of her top.

A minute later the front door swung open. Four men entered the room, one in overalls with a sign on the pocket that read Don's Lock and Key.

Four pairs of eyes rounded in astonishment.

Rick stayed where he was and made certain Audra didn't move. "I thought everyone knew it was against the law to break and enter a private dwelling."

"This is our house," Tom blurted. "We thought Audra had moved out."

He flashed Tom a wintry smile. "She owns this house, too, and has been living here. You should have knocked first. Don here is witness to the fact that you didn't. An attorney will use that in a court of law against you boys."

The other man seemed to consider his options, then he walked back outside. Pretty soon an engine started up.

One down. Three to go.

"Seven people in the living room of the main house on Thursday evening, three of whom are in this room, will have to testify under oath that Audra stated she wouldn't be moving out until her cast came off. Isn't that right, Jim? Greg?''

They both looked taken aback. After a long hesitation, they filed out the door.

Good. Two more down. In another minute two more engines fired.

Tom's stance remained aggressive. "This has nothing to do with you, pretty boy."

"Tom—" Audra half gasped her cousin's name.

Rick rose to his full height. "Since I'm a guest in this house and we're in front of a lady, I'll let that slide…for now."

"You're hiding behind her skirts and you know it!"

"Shall we step outside to finish this conversation? Don't let my injury worry you."

"Go to hell!"

Tom stormed out, slamming the door behind him. Rick waited until he heard the rev of an engine followed by the squeal of tires. Before long, the truck was barreling down the road.

When quiet reigned, he turned to Audra, who'd gotten to her feet, hugging her crutches. She'd lost some color.

"I don't think they'll be back anytime soon."

"Tom's behavior is terrifying," she whispered. "What if he and the boys decide to take this out on Pam and Clint?"

"I'm calling them now."

He pushed the button for the preprogrammed number. His father picked up on the second ring.

"I've been waiting for your call. The boys were here earlier to transport the horses. I figured they'd head over to the bungalow when they'd returned the horse trailer. Just now I saw the third truck pass in front of the ranch house. Tom was going at a maniacal clip toward the highway."

Rick turned his back on Audra and headed down the hall for his bedroom. "The boys are out for bear, Dad. They brought along a locksmith to get inside and found us sitting in the living room."

"That's breaking and entering."

"Exactly. I threatened them with a lawsuit. They didn't have a leg to stand on, not when the locksmith took off after he realized he could be called as a material witness."

"It's clear Tom's out of control," his father mused aloud. "Unfortunately he's the one who initiates all the trouble. Greg and Jim only do what they're told."

"They bolted on the heels of the locksmith."

"That's not surprising."

"You can bet they're huddled somewhere with Tom while they plan their next move. Audra's petrified."

"I don't like it either, especially when the new owner is coming next week. Since the boys have proved they're willing to hurt the people I love, it's time to get an attorney and start documenting everything. One more violation and I'll take them to court. First thing in the morning I'll get on it."

"Let me know how I can help."

"You already have by simply being here. Let's be thankful David was out of firing range."

"Agreed. Thanks, Dad." He clicked off.

As far as Rick was concerned, it was time to bring in a security man. Someone who needed work and had a vested interest in what was going on at the Jarrett Ranch.

No doubt David had entertained the same thought when he'd asked Rick if he wanted a job.

What was it? To provide company and protect Audra while he recuperated?

In another twenty-four hours Rick would be strong enough to walk around the bungalow after dark and keep an eye on things. Give him another few days and he'd be able to check out both houses and the barn during the night with no one the wiser.

For the first time since he could remember, Rick felt useful.

Being a driver for Mayada was good honest work. He derived great satisfaction when he placed in the number one or two spot in a race.

There was a certain pleasure in knowing he ranked high as a Formula One driver among his peers. Many enjoyable moments had been spent with crew chief Wally Sykes, who'd become a lifetime friend.

He'd be a liar if he didn't admit it felt good to know his financial situation would take care of him for life if he were unable to work again.

There was no way to deny that until his midtwenties, the perks of traveling around the world, of being presented to kings, queens, dignitaries, of dining with the rich and famous, of dating beautiful women had gone to his head.

But taking all that into consideration, he'd never

felt that what he'd done with his life counted for anything significant.

He'd never felt needed before.

Not until Audra had trembled in his arms out of fear.

He couldn't comprehend the years of abuse she and Pam and their uncle had suffered.

Rick had never known abuse. He'd been raised with gentility and grace. His noble parents had made his world safe and beautiful. He'd been loved, and he'd been able to give love in return. No two brothers could be closer.

He felt his eyes prickle beneath their lids.

The boys' heinous treatment of the Jarrett family was an offense to him. He couldn't, wouldn't tolerate it.

No more abuse. Today marked the end of it.

CHAPTER EIGHT

RICK ATE three helpings of beef tenderloin roast along with some roast potatoes and carrots. Audra toyed with her food. The shock of realizing her cousins held nothing in reverence had broken something inside her.

After dinner he didn't argue with her when she suggested he go back to his bedroom and lie down. She turned on the television and handed him the remote. He flicked to a station showing highlights of a pro golf tournament while he rested on the bed.

She wondered if he played the game or simply enjoyed watching it. There were a lot of things she wondered about where he was concerned. Too many things.

The way her patient had dealt with the break-in filled her with awe. Three riled-up, adrenaline-driven members of her family ready to have their way had been thwarted by a man who had used his brain and kept a cool head.

Rick Hawkins wasn't one of the top race-car drivers in the world for nothing. He'd sat down next to her. She'd felt his arm go around her shoulders in a protective gesture.

Audra would have known if that invincible exterior he'd presented to her cousins had been a mere facade.

In an instant, she would have detected any sudden change in heart rate or breathing.

He'd been as calm as a beautiful spring morning.

Her admiration of him was beginning to make her panic.

Out in the kitchen she put the little bit of leftover roast into the fridge. She could make Rick a sandwich with it tomorrow. Once the dishes were done, she returned to his room with ice water and another pill.

"Call out if you need me," she said, avoiding his eyes. "I'll be in the other room planning my radio show for tomorrow night."

It was a good thing she had a job that required a certain amount of preparation. With three programs to do next week, her mind was kept occupied. She worked undisturbed until eleven-thirty.

On her way to bed she peeked in on Rick. At some point he'd turned off the TV and was sound asleep. After the shock his system had received because of his accident, he needed rest more than anything else.

For the time being, her greatest fear was that she'd have a nightmare and wake him up. Anxious, she swung herself across the room to look out the window. The moon had come up. If she didn't have this cast, she'd saddle Prince and go for a ride.

Once the cast came off, she assumed she'd be able to do all the activities she'd done before the crash. Except for telling her she'd have to go for some physical therapy, the doctor hadn't said whether there would be restrictions.

So far she'd been afraid to ask....

On the Internet she'd read that when your leg had

to be pinned, you could end up walking with a limp. Not always, but sometimes.

She could hear her cousins' hateful, mocking voices. ''There goes old maid Red with her gimp leg!''

Though it had been years since she cared what they thought or said about her, she did worry about performing in public if her leg dragged as she walked out on stage.

Before the crash, she'd committed to doing a four-week tour with her harp ensemble group starting mid-July.

Her boss at the radio station had told her they would repeat some of her older shows during her absence.

Along with scheduled performances with the Utah Symphony, the Denver Philharmonic and the Los Angeles Philharmonic, she and the other harpists would be doing a series of summer concerts at The Canyons in Utah, Red Rock in Colorado and the Hollywood Bowl in California.

Though her colleagues would tell her it didn't matter, she would hate to be singled out as the one in the group of four harpists who was different. No matter what, when you saw someone who limped, you wondered why.

A harpist would arouse even more speculation because of her body's attitude while playing her instrument. So much for blending in with the others.

But maybe she was getting ahead of herself.

Part of her was ashamed for her thoughts. She knew she should be thankful she still had her leg.

She *was* thankful.

God knew she was. She'd been talking to him non-stop about it for a long time now.

Next Sunday she would ask Pam to drive her to church over in Hill Grove where she'd been attending for years along with Uncle David and Pam. She felt well enough to start resuming her normal activities.

Many of the people in the congregation, including the pastor and his wife, had brought in food and sent flowers when they'd heard about her accident.

They'd prayed for her. It had touched her heart. She'd sent out thank-you notes, but she was eager to express her gratitude in person.

After expelling a sigh, she turned from the window determined to get back in her old habits. First thing tomorrow she would start practicing for her tour. A half hour twice a day. She would build from there so she'd be ready.

Filled with resolve to stay so busy she wouldn't have time to think about Rick Hawkins and how he made her feel, she lay down without that accompanying sense of dread for the night ahead.

RICK HAD EATEN a big lunch. While Audra was practicing on her harp, he'd decided to take a stroll around the bungalow to walk it off and do a little reconnaissance work.

Nothing seemed amiss at the moment.

The fact that Audra didn't have any nightmares again last night was a good omen. Since he'd only needed one pain pill in the last twelve hours, he was feeling more like his old self. The area around his collarbone and shoulder was still tender, but the pain wasn't nearly as intense as before. After the incident with the boys yesterday, he needed to keep a clear head.

It was a nice day out. Warm. A few high clouds.

When he came to Audra's bedroom window he could hear her playing and he paused to lounge against the bungalow's yellow siding and listen. His eyes closed, all the better to enjoy the piece.

Strange to think how during the many years he'd been immersed in the world of racing and everything that had led up to it, she'd spent the same amount of time out here on the ranch perfecting her musical talent. Neither of them had had any knowledge of the other's existence.

He'd enjoyed relationships with three women whom he'd come close to marrying, most recently, Natalie. But he could never bring himself to propose. Now that he'd met Audra, he knew why....

As different as each woman had been, there was one drawback they'd had in common. They didn't have lives of their own. They'd lived for Rick to make them happy.

No person could do that for another person. In the end, he'd been forced to walk away.

None of those three women were like Audra, who had every reason to be needy and look to someone else for all the answers. Yet she found joy from within despite personal tragedy and sorrow. In that joy lay her great strength and charm. Her compassion for others.

Deep in contemplation, he hadn't realized a car had

pulled into the driveway until he heard a door slam. His eyes opened in time to see a guy close to his age, maybe a little younger, walk toward her front porch. He was dressed in shirtsleeves and jeans.

Someone else sent by Tom and the gang?

Rick moved fast to intercept him. Closer to the vehicle now, he saw that the sandy-haired stranger was driving a rental car.

"Can I do something for you?"

The other man turned in Rick's direction, taking in the sling securing his arm. "I hope so. I'm Hal Torney, Ed Torney's son, the man who bought the Jarrett property."

In a few steps Rick reached him. "My name's Rick Hawkins." They shook hands. "I'm the son of Clint Hawkins, the man who's married to Pam Jarrett. They own the main ranch house. We heard your dad would be coming sometime this week."

The guy nodded. He stood about six feet, with a golfer's build. "Dad asked me to take a look around and make certain everything's a go for me to fly him in on Wednesday. He'll be bringing an architect with him. No one answered the door at the main house, so I drove here. I need someone to show me the location of the hangar and runway area."

Rick's father and Pam could be anywhere. "Are you a commercial pilot?"

He flashed Rick a friendly smile. "Not yet. I'm logging all the hours I can get and then some. While I'm here, I'd like to check out the plane."

Before Rick could respond, Audra emerged from

the house and stood on the front porch with her crutches.

"Hello," she said. "I heard voices. Can I help you?"

Rick didn't like the way the guy's brown eyes lingered on her face and figure. She was dressed in a simple white skirt and pale orange top. Her feminine appeal stuck out a mile.

"Hi."

Just the way he said the word caused Rick's teeth to clench. It sent pain down to his collarbone.

"I'm Hal Torney, the son of the new owner. I was just telling Mr. Hawkins I'm here to take a look at the plane and check things out before I fly Dad in on Wednesday."

"So *you're* the pilot."

"That's right." He grinned.

"I'm Audra Jarrett, David Jarrett's niece. My cousins and I own this bungalow and the adjacent property."

"Do you live here all the time?" The other man looked hopeful.

"No," Rick answered before Audra could. He flashed her a benign smile. "Hal was just telling me they're bringing an architect with them."

Audra's pleasant expression didn't change, but he knew what she was feeling inside. The Windshield Rancher had arrived, shattering her world.

"I see. If you'll give me a moment, I'll get the keys and drive with you out to the south thirty."

"Great."

This was a job for Pam, but Rick knew Audra

would never disturb her cousin. Pam and Clint weren't home anyway. Since Rick had no intention of letting her be alone with the guy, he walked over to the rental car and got in the back seat.

"*You* can't come," Audra cried when she approached the car a minute later and saw Rick already there. "It could jar your bones and do damage all over again."

"I'll chance it," he murmured. In truth, he was taped so securely, it would take another fall to injure him again. "If you're able to ride out there in your cast without a problem, then I'm in no danger either. Hand me your crutches, Audra."

He'd left her little choice but to comply. He used his right hand to lay them across his lap.

Hal Torney closed her door, then walked around to the driver's side and got in.

Rick didn't know where in the hell the south thirty was, but he intended to find out, and now was as good a time as any. Part of his new security job was to learn everything he could pertaining to the Jarrett property.

The next half hour turned out to be instructional. Audra explained the lay of the land as they drove along. The road they were driving on was the public access road and dividing line between their ranch and the Tilsons' who owned the Circle T to the left. All the fenced property on the right between the two ranch houses was Jarrett property. It went as deep as the farthest edge of the bluebonnets. The seven hundred and eighty acres of land beyond the carpet of flowers comprised the south thirty. A hangar that looked to be in excellent repair sat on a flat piece of ground at the west boundary, where another Jarrett ranch house had once stood before the tornado had obliterated it.

While Audra undid the lock, Rick walked around the grassy runway near the hangar, contemplating what the devastation would have been like.

Once she showed the other man inside, Rick followed at a distance. There sat David's four-seater Cessna.

Not too long ago he'd flown Rick's father to Odessa in this plane so he could make the commercial flight to Denver and beat Nate home from Philadelphia.

What a night that had been. Thanks to David, Clint had been waiting at the airport to talk sense into Nate, who'd just broken his engagement to Laurel. It was a talk that had changed the course of history for Rick's only brother. He was now a happily married man.

"Everything looks great," Rick heard the guy say as he jumped down from the plane.

"This was my uncle's pride and joy."

"You can tell that by the way he's kept everything in perfect order. Did you like to fly with him?"

"I loved it."

The tremor in her voice tore at Rick's heart.

"When that cast comes off, I'd love to take you up in the Cessna. In the meantime, how would you like to go to dinner with Dad and me in Austin on Wednesday night? We want to be friends with our new neighbors. Later on, you'll meet the rest of the family.''

"How many of you are there?"

''My parents have five children. I'm the youngest. They're all married except for me, but everyone will be flying in for visits once the house is built. I'll be living with them for a time.'' His eyes swept over her again. ''So, what about dinner?''

Rick's right hand tightened into a fist. He knew exactly what Hal Torney was after. The man didn't waste any time.

''That's very nice of you, Hal. Can I take a rain check? I'm a disc jockey and do a radio broadcast from the ranch at night.''

"You're kidding!"

"No."

''*That* I've got to hear.''

''Until my cast comes off, my doctor doesn't want me driving long distances to do my show.''

"In fact, your doctor wouldn't have approved of your riding this far and back,'' Rick asserted. Audra darted him a surprised glance. ''You should be home resting that leg.''

Her chin lifted. ''If anyone should be in bed, it's you.'' She turned to the other man. ''Rick was barely released from the hospital after suffering a broken collarbone.''

''That's no fun,'' Hal said, but he continued to stare at her. ''How did you break your leg?''

''I'm afraid it'll have to wait for another time,'' Rick muttered. ''We both need our rest. You understand, don't you, Hal?''

"Sure."

Rick forced the other guy, clearly miffed, to walk outside with him while Audra locked up.

On their drive back to the bungalow, he waited for Hal to say something about the bluebonnets. Though the flowers had reached their peak last week, they were still a beautiful sight.

People came to Texas from all over the U.S. to see the bluebonnets in spring, yet the other man made no comment. Rick imagined Audra was waiting for Hal to make a remark about them, too, but he never did.

When he pulled to a stop in the driveway, Audra turned to him with an enigmatic look. "You take the keys, Hal. These are extras, but they belong to your family now."

Hal could have no understanding of what was going on inside of Audra, but Rick knew. He got out of the car and opened her door before Ed's son could come around.

"It was nice to meet you, Hal," Rick said as he handed Audra her crutches. He could tell the man was hoping to be invited inside the house. "Enjoy your flight back to Cleveland."

"Thanks." He didn't sound as friendly as before.

His gaze swerved to Audra. "I'll see you again soon then."

Rick had to give him credit for making one last stab at contact with her.

Audra nodded, causing her dark red curls to bounce. The overwhelming urge to fill his fingers with them and draw her into his arms drove Rick to start for the porch first.

Behind him he heard Audra say goodbye to their visitor.

Rick held the front door open for her. The second she'd swung herself past him, she headed straight for her bedroom. He closed the door and followed her.

"What do you think you're doing?" she demanded when he appeared at her door before she could close it.

"I thought you might like a friend to talk to. It isn't every day you give up the keys to your past life."

Her lower lip quivered, the only outward sign of the turmoil within.

"I've been doing it in my mind for a long time."

"I know. I heard your song," he murmured. "But no matter how hard we try to anticipate something terrible, we're never truly prepared for the dreaded moment until it arrives."

Without asking her permission, he took the few steps to reach her and gathered her against him with his good arm, crutches and all. His chin sank into her fragrant curls.

He absorbed the tremors from her body, though she never made a sound.

"Now I know another reason why Uncle David went to stay at the club. He couldn't face going out there a second time."

"No. He left his brave little Audra to handle it with her usual grace."

"I don't have any more brave left in me."

"Yes, you do," he whispered in the silk of her hair. "You're the strongest woman I know."

RICK MADE the word *strong* sound beautiful.

She didn't dare listen to anything else he had to say.

She didn't dare stay folded in his arm like this. She would start to like it too much.

She already did like it too much.

One day soon he'd be going away. Only a fool would pretend otherwise. Audra had been a fool once before. Never again.

She moved her right crutch to take the necessary steps away from him. "Thanks for the shoulder to cry on." She smiled up at him. "Now I think it's time you were back in bed."

"I admit I'm tired. How about a game of poker before I fall asleep?"

His suggestion was exactly what she needed to shake off certain tormenting thoughts. "Are you a good loser?" she teased.

"No."

Audra chuckled. "I should have known better than to ask Lucky Hawkins a question like that."

His white smile caught her by surprise. She felt like the time Prince missed a fence and she flew over his head into a patch of wild strawberries.

"The cards are in the kitchen. I'll look for them while you get settled in your room. Do you want me to bring you anything else? A—"

"Cola."

They'd both said the word at the same time and laughed.

"What stakes are we playing for?" he asked a few

minutes later. She'd seated herself on the side of his bed to rest her leg.

"You're the patient. I'll let you decide."

"If I win, you have to promise never to go flying with Hal Torney."

Audra lifted her head. She studied him briefly. "You don't need to win for me to make a promise like that. Uncle David is the only person I trust to take me up in a small plane."

"Good."

They started playing.

"You were kind of hard on Hal."

"I was?"

"You know you were." She couldn't stop herself from smiling.

"He's not your type."

"How do you know that?"

"I can't see you being attracted to a man whose interest in checking you out along with the property was greater than his concern over your leg."

Don't say any more, Rick.

She looked down at the hand she'd been dealt.

"When did your uncle learn to fly?"

"He was a pilot in Korea."

"Nate's going to have to meet him. They'll be swapping stories into the night."

"That's what Clint said."

"My father knows a lot more about you than I do. I think I'm jealous. Why don't you tell me about the beginnings of Audra Jarrett? I want to know when your uncle discovered he had such a talented niece."

Rick had asked her that question once before. She

supposed she couldn't avoid answering it a second time.

"Pam's mother insisted all of her children take piano lessons. I think Pam started when she was about seven years old. She's the talented pianist in the family."

"Is my dad aware of that?"

"I'm sure Uncle David made her perform in front of him, but she'd be the last person to show off. After the tornado, he bought her the baby grand. She gave lessons to some of the kids in the area and taught me to play. The boys refused."

"Did you like it?"

"Um, so-so. When the grade school started a music program for children who were interested, Pam encouraged me to learn to play another instrument, too. She could see I wasn't that enchanted with piano."

Rick smiled. "My folks had an upright they kept in a basement room they called the music room. There's still an old set of drums Nate thought he wanted and then didn't. I'm afraid neither of us showed promise."

"A lot of people tell the same story. Anyway, I tried a variety of instruments and ended up enjoying violin the most. In junior high I signed up for orchestra. Uncle David insisted I join the choral group, too. He always liked to sing and thought it important that everyone did. I guess my teacher thought I had a natural singing voice and she told the family I should take private lessons."

"Did you?"

Rick's flattering attention was going to get her into trouble.

"No. By that time I was listening to country music like all my friends. I wanted to learn how to play guitar, so the teacher who taught orchestra and band let me use his old electric guitar to fool around with at home."

"Did you ever get formal training on the guitar?"

"No."

He shook his head. "You're unbelievable."

"Uncle David and Pam didn't know what to make of me. I still practiced my violin and did my chores. When it was time for bed, I went up to the attic with the guitar. I'd hook it up and then work out harmonies while I listened to the country and rock stations on the radio. The lyrics could be pretty heart-wrenching sometimes. I found myself making up my own songs just for the fun of it."

She eyed Rick. "Your father told me you did the same thing. You'd hibernate in the garage after dark, no matter how freezing it was. I understand you bought a little heater with the money you earned from doing chores, and then you'd work on your go-cart while you listened to Mozart."

His eyes softened. "Let's stick to you for now. I want to hear the rest."

"The rest, huh?" She sighed. "My freshman year in high school the orchestra and a cappella students went on a field trip by bus to attend a performance of the Austin Symphony Orchestra. My world changed that day. I heard Saint-Saën's *The Swan*. It was a composition for harp and violin."

"I know the piece," Rick replied. "It was one of my mother's favorites."

Audra nodded. "It became mine. As soon as I got home, I told Pam and Uncle David I wanted to stop the violin and take harp lessons. I promised to earn all the money myself and do whatever I had to do because I knew the harp was my instrument. Pam arranged to drive me into Austin twice a week for lessons with a local harpist. The first time I was able to play a piece, the experience was magical. The only thing I can liken it to would be the way you must have felt when you suited up, sat in a real race car and did a few laps around the track."

"You mean like you'd died and gone to heaven?" His facial expression reflected that moment of epiphany.

"Yes. That's exactly how it felt. I wanted to play the harp all the time and made arrangements to rent one. A month before my graduation, my uncle bought me my own harp."

Her eyes filled. "You'll never know how much it meant to me."

"I think I do," he said in a low voice. "He believed in you and wanted you to know it."

Audra sniffed. "I played a harp solo on it at my graduation. It was Debussy's *Girl With the Flaxen Hair.*

"My harp teacher was in the audience and she'd brought a friend with her, Clea Marks. Clea played the harp with the Austin Symphony Orchestra and was a faculty member in the fine arts department at the University of Texas at Austin.

"After hearing me play, it was decided Clea would

start giving me lessons in her spare time. So I attended the university in Austin and received my fine arts degree. We became very good friends.''

''That happens with a special mentor,'' Rick mused aloud. ''I had one in my crew chief, Wally. He'd been a racer. He knew the ropes, and knew how to help me.''

''Clea was wonderful in that same way. She urged me to continue studying harp at the Paris Conservatory.''

''How long were you in France?'' He acted as if he really wanted to know.

''Two years.''

''We would have been there at the same time. I was in Europe for a lot of races. When I had time off, I often went to concerts. I must have been in Paris at least six or seven times to hear various performances.''

She stared at him. ''Do I dare admit I've never been to a Formula One race?''

''Dare all you want. What you were doing with your time couldn't be compared to watching a bunch of testosterone-filled drivers try to beat each other around a track with the fastest time.''

''It's all important if it's what you *have* to do with your life, Rick. Of course, I didn't spend every second of my time studying music,'' she admitted.

When she thought of Boris now, it didn't hurt.

Before Rick could jump in with the one question she didn't want to answer, she said, ''Upon my return home, Clea asked me to join her harp ensemble.

''She was friends with two other renowned harpists

from New York and Boston. The four of us did some television appearances that aired nationally. Last summer we went on a summer concert tour back East. A local radio station host in Austin did an in-depth interview with me and Clea over the air before we left.''

Rick crossed one ankle over the other. ''He knew he'd struck pure gold. I bet the second the broadcast ended, the owner hit you up with a radio spot of your own and a monetary offer you couldn't refuse.''

Her cheeks went warm. ''Something like that.''

''Have you made your own CDs to sell?''

''Only for the listeners when they call in and request one. My boss insists on having some available.''

''How many agents have come along begging you to let them make you a film star?''

''Oh, three or four,'' she teased. ''But that was before my accident. The camera wouldn't be kind to a gal with a gimp leg.'' She winked at him before reaching for her crutches.

His expression sobered. ''When's your next tour with the ensemble?''

''This summer, provided I've finished my physical therapy by then.'' She got off the bed and gathered the cards.

''What are you doing? We haven't had our poker game yet.''

''Your eyelids are fluttering like a baby's. All this talk about my job has reminded me I've got to phone the station manager before I do my program tonight. I'll wake you for dinner. Go to sleep.''

''I will on one condition.''

''What's that?''

''Put on a CD of you playing *Girl With the Flaxen Hair*.''

''I'll see what I can do.''

CHAPTER NINE

"THIS IS 580 on your AM dial, the Hill Country station out of Austin. You're listening to the *Red Jarrett Show* and I'm taking requests. My producer, Jack, tells me Theresa is on the line. Hi, Theresa."

"Hi, Red. You have a super show."

"Thank you."

"Man, it's been hard to get in. We've tried since Christmas. Anyway, my friends and I were closing up the restaurant a long time back and you sang a great song called 'Hey Wanda? Bring The Blue Plate Special.' We'd all like to hear it again, and we want to know if we can order it on CD."

"You bet. Stay on the line and the producer will tell you how to get it. What's the name of your restaurant?"

"The Longhorn Steak and Grill."

"I've eaten there. Great steaks by the way. Don't you serve those nummy little deep-fried mashed-potato balls?"

"Yes ma'am. The chef's going to love it that you remembered."

"They're *good*."

Rick grinned at the way Audra exaggerated the word *good* with that sexy Texas accent. He'd been lying on one of the twin beds watching her do her show. He never wanted her to stop.

"This song is dedicated to all of you hardworking people at the Longhorn."

He watched her pick up her guitar and put in a backup tape. While she was occupied, he kept pressing the redial button on his phone to get the station.

It was only quarter after twelve. He was starting early because he had a request of his own to make. In case he got through, he'd opened his wallet to pull out his credit card and another card with some addresses and telephone numbers on it.

Hey Wanda?
Bring the blue plate special,
I'm eating alone tonight.
Put me in the corner,
Away from all the light.

If anyone should ask for me,
You know what to say,
All I want's the blue plate special,
Everyone else just stay away.

Don't come any closer,
Don't sit down with me,
Don't tangle with me, honey,
Just leave me be.
I want the blue plate special,
Without the company.

Other guys have tried,
Much braver than you,
Save yourself the trouble,

I'll give you a clue.
I want the blue plate special,
I don't want you.

You don't want to be around me,
You don't know who I am,
You think you have the answers,
But honey, I don't give a damn.
I want the blue plate special,
Did you hear me? Scram!

Hey Wanda?
If anyone should ask for me,
You know what to say,
All I want's the blue plate special,
Everyone else just stay away.

Audra's songs not only came from the gut, they hit you in the gut. How many times after a race had Rick walked into a place to eat and just wanted to be left alone to think without some woman from the track coming up to his table to join him.

More than once when he'd been in a mood, whether reflective or foul, he'd paid a waiter or a waitress to find him a place in a corner well out of sight.

Audra, Audra.

Where have you been all my life?

Enchanted by the fabulous show she was putting on, he was stunned when he finally connected with the producer at the station. The time had almost gone and he hadn't noticed. It was quarter to three.

She hadn't looked at him the whole time. At the

moment, she was busy playing the taped commercials. With her headphones on, she had no idea what he was up to.

"You have a request for Red?"

"Yes. It's 'Racetrack Lover.' I'm Rick, the guy who had the accident on the horse."

"Oh yeah. I remember. I'll tell her. She didn't know if you were listening or not. This is going to make her day."

Audra knew now, but her reaction hadn't told him much at the time.

"I'd also like to order some CDs she's made."

"Hang on. After she takes your request, I'll get the information."

Rick was put on hold. He could hear Audra speaking into the mike.

"We're coming up on three o'clock. Time for one more request. My producer says...Rick is on the line."

Rick heard the slight pause before her shocked blue gaze darted to his from across the room.

"Hello, Rick."

"Hello, yourself." He'd never had this much fun in his life. "May I make a comment before you sing 'Racetrack Lover'?"

"Go ahead."

"Race-car drivers are just like other men. They have their good and bad qualities. They can be afraid and lonely. They want what every man wants."

"And what's that?"

"A chance to be understood."

"Did the listening audience catch what he said?

You've just heard from the living legend Lucky Hawkins, one of the greatest Formula One race-car drivers in the world.

"The station is honored you would call in, Rick. After such a frank confession, no one in the audience could accuse you of being like the racetrack lover in my song.

"May I take this opportunity to wish you a speedy recovery after your accident? Those who heard my program the other night learned that Rick's horse fell on him. He's out of commission at the moment, but not for long. One day soon we'll hear he's won the Laguna Seca for the fourth time."

His pulse started to race. How did she know about that unless she'd plied his father with questions?

Rick watched her reach for the guitar and put in another backup tape. While she let it rip, the producer started talking into the phone.

"I'm Jack, Audra's producer. I can't believe you're Rick Hawkins!" He sounded as excited as Brent Marsden did the first time they were introduced.

"I watch you race every chance I get. You're the best, man. Did you and Audra meet in Europe? Because if you did and she's been keeping this from us, she's in deep trouble. Our boss is a big fan of yours, too!"

"Thank you. Actually, Audra and I met very recently. It's a long story. I'm anxious to collect everything she's put on CD. Would you be willing to Express Mail whatever you've got?"

"I'll send it tomorrow. You'll have it Wednesday afternoon if you're within the U.S."

Rick gave him his father's address at the main ranch house.

"I'd like another set sent to a Nate Hawkins." He read off his brother's address in Colorado Springs, then gave Jack the credit card information.

"That's it. Don't be a stranger, Rick. Call in again anytime."

"I promise."

"Can I quote you on that to the boss?"

"You can." Most definitely you can.

He hung up in time to hear Audra say her closing comments before the show went off the air.

AUDRA REACHED for her crutches and stood up. She wasn't as exhausted as she'd been last week after doing her program.

By now Rick was on his feet. He moved faster than before. His color was good. The two patients were getting better.

"I didn't know you were a masochist," she said.

The corner of his mouth lifted. "You mean because I wanted to hear 'Racetrack Lover' again? I find I've developed a fondness for the song."

"You're a nice man, Rick Hawkins. Knowing your father, he couldn't have raised any other kind. Now it's time we were both in bed. Let's agree to sleep in. I'll fix us a big lunch."

"You'll get no complaints from me."

She followed him out of the room and turned off the light. "Can I bring you anything from the kitchen?"

"I was going to ask you the same question."

Audra shook her head. "All I want is sleep."

"In other words, the blue plate special."

She laughed. "Please don't take everything I say or do literally. I'm feeling bad enough to think I might have hurt your feelings when I wrote 'Race-track Lover.'"

"Maybe my pride took a little beating."

It was hard to tell if he was teasing or not. "Am I forgiven?"

"Do you want to be?"

What kind of question was that? "Of course."

"When we're both free of our restraints, how would you like to watch a Formula One race with me? Purely as spectators. I'll go incognito. We'll watch from the bleachers and you can ask me all the questions you want so you'll have some understanding of the sport. Understanding takes away fear."

Her heart gave a tremendous thud.

She knew all she needed to know about racing. It could kill a driver instantly. Rick planned to return to the sport the minute he got better.

The last thing she wanted to do was learn all about it from him. She would never know another moment's peace.

But what she said to him was, "Ask me that question again when we've both been given a clean bill of health from our doctors." By the time she'd finished her physical therapy, he'd be long gone.

His eyes had narrowed until she couldn't see the gray irises. "You can count on it. Good night, Audra. Your program was superb."

"Thank you for being such an appreciative audience."

He turned away from her and disappeared down the hall to his room.

Within five minutes she'd climbed into bed wearing a loose-fitting T-shirt and her cutoffs. After such a long day, she would sleep tonight.

Or so she'd thought.

When we're both free of our restraints, how would you like to watch a Formula One race with me? Purely as spectators. I'll go incognito. We'll watch from the bleachers and you can ask me all the questions you want so you'll have some understanding of the sport. Understanding takes away fear.

If Rick had asked her to go anywhere else but the racetrack, Audra would have been thrilled to her bones.

It was unfair of her to feel the way she did. She made her living through her music. He made his through racing. She'd shown him her world. He wanted to show her his.

No matter what the future held, their lives would always be connected because of Clint and Pam. It was critical for her and Rick to get along. He had understood that sooner. Being the more pragmatic of the two, he'd issued the invitation as an olive branch of sorts.

Being the more prickly of the two, Audra hadn't chosen to take hold of it. Not yet. Maybe not ever, she thought as her eyes closed.

"PAM? Did you see that crash? No— It's Rick— Help me get to him— Help me— So many people.

Let me through— I'm coming, Rick—it's Audra. Can you hear me?

"Rick— You're bleeding— Dear God, there's so much blood— Don't die, Rick— Please don't die.

"Somebody help him— He's trapped inside the car— Pull him out— Get him out— Don't let him die— I couldn't bear it— Someone save him, oh please God, save him— Rick—"

"Audra? I'm right here. I'm all right. Audra. Wake up."

She could hear Rick's voice reaching down inside her.

"Rick?"

"Yes, Audra. You were having a bad dream."

"It was a dream?" she cried. "It seemed so real. You were in this crash. Your race car rolled and landed upside down. No one could get to you, and—"

"I know, but it didn't happen. I'm here with you. Go back to sleep."

"I thought you were dead." She broke down sobbing. "You were trapped and your face looked so white—"

"It was just a dream. Shh." She felt his lips against her closed lids, her cheeks. He was real and alive. "I'm right here and I'm not going to leave you."

"Don't ever leave me—"

"No, Audra—I'll never do that."

WHAT ON EARTH?

Something had happened to her pillow.

Audra turned her head. It felt as if she was lying against someone's shoulder.

Her eyelids flew open to discover a pair of gray eyes only inches away from hers. They were studying her features rather intently.

"Don't scream and spoil the moment. It's only 11:00 a.m. I'm not ready to get up yet."

She swallowed hard. They were lying side by side. "I must have had a terrible nightmare."

"Yes. You asked me not to leave you."

"I'm sorry you had to come to my rescue again."

"I'm not. When I told you I'd stay right here, you went back to sleep and have been peaceful ever since."

She moistened her lips. "Uncle David wants me to see a doctor. I guess I'd better if I'm going to keep dreaming about Pete."

Something flickered in the recesses of his eyes. "Tell me about him."

"Pete? There's very little to tell. He worked as a technician at the radio station. He was two years younger than I am. I knew it had taken a long time for him to work up the courage to ask me out. When he finally did, I couldn't turn him down. I didn't think one date could hurt."

Rick made a sound in his throat. "My brother and I have always had the philosophy that we leave this earth when it's our time to go. It was the only thing that helped me get through my mother's death."

"Uncle David feels the same way you do. He has a strong belief in the hereafter."

"What about you?"

"I believe the Jarretts are all together somewhere, and that they're happy."

"Then why not Pete?"

Her chest heaved. "That's a good question." Her eyes stung with tears. "Maybe it's because he went alone."

"He had to have relatives who'd gone before him. Have you ever thought that your family has been watching over you, and they were there to greet him?"

She stared at Rick. "That's a wonderful thought." Her voice trembled.

He nodded. "My mother died with her two best friends. I like to think of the three of them waking up together on the other side."

"I would love to have met her. Pam happened to see a picture of her in her wedding dress."

"I know the one," Rick murmured. "Dad kept it in the study on his desk."

"My cousin said she was the most beautiful natural-blond woman she's ever seen in her life. Tall and statuesque with eyes like sapphires."

"You have the same color eyes."

His comment trapped the breath in her lungs. A moment passed before she forced herself to sit up and reach for her crutches.

"Where's the fire?"

Without looking at him, she said, "If I'm hungry, you must be starving."

"Frankly, food's the last thing on my mind. It's been nice to lie here and talk."

Too nice, Audra's heart cried. I could make it a habit. A minute, by hour, by week, by month, by year, by lifetime habit!

"When am I going to hear about the man who hurt you?"

She got to her feet. "You don't really want to know. It's not important anymore."

"Then you shouldn't have a problem telling me about him."

"What happened, Rick? Did I say something about Boris during my nightmare?"

"No," he murmured. "Boris wasn't the name of the man you were begging God to save."

"Good."

The minute she said it, they both smiled.

"I'd been at the Paris Conservatory for a year and a half taking master's harp classes. Then came spring and it was time to perform. That's when I met Boris. He was a gifted young conductor. For a season we lived and loved in a world of culture and music. We did concerts together in Strasbourg, Lyon, Dijon. Everywhere we went, we were treated to soirees after our performances.

"It was flattering to be asked to play in front of private groups of music lovers and critics. I'd never known such a high, and all because Boris was there giving his nod of approval. That's the trouble when you're a naive little gal from Texas. I believed he was proud of me. When the season came to an end, so did our relationship. He found reasons why I couldn't join him in the south of France to meet his family after all. A mutual friend who'd been on tour with us set me straight. He told me Boris was jealous of me. I couldn't comprehend it."

Rick moved off the bed. "You're a musical prodigy, Audra. No doubt Boris was a very good conductor. But he wasn't secure enough within himself to watch you receive the acclaim over a lifetime of being married to a brilliant musician."

"It took a year for me to understand that."

He came closer. "Remember the film *Amadeus?*"

She smiled. "It was wonderful."

"I agree. Mediocrity versus genius. Solieri was so jealous of Mozart, it drove him mad."

Audra cocked her head. "How many drivers have been jealous of you?"

He pursed his lips. "One or two."

"At least they weren't female."

"No."

"So, now that it's true-confession time, let's hear about the mystery woman in Lucky Hawkins's past. The one who turned you into a bachelor."

"There've been three."

Somehow Audra hadn't been expecting that kind of blunt honesty.

"Did they all hate what you do for a living?"

"No."

Obviously there was something wrong with Audra.

"At the age of twenty-two, I met Gina, who was the daughter of a wealthy Italian industrialist. I was a guest at their villa in San Marino for a while. We lived our version of what you lived with Boris. There was just one problem. When I had to go to work, she pouted, and we ended up fighting all the time."

Audra would have been twenty back then, a student at the university in Austin.

''So when did a wiser, older Lucky Hawkins fall in love again?''

His eyes smiled. ''Three years later I wasn't any wiser. I fell for the sister of a racer on one of the German teams. We'd become good friends on the circuit and I was invited to spend some time at his parents' summer home in Heidelberg. Elke was there with her girlfriends. It was a continual party. When Eric and I had to leave for the track, she'd come and watch. But as time went on, she'd beg me not to go.

''One morning I asked her what she was going to do all day while I was gone. She said she had no idea. Probably sleep some more, then do shopping until I returned. I asked her again in all seriousness. Didn't she have something important to do with her life? Something she was excited about? That's when she got angry, and I could see history repeating itself.''

''Two down, one to go,'' Audra quipped.

After a pause, ''Natalie lives in Phoenix where I train for Mayada. I met her while we were both doing laundry in the apartment complex where I lived. She'd graduated from college in resort management and was in charge of the sales department of a hotel there. We were in a relationship when I made the decision to leave racing and go home to help my father run the business.''

Audra frowned. ''How come she didn't join you in Colorado?''

His face held a pensive expression. ''Because I didn't ask her.''

''Why?''

''She had many needs I couldn't fill. I disappointed her time after time. The thought of trying to make her happy in a marriage when I knew it wasn't possible kept me from proposing. Nate said it best when I asked him about the girl he'd left behind in Holland after he'd resigned his commission. 'It just didn't feel right.'''

''And I thought *my* love life was complicated,'' Audra muttered. ''Come on. Bring your battle-weary body into the kitchen while I fix us lunch.''

Rick followed her out of the room. For some reason, what she'd just said caused him to look like an excited little boy. ''What song are you writing in your head now?''

He asked the question while she was poking around in the fridge for the ham and cheese.

She shut the door, trying not to smile. ''Do you mean 'Battle-Weary Warrior,' or 'It Never Felt Right'?''

His rich laughter filled the kitchen. She loved it. ''Admit you've got a song halfway composed already. How does it go? Come on. Sing it for me.''

He'd anticipated her next move and put the bread on the counter in front of her, trapping her so she couldn't take another step.

''Mind you, it's only a rough draft,'' she teased.

''I knew it,'' he whispered.

It never felt right,
In broad daylight,
It never felt right,
In the dead of night.

It never felt right,
In the middle of the day,
There wasn't any reason,
For me to stay.

It was better I left,
Before things fell apart,
I'd rather hurt her now,
Than one day break her heart.

By walking away,
We're both set free,
We've only got one shot
At living happily.
So I'll do it again,
If that's the way it has to be,

I'm giving fair warning,
To everyone in sight,
I'll be long gone by tonight,
If it doesn't feel right.

In the next breath Rick cupped her chin with his free hand. "Your battle-weary warrior's not going anywhere, and this feels right."

His head descended and he covered her mouth with his own.

Audra's moan of pleasure filled the air.

She couldn't remember a time when she hadn't wanted him to kiss her.

It *did* feel right.

She tightened her fingers on the handles of her crutches so she wouldn't throw her arms around his neck and cause more damage. That didn't seem to present any problem to the man whose strong male body molded to hers while he kissed the very daylights out of her.

"Audra?"

"Rick?"

"We rang the buzzer and knocked. Anybody home? We've brought barbecued ribs."

CHAPTER TEN

RICK SAW HIS FATHER out of the corner of his eye and tore his lips from Audra's.

There was only one difference between this moment and the one in the Hawkinses' kitchen in March. His father didn't go back outside and announce his entrance the way Rick had done. He just kept coming, setting the ribs down on the counter.

Pam was right behind him, holding a large bowl of something he suspected would taste delicious. The Jarrett women could cook like nobody in this world.

Rick shielded Audra as best he could while she fought to recover by filling a pitcher with water at the sink. As soon as her red blush started to fade, he turned to face his father, who stood there with his hands on his hips in that familiar stance of his.

"It looks like you two are managing to get along fine." His deadpan expression didn't fool Rick.

"We were almost ready to send for you and Pam. As you can see, we're down to a couple of ounces of cheese and a few slices of ham. Those ribs are making my mouth water. How about you, Audra?"

"Pam knows how much I love them," came a tiny voice. It didn't sound at all like the one belonging to the woman who'd been singing to him moments ago. "Will you stay and eat lunch with us?"

"I thought you'd never ask," his father drawled.

With her back to everyone, Audra said, "Why don't you put the food on the table."

"I'll get the silverware," Rick volunteered. His dad found the plates. Pam got the glasses down from the shelf.

The domestic scene took him back years, to a happy time when he and Nate were still in high school and the kitchen was the place where the family would congregate. Everyone had their little jobs. His mom hummed while she stirred the gravy. His dad stood there telling him and Nate something funny that had happened at the store. Then their parents would ask them about their school day. Nate always aced his exams. Rick's grades left something to be desired.

After dinner he'd head for the garage, a place he'd taken over to support his racing mania. To his parents' credit, they never complained.

He could picture the house at Copper Mountain nestled in the pines, with the snow piled high and Eagle's Nest Mountain looming behind it.

By anyone else's standards, it was simply an older two-story house. Nothing special. But it was home to him. A place of contentment and peace.

For a few minutes the atmosphere in this kitchen brought back those heartwarming feelings.

"Rick?" Pam prodded. "Do you want potato salad?"

"Please, and lots of it."

Soon everyone was served and they tucked in.

"We've got some news," his dad began.

"So do we," Rick said. "You go first."

His father gave him a searching glance. "Does it have to do with the boys?"

"No. We had a visitor yesterday."

"Who?"

"Audra will tell you what happened."

After Audra explained about Hal Torney, Pam said, "I'm sorry we weren't home to show him around, but we had a meeting in town with George Cutler, an attorney Uncle David's lawyer referred us to."

Clint nodded. "He's coming out to the ranch to-morrow morning to talk to you two about the details of the boys' break-in. He'll take formal depositions."

"We'll be ready."

"After Pam and I returned from Austin yesterday, we rode over to the Tilson place to make sure everything went all right when the boys transferred the horses to be boarded. It seems the Tilsons' fourteen-year-old granddaughter Amy happened to be in the barn when your cousins arrived.

"They didn't know she was visiting, or that she'd just come in from riding and was currying her horse. She overheard them talking about making me sorry for the day I ever set foot on Jarrett property. After they left, Amy told her grandpa."

Rick grimaced. "When Mr. Cutler leaves here, he needs to have a chat with the Tilsons."

"That's his plan. I phoned him from Mervin Tilson's study. He'll take a statement from Amy."

"What about Tom's threat that your bed-and-breakfast guests can't ride past the creek?'' Rick questioned.

''I've already thought of a way around that,'' Audra interjected. ''While we were out at the hangar yesterday, an idea came to me. The creek runs through the whole property, so I'm going to take the thirty acres closest to the main house and barn. They'll include a portion of the bluebonnets. We'll just move the fencing to the border between my property and the boys'. Let them have the other ninety acres that take in the rest of the bluebonnets. It's perfectly fair to everyone.

''When Mr. Cutler comes, I'll ask him to talk to Uncle David's attorney so the land can be surveyed and recorded in my name. That way your guests can ride all over my property and never have to deal with the boys.''

Rick had to admit her plan was brilliant.

''You don't have to do that for us, Audra.''

''Pam, I'm going to be living in Austin. Most of the time I won't even be out here. Part of the attraction of your bed-and-breakfast is the taste of ranch life on the back of a horse. The bluebonnets are a tremendous draw in the spring. So, no more discussion.''

Pam got out of her chair to hug her cousin.

''Like I've told you before, you're one in a million, sweetheart,'' Clint said in a tremulous voice.

Rick had the strongest hunch David Jarrett had known his little Audra would make everything right in the end. Deep in contemplation, he barely noticed that the man next to him had gotten to his feet.

"I'm going out to the truck and bring in the groceries. We bought some doughnuts for dessert. They're your favorite. Raised, with chocolate icing."

"NATE?"

"Dad, I was just about to call you."

"I figured you'd be home from work by now."

"Your timing's perfect. I'm pulling into the driveway. How's our one-armed bandit?"

"Doing better than a man with two."

Nate smiled. "You had a reason for saying that. What is it?"

What Nate heard next made him so happy he couldn't wait to tell Laurel.

"It appears Audra is recovering from her broken heart. This is great news, Dad."

"It looked like it from my vantage point. They had no idea Pam and I had to go back to the living room and come down the hall again to announce we were there."

Rick had been forced to do the same thing when he'd walked in on their father and Pam in March, but this situation was entirely different. Nate had been so worried about his brother's recent state of mind, this kind of news couldn't be more welcome.

"I can tell you this much. Rick's not the same depressed person I met on the road to the ranch in the middle of the night last week. That man has disappeared."

"Let's hope it's for good."

"This is a day-at-a-time kind of thing."

"It's providential their injuries will keep them under the same roof for another three weeks anyway."

"We can hope."

"Why do you say that?"

"David's moving into his condo this Saturday. Audra's not going to let him stay there alone."

"A lot can happen in three more days, if you know what I mean."

"I do."

"What's the latest on Pam's cousins?"

Nate listened while his father told him he'd hired an attorney. The news that Audra was going to take legal steps so her property would be available for the bed-and-breakfast revealed a lot about her character. All of it impressive.

"Everything sounds good, Dad, but do me a favor?"

"What's that?"

"Fly high and watch your tail."

"I'll be careful. Talk to you tomorrow. Give the women in your life a hug from me."

He could see Laurel and Becky at the front door of the house waiting for him. Something told him he would never get over the wonder of coming home to them every night. "That's going to happen in about thirty seconds. Give everyone there my best."

"Will do."

IN ANTICIPATION of Mr. Cutler's visit in the morning, Audra dusted and vacuumed the living room. Satisfied with the result, she only had one more project to accomplish before bed.

She swung herself down the hall and found Rick lying on top of his bed talking to someone on the phone. The second he saw her appear in the doorway he hung up and subjected her to an intimate appraisal. At least it felt intimate to her.

Since that kiss in the kitchen, she'd sensed a heightened tension between them. It shouldn't have happened, but she supposed it was inevitable with them living in such close quarters. He was a normal male with normal desires.

Audra wished she could blame her ardent response on the fact that she was a typical female who played around when opportunity knocked and didn't take one little kiss seriously.

"You've been a busy bee, even without your nightshirt."

She looked down at her shorts and T-shirt. "I would have put it on, but I didn't want you to think you were hallucinating again."

"No chance of that happening. I haven't had a pain pill all day."

"You're healing fast. That's good news for the people at Mayada waiting for you to get back on the team."

"Sounds like my nurse is growing weary of taking care of her patient."

"I didn't say that and you know it. In fact, I came in here to tell you it's time I took care of you properly."

He got that excited look on his face again. "I'm all yours. What did you have in mind for starters?"

"Meet me in your bathroom and you'll find out."

"Now?"

"There's no better time. Come on."

On her way to the master bath, she grabbed a clean pair of navy sweats from the drawer. He was right behind her.

"Do you know how to do CPR in case I have a heart attack?"

"Is that what happens when you get your hair washed? I know you want to feel your best self when Mr. Cutler arrives in the morning."

A strange quiet filled the bathroom.

"Except for my mother when I was a little kid, I've never let a woman do that for me."

"Pretend I'm your nurse," she said, pulling his shampoo and deodorant from the cabinet.

"That would be impossible."

Ignoring his comment, she rested one of her crutches against the wall and leaned on the other to start the shower. When she'd adjusted it to the right temperature on low pressure, she said, "Okay, here's what we're going to do.

"After you get in the tub at the dry end, I want you to lean over so I can get your head wet and nothing else. Then I'll turn off the water and ask you to sit on the side of the tub while I shampoo you. When we're ready, you stand up and away while I turn the water back on. Then lean over again so I can rinse you."

"I've dreamed about moments like this."

"Let's hope the experience lives up to your expectations."

He placed his right hand on her shoulder to support

him while he stepped inside. A few minutes later her fingers were scrubbing his scalp. He kept letting out groans of pleasure.

"I'll pay you a thousand dollars to do that for five more minutes."

She'd pay him double that to be able to perform these kinds of tasks for him for the rest of her life. "Make that a thousand a minute and I'll oblige you."

"Agreed."

Before long she'd rinsed him off and dried his vibrant black hair as best she could. He was a beautiful man—by anyone's standards, but especially by her own.

"Where'd you get that tiny scar at the edge of your eyebrow?"

"Skiing. Nate crashed in front of me while we were shushing down Eagle's Nest. The tip of his ski pole nicked me."

"How old were you?"

"Eight."

She had an idea he and his brother were inseparable growing up.

"I see another small scar on the back of your neck."

"A pellet from Chip Warner's beebee gun got lodged in there. If you're looking for signs of race-car injuries, I don't have any."

Not yet.

No wonder Clint was terrified.

"Stay where you are." She filled the sink with warm water, then took a cloth and soap to wash the part of his body he couldn't reach. After rinsing him off, she dried him and applied the deodorant for him.

"All done. I'll leave you alone now to finish up."

Fitting her other crutch under her arm, she turned toward the doorway in time to hear, "When your cast comes off, it'll be my pleasure to wash that leg and give it a good massage."

The thought of his hands on her body took her breath away.

She hurried into the kitchen to fill a pitcher of ice water for him. Once she'd returned to his room with a clean glass, she put both items on the nightstand.

While she was plumping his pillows, he emerged from the bathroom clean shaven, hair brushed. He wore the sweats she'd provided for him. Besides his own wonderful male scent, he smelled of toothpaste and shaving cream.

"How about a game of cards before we go to bed?"

"Maybe tomorrow night before my show? It's getting late. I need to call Uncle David."

"In that case, I'm going to take a walk outside and stretch my legs. I'll lock up when I come back in so you don't have to."

"Thank you."

"Audra?"

She didn't dare look at him. "Yes?"

"You've made a new man of me."

"Washing your hair always makes you feel better. Good night."

RICK WATCHED her disappear from his room.

I have news for you, Audra Jarrett. I'm talking

about a lot more than the personal attention in the
bath, an experience I intend to return one day soon.

He found his sandals and started for the front of
the house with his phone in hand. Audra had shut her
bedroom door. Resisting the temptation to join her,
he headed out of the house into a warm night. Earlier
in the day the temperature had climbed to the high
eighties. It felt much more humid than usual.

A tour around the bungalow revealed nothing
amiss. He couldn't see anyone on horseback. Since
Sunday, when Tom had left the house in a rage, Rick
had kept an eye on the road when he could. So far
he hadn't seen any of the cousins drive by, but something had to be brewing.

Tonight he'd sit on the porch and keep a vigil until
dawn. Right now he felt too alive from Audra's min-
istrations to go to bed.

No doubt his father was on the lookout at the main
house, trying to gauge the form of retaliation he could
expect. Amy Tilson's input had only verified what
was common knowledge to the rest of them.

To pass the time, Rick phoned Chip Warner and
told him about his accident. Since Rick had been on
the phone earlier with Wally to let him know why
he'd never made it to Arizona, they talked track stuff
for a good half hour.

Then he listened while his buddy broke down and
wept over his marital problems. He and Jackie were
separated. She'd gone to Denver with their daughter,
Angie, and son, Devlin. She had a job in a hospital
as a nurse. He was still in Colorado Springs working
odd jobs at the track.

"What does Jackie want, Chip? What's the bottom line if you're going to make this marriage work?"

"She says I'm a pathetic has-been. I'm like the guy who was replaced by new management, but who still hangs around the office trying to pretend he's important."

Rick winced.

"Bottom line? I've been given three months to find real work. 'Go to an employment agency,' she said. 'Find something full-time that brings in a steady income to send the kids to college and gives us a pension.' Maybe then she'll talk to me. Hell, Rick—I don't know where to start. I don't know how to do anything else!"

Rick lowered his head.

Chip lived and breathed racing, but he was a guy who'd stressed too much to be a top racer. Now he was too old. There were younger, better racers on their way up who didn't let anything get to them.

Rick had always believed that his buddy's expertise lay in his ability to come up with brilliant strategies to win races. He was like an offense coordinator in football. Rick had won many a race by applying some of Chip's techniques, and he would always give his friend credit.

When he thought about it, he decided that Chip ought to be a teacher for someone who owned a racing school. Nobody would do a better job. He'd be happy.

The only problem was, that kind of job was almost impossible to come by unless you'd had a brilliant racing career first and knew powerful people in high places. It helped to be married to the owner's daughter.

Jackie would take him back if Chip could wangle a job like that.

She only despised racing because she knew Chip had never achieved his dream. His wife was exhausted from living with an unhappy man.

It all boiled down to that…being happy with yourself.

His thoughts returned to Audra, who'd taken up permanent residence in his psyche. She was different than Jackie. She despised racing because it killed. Her last nightmare had convinced him of that.

There was a time when Rick had lived and breathed racing, but something had changed for him in the last year.

A lot had changed since he'd stopped off in Texas.

"Listen, Chip, I'm going to call you again next week. In the meantime, I'll think about your situation and see what I can come up with to help you."

"Thanks, Rick, but it's not your problem. Jackie was wrong. I'm not even a has-been, because I never made it to the big leagues in the first place. What I've done doesn't count for anything. The kids don't deserve a dad like me. I'm scared silly."

His buddy was drowning. At thirty years of age, Chip was drowning. Rick understood. On the drive down to Texas, he'd felt as if he, too, was going under for the third time.

But since his arrival, something had happened. He

could see light shimmering overhead. He could feel himself rising toward it. A short distance more and he'd break the surface to fill his lungs with life-giving air.

"Hang in there, buddy. I swear things are going to get better."

I've got an idea. One I can't talk about yet. When I'm ready I'll tell you all about it.

"Thanks for listening, Rick."

"Anytime."

When they'd clicked off, Rick was too energized by his thoughts, flying hard and fast, to sit there any longer. He found himself walking along the road to the main house, keeping an eye out for anything that moved.

Halfway there he worried Audra might be in the middle of one of her nightmares. He started back, noting that only one truck had driven by so far. Rick had heard the rock music blaring before he'd seen the teenager with his arm around his girlfriend.

Four o'clock in the morning.

Rick and Nate had never come in the house that late after a date. They knew their father would be up to say good-night to them. The thought of having to face the excruciating look of disappointment in his eyes was enough of a deterrent to prevent that from happening.

Funny how circumstances had changed.

His dad seemed fine about Rick keeping an eye on Audra for the next few weeks. When he was a teen, he couldn't have imagined the day dawning when his father would condone a son of his living alone with a woman for days and nights on end.

Audra's a sweetheart.

Those were his dad's words, said with an affection that ran deep.

In the last week, Rick had come to believe the same thing about her.

With as much stealth as he could muster, he let himself back in the house, locked up and tiptoed down the hall. All was quiet. There was no light under her door.

If she'd had a nightmare, he imagined she'd be up composing another song to calm herself. He fought not to open the door and look in on her just to be sure she was all right.

His thoughts flew back to the first time he'd laid eyes on her staring up at him from the bed in fright and confusion. He didn't have the words then to describe what he was seeing.

He had them now.

She was a beautiful Texas bluebonnet, broken off in the wind and carried a long distance from home.

Rick needed to capture her before she was lost forever. His whole desire was to plant her in his heart where no wind could find her. Where she would be safe and adored.

AUDRA WAS AWARE of the muggy heat as she pulled two letters from the mailbox. Bills.

Yesterday had been warm, but this afternoon the temperature had to be in the nineties and climbing. The air felt unusually heavy.

She looked up at the sky. The fair cumulus clouds she'd seen this morning when she and Rick had walked out to Mr. Cutler's car to say goodbye were gone. In their place, fast-moving cirrus clouds from the west filled the sky.

Had Pam noticed? The hairs stood up on her arms.

She grabbed hold of her crutches and hurried into the house as fast as she could go.

"Rick?" she cried from the hallway. "Turn on the television to the weather station, quick!"

When she reached his bedroom, he was on his feet with the remote in hand, but he hadn't found the right channel yet. His eyes pierced hers. "What's wrong? You look like you're going to pass out."

"Here. Let me."

"…storm system has moved in from the west. The National Weather Service reports a strong south wind blowing in moisture from the Gulf of Mexico. There's a dry line moving across the state from West Texas.

"Heavy amounts of rainfall have been reported east of Fort Davis. Hail is coming down the size of golf balls in Fredericksburg and Kerrville, where a storm cell has formed. A severe thunderstorm warning and tornado alert is now in effect for all areas of Austin County."

Sickness welled up in her throat. "Call your dad, Rick. Find out if he and Pam know about the storm. I'll phone Uncle David. He'll get hold of the boys." She hurried into the kitchen for her cell phone, lying on the counter.

It rang until she got his voice mail.

By now Rick had joined her. He put his hand on

her shoulder. "They're in Austin. While they were talking to some people about obtaining a food handler's permit, the alert went out. They're on their way to the Cattlemen's Club to find your uncle."

"Thank God."

"I'm going to run to the ranch house and get my car. I'll be back for you as soon as I can and we'll get out of here."

"There isn't time for that, Rick."

"What do you mean?"

"I've seen the sky." Her voice shook. "Listen to the wind. The storm's here."

"Then we'll get in the bathtub and cover up."

"No. If the house were made of bricks, we could take our chances here. But it's a postwar wooden bungalow. We've got to get away from it and into the creek bed now!"

After helping her down the steps of the back porch, they both looked up. She felt the splash of a gentle raindrop on her face.

Rain, hail, then the tornado. This was how it began.

He took her left crutch away and laid it on the ground. "Come on, Audra. The creek's not that far."

Using his right arm, he told her to use him for a crutch. Together they made faster progress than she would have believed possible. She was too out of breath to talk. Rick didn't seem at all winded.

They stuck to the access road until they came to the culvert. By now the rain was coming down in sheets driven by the wind. "Here. Let me help you lie down so you can crawl underneath the crossbridge.

"Just use your left leg and drag your right one.

That's it. Now stay close to the side of the culvert and you won't get wet from the creek.''

Audra was so terrified, she wouldn't have been able to do this without him. Once she'd inched her way inside and was out of the rain, she felt his body cover hers so she was protected from the water.

"You're going to be soaking wet, Rick."

"I couldn't care less."

"But your sling and bandages—"

He kissed the tip of her ear. "They'll dry out."

"Rick—" She cried his name before she broke down sobbing. "I should never have invited you to come here to recuperate. This is my fault."

"What are you talking about? If I'd been at the main house instead of here, I would have jumped in my car to come for you."

"But if anything happens to you, your father will never get over it. Pam won't be able to console him. He loves you so much. Your brother loves you so much.

"All these years you've been safe racing cars. Then you come to Texas for an overnight visit and meet up with three men I'm ashamed to call members of my family.

"You go for a ride on Pam's horse and end up dueling with a water moccasin. Then Marshmallow falls on you and breaks your collarbone.

"B-because you're the gentleman you are, you accept my offer to take care of you in a house that doesn't have any air-conditioning or a basement," she stammered.

"I should have acted on my instincts this morning.

There was a different feel in the air when I got up. I didn't want to admit I was nervous, especially not in front of Mr. Cut—

"Oh no— The hail's starting!"

He'd never seen golf ball–size hail before. "It's all right, Audra. We're going to be all right. I swear it."

"What if I never see you again?"

"I'm not going anyplace without you."

"If—if we wake up on the other side, will you come and find me?"

CHAPTER ELEVEN

AUDRA, AUDRA.

"I won't have to look for you because we're staying right here." He kissed her temple.

I've got you in my arms. I'm never letting you go.

"L-look at the size of the hailstones now!" She burrowed against him, totally traumatized.

He was looking, but he didn't believe what he was seeing. They might as well have been baseballs falling like bombs from his brother's F-16. They filled the creek. It surprised him that their impact didn't dent the crossbridge.

"Don't watch."

No sooner had he shielded her eyes than the hail stopped abruptly. He got this eerie feeling and lifted his chin from her curls to see what was happening.

Out of the end of the culvert he glimpsed a giant gray pinwheel swirling above the land. Maybe three miles away he saw a little black finger descend from the southwest end of the formation.

Dear Lord. He swallowed hard.

It wiggled its way down until it reached the ground. Rick held his breath at the thickness of the column.

It seemed to stay there forever. Audra tried to lift her head. He wouldn't allow it.

She'd be plagued by new nightmares imagining thirty members of her family disappearing in a funnel like that one. If he didn't miss his guess, it was in an area close to the place that had once been the town of Hillmont.

"What's happening?"

"Shh." He covered her cheek with kisses. "Just hold on to me," he whispered.

The funnel was moving their way.

He'd seen video footage of tornadoes. Now he understood why tornado watchers said the sight of one up close was beautiful and terrifying in the same instance.

If it kept coming in their direction, the tornado would sweep up the bungalow, the fencing, the main house, the trailer, his car, the barn. The horses...

He groaned when he thought about the animals.

There'd be nothing left for the boys to contest.

That was Rick's last thought before the dark column suddenly switched directions and headed north out of his line of vision. He didn't think his eyes were playing tricks on him. Like Nate, he had perfect vision.

"Stay where you are, Audra. I'm going to move to the edge of the culvert to look out." He removed his arm.

"Don't!" she begged and clung to him.

"It's okay. I promise I won't leave you."

She reluctantly released him so he could creep to the end. When he looked to the right, he could see the funnel way off in the distance. It didn't look as solid as before.

He crept out among the icy white balls and got to his feet to survey the landscape. Except for the air being cooler, everything appeared to be the same. Three or four miles away he knew massive devastation had been left in the tornado's wake.

For Audra's sake he would always be grateful the Jarrett Ranch had been left untouched this time.

"The danger's over," he assured her after scanning the sky. It would be evening before they knew it. "Stay put for a minute while I call Dad and find out what the weather service is saying."

He pulled the phone out of his jeans pocket and punched in the number. His father picked up before the second ring.

"Rick, we're almost to the ranch. That tornado missed you by four miles."

"I know." He walked around the other end of the culvert to get her crutch. "It was headed straight for us. At the last second I watched it shift north."

"Thank heavens you're all right. The funnel dissipated northwest of Austin. We've been listening to the radio. They're saying it was an F-3. How's Audra?"

"Tell David she's fine."

"I'll phone him right now."

"We're leaving the creek to go back to the house."

"How much damage have you done to your injury?"

"None."

He could tell that his father wanted to say something else, then thought the better of it. "Pam and I should be joining you in about fifteen minutes."

"Fine."

Rick put his phone away and went around to the other end of the crossbridge. He got down on his haunches. "The alert is over, Audra. Crawl toward me and we'll go home."

"D-did you see the tornado?" Her teeth were chattering.

He couldn't lie to her. "Yes, but the storm has passed and the funnel broke up. Come on." He helped her to her feet and fit the crutch under her arm.

They worked as a team to walk back to the house. She faltered several times from weakness. He gripped her waist to support her. No word passed between them. Soon they reached the bungalow. He handed her the crutch by the back door and helped her inside.

"When we left this kitchen, I didn't think we'd ever see it again." A shudder passed through her body he could feel.

"Try not to dwell on it."

"That's asking too much. You must be in terrible pain."

"I didn't injure myself."

"Don't lie to me. Your bandages and sling are sopping wet," she cried in an anxious tone. "If you've dislocated your shoulder again—"

"Listen to me, Audra. I swear to you nothing's wrong."

"We still have to call your doctor and find out what to do."

"I will later. Right now I'm assuming the phone lines to the hospitals are jammed. Let's clean up your cast first. Come and sit down on the chair."

Once she was settled, he took a cloth from the drawer and got down on his haunches to brush away the dirt that clung to it. He wiped off her other leg, too. "Your skirt and blouse need to be washed."

"So do your jeans, but I don't really care." Her eyes sought his. "I'm so thankful we're both alive, nothing else matters."

"I agree."

"Thank you for being there for me, Rick. I don't know what I would have done if I'd been alone. Probably fainted dead away from fright before I ever reached the creek."

Rick was ready to take her in his arms, when his cell phone rang. He put the cloth on the counter and checked the caller ID. "It's my brother."

"I'm sure he's worried sick about you. Talk to him while I change."

"Are you sure you don't want to sit here awhile longer?" She looked pale.

"I'm fine. Don't keep him waiting." She got up and made a quick exit from the kitchen on her crutches.

He put the phone to his ear. "Nate?"

"Dad already told me you and Audra are all right, but I needed to hear your voice. Laurel called me while I was on my way home from work. She happened to have been watching something on cable and heard about a tornado touching down in Texas. I don't know the details, but Dad said you were an eyewitness."

Rick leaned against the counter. "I've seen things that put the fear in me before, Nate, but this was different. The sight of nature doing something only a higher power could stop was so unbelievably awesome and terrible, I'll never view life the same way again.''

After a long silence, ''Did Audra see it, too?''

''No. I crushed her against me so she wouldn't be able to watch. She already has nightmares from the crash she was in. I'm not sure I won't be having some horrific dreams myself. Their family lost thirty people in a funnel just like that one.''

''I heard,'' his brother murmured in a solemn voice.

''It happened almost in the same place! Can you comprehend it?''

''No.'' There was a silence before Nate added, ''We're lucky none of us saw the avalanche.'' Nate had just read Rick's mind.

His eyes smarted. ''As you told me after you held Becky in your arms at the hospital, life is precious. While Audra was clinging to me in the culvert, I realized it like never before. I also understood how puny man's power is, how helpless I was to protect her. All we could do was hold on to each other and pray we weren't going for our last ride around the track.''

''Don't even think it. Are you guys okay now? You know what I mean.''

He did. ''We're alive. That makes us perfect.''

''And here I thought all clear and present danger was confined to the skies over the Middle East.''

Rick made a noise in his throat before wandering into the living room out of earshot.

"Welcome to Texas. It's been a wild ride so far and getting wilder all the time."

"Dad said he's waiting to see what Pam's cousins are going to pull next."

"We're both doing reconnaissance during the night to keep an eye on things."

"You're getting reinforcements. Laurel and I will fly down in the morning and drive to the ranch from the airport."

"That's music to my ears."

"Speaking of music, Laurel received your express package while she was watching the news. We haven't had a chance to play any of the CDs yet, but we will tonight. I had no idea Audra was a singer."

"She's so many things, I don't even know where to start." In the next breath he found himself bragging about her radio program and her studies in France.

"When you're listening to the country music, remember every part of what you're hearing is one hundred percent original Audra Jarrett. She's self-taught on the guitar. This summer she's doing a tour with her harp ensemble. She'll be playing with the Denver Philharmonic at Red Rock."

Rick could hear his brother trying to absorb everything.

"How come Pam never said anything, or Dad? All we knew was that she'd been in a terrible car crash."

"That's a story for another day. I've got a ton to tell you when you get here."

"We'll catch up on Friday."

Excited his brother was coming, he hung up and went in search of Audra. They met in the hallway.

She'd changed into another skirt and top. He could tell she was still shaken and probably would be for a long time to come.

His eyes searched hers. "Pam and Clint will be here any minute."

The relief on her face made him realize she needed to talk this out with her cousin. "I'll make some sandwiches."

"We'll do it together."

At this point Rick was starving and ate while he helped prepare the food. They worked in companionable silence until she said, "There they are, but they're driving your car."

Rick walked through the house to the front door and opened it. Audra followed. To his surprise, Pam was at the wheel. He noticed his father get out and walk toward them.

When he reached Rick, he patted his good shoulder. "Pam's driving you over to an Instant Care clinic about five miles from here."

"I don't need help."

"Do it for us?" That pleading look in his eyes got to Rick every time. "I'll stay with Audra."

"Please go with her, Rick," she urged.

Not wanting Audra to worry about him on top of what had just happened, he nodded. "Okay. We won't be long."

Famous last words.

It was close to eleven before they returned to the bungalow. A surge of people had descended on the clinic in Marysvale, some who'd been injured by flying debris during the tornado, others with problems unrelated to the weather.

He came home taped clean and dry, with a new sling. Because he hadn't hurt himself in the culvert, he'd opted not to wait for an X ray to be taken. All he wanted was to get back to Audra.

"Don't let her be alone tonight after her program," Pam murmured before they got out of the car.

Audra had been on both their minds. Rick had already planned to stay close to her, but it was nice to be given permission. "I have a plan that will help us to relax."

"SO IF YOU'VE JUST JOINED us, you need to know the station is donating a hundred percent of the money made from the purchase of CDs to the Red Cross to help the injured.

"From what we've learned, the tornado took one life today. That's one loss too many, but thanks to the alert system, hundreds were spared.

"There's time for one more phone call before the top of the hour. If you just want to talk about the storm, that's what we've been doing. My producer tells me Mark is on the line.

"Good morning, Mark."

"I don't think there's much good about it."

It was Tom.

She would know his voice anywhere.

"Frankly I'm not so certain that money will make it into the right hands. In fact, I find it downright offensive that you use this program to promote yourself in the name of the tornado survivors."

The venom in his tone chilled Audra.

Her gaze flicked to Rick, who'd been lying on the bed watching her throughout the program. Now he was on his feet. His eyes held a dangerous glitter.

She took a deep breath. ''When the town of Hillmont was struck by a tornado years ago, the remaining members of the Jarrett family were the recipients of many outpourings, financial and otherwise, from all over the state of Texas.

''I consider it a privilege to be able to pay back the community in some small way for the groundswell of support we received. It isn't as much as I'd like to give, but it comes straight from the heart.

''That's all the time we have for tonight. Join me again on Friday at midnight for the *Red Jarrett Show.*''

Audra made her closing remarks and signed off.

By the time she'd taken off her headphones, Rick had moved behind her where she was perched on her stool. He put his free arm around her neck and buried his lips in her hair. She felt his touch radiate through her body.

''You handled Tom with such grace, I respect you more than I can say. To think after all they've done, you were so worried about them, you wanted them to know a tornado might be on the way. Come on. Let's go to my room to unwind.''

Her heart began to thud. ''You need your sleep. So do I.''

''Sleep can wait. Talk can't.''

He helped her with her crutches.

''I don't think—''

"I do."

Audra experienced new fear as they left the room and walked down the hall. It was too easy to turn to Rick whenever she felt like it. She couldn't comprehend the thought of him leaving for Arizona.

If this was the way Pam had felt after spending a few short days with Clint in Colorado, Audra understood why her cousin would have done anything to hang on to her newfound happiness.

But her situation and Audra's weren't the same. Though Clint and Rick were father and son, they were two different men with two different agendas.

Clint wanted the same joys that his first marriage had brought him.

Rick was still single. He was a world-famous sports figure. He had places to go, more records to break.

He was a wonderful, kind, gentle, intelligent, exciting, masterful, sensitive man. She would die if anything ever happened to him.

She'd fallen in love with him.

It had happened without her realizing it. She couldn't name the moment. There were so many.

Audra had never envied Pam until tonight.

Marriage for her cousin may have come in the summertime of her life, but it had been worth the long wait to end up being loved by Clint.

The Hawkins men were exceptional.

"You need some pampering," Rick said after he rested her crutches against the wall. She lay down on one side of his bed while he found a pillow to prop her leg.

Somehow, with the coming of the tornado, their

roles had reversed. He was now the caregiver. Her eyes followed him around until he'd settled back against a couple of pillows. When he turned on his good side to face her, Audra's breath caught.

This close to each other it was a constant struggle not to study his attractive features.

"Did I tell you I saw a teenager and his girlfriend drive by the house about four o'clock yesterday morning?"

She blinked. "No. Were you outside?"

"Yes. I couldn't sleep. They were cuddled together listening to music. It took me back to my teens when I seemed to have a crush on a different girl every other week. I would have given anything to be out that late with one of them."

Audra smiled. "It's a good thing you had vigilant parents. Uncle David was just as bad. 'Eleven o'clock, Audra.'"

"Do you know what's so nice?"

Her heart yearned toward him. "What?"

"It's four in the morning, and unlike that teen out in the truck, I have my dad's permission to be alone with you for as long as I want."

She averted her eyes. "You didn't have much choice, since I'm the one who invited you to stay here."

"Do you honestly think I would have taken you up on your offer if I didn't have an enormous crush on you?"

Careful, Audra.

"What I think is that you've been endowed with a

strong sense of chivalry. It helps you make the most of a bizarre situation with an oddity like me.''

His dark eyebrows lifted. ''You see yourself as an oddity?''

''Perhaps that's a slight exaggeration. I'm normal enough to have a crush on you, too, but unlike the other females you've met, I realize that's all it is.''

''I like the way you think,'' he murmured. ''Shall we pretend we're in my dad's truck and do what we're dying to do?''

She eyed him through narrowed lids. ''We're not teenagers anymore.''

He flashed her a mischievous smile. ''That's right. Scared?''

''In our condition, no.''

''Sure?''

Heat spiraled up her body to her cheeks. ''Take your best shot and we'll see.''

''My best shot...''

She was dying all right, and he knew it!

''Meet me halfway.''

''It's kind of hard with this cast.''

''Try.''

In the process of inching closer, Rick kissed the corner of her mouth. She strained toward him only to find herself being tantalized by little kisses that followed the outline of her lips from top and bottom.

Audra did the same thing to him, then went further afield to relish the rasp of his chin and jaw. His lips chased after hers in an exciting duel of the senses. Seduced by his mastery, her heart leaped when she felt his mouth close over hers.

They couldn't wrap their arms and legs around each other the way their bodies were straining to do. Somehow it didn't matter. Their mouths became the focal point of their existence. Each kiss grew longer, hungrier. Unable to distinguish between them, she forgot caution and let desire take over.

"I want you, Audra," he whispered against her lips. "I want you more than anything I've ever wanted in my life."

She knew he meant it for the moment. At a time like this, a man's body, a man's passion didn't lie. But hearing the words brought her back to some semblance of reality.

"I want you, too, more than you can imagine. However, next month, next year, we'll both be in different trucks at four in the morning. What's nice is we'll be able to wrap our arms and legs around the next person we have a crush on.

"But I'll be honest with you—" She kissed the end of his straight nose because his mouth had formed a grimace. "I've had a fabulous time this morning. I wouldn't have missed it for the world.

"One day years from now, I'll be able to tell my children I took a spin around the track with Lucky Hawkins. It was only one lap, but it contained enough thrills and chills to last me a lifetime.

"Good night, Rick. Thank you for helping me get my mind off the tornado. Your strategy worked, big-time."

She reached for her crutches and got to her feet. Within seconds she'd made it to the door of his room, which was shrouded in darkness.

He'd let her go too easily.

He didn't mind that she'd left him.

The guy had done his duty, no doubt at Pam's urging. Now he craved much-needed sleep.

Rick had been the one who'd witnessed the tornado. Audra had been too much of a coward to watch. After his rather extraordinary experience, he was exhausted.

This was how the end of her relationship with Boris had started. He'd slowly distanced himself from Audra without her catching on. When she'd asked him how soon he wanted her to join him in Cannes, he'd told her it wasn't a good time. But he'd be in touch.

Audra would never give Rick the opportunity to say, "My racing schedule won't permit me any free time for a while, but I'll probably see you at Christmas when the fam—"

Her thoughts were cut off by a loud crack and the sound of glass shattering. It came from her bedroom. She cried out in surprise.

Quick as lightning Rick joined her in the hall. "Tom sent you a message with that phone call tonight," he said in a low voice. "Enraged by the way you dealt with him over the air, he has now resorted to using a rifle to make certain you get the point. Don't move, Audra."

"Please don't go in there," she begged. "You can't take on all three of them in your condition." But her words were wasted on him.

It was a surreal moment as she watched him get down on his haunches and disappear into the room.

To her heartfelt relief he came back in the hall a minute later carrying one of her chairs.

Without saying a word, he took the crutches from her and forced her to sit down. "The hall is the safest place for you until the police get here. What's your address?"

In a dazed state she gave it to him, then he was talking to the 9-1-1 dispatcher.

"An attempt was made on Ms. Jarrett's life. There's a bullet lodged in her bedroom wall. We don't know if the gunman is still out there. He could be family."

Before Rick rang off, he'd given the dispatcher the names of her cousins, along with a description of the boys' trucks and cars. Considering what Rick did for a living, it shouldn't have surprised her he knew the make, model, color and year of each vehicle.

"The police are on their way," he told Audra before she heard him relating everything to his father. Pretty soon he was on the phone to his brother, but he walked into his bedroom during their conversation.

It wasn't long before three officers arrived at the bungalow. At this point, Rick was off the phone and let them in the living room. While one of them stayed in the hall to get statements from her and Rick, the other two went into her bedroom. Another one was outside the house.

Soon Pam and Clint arrived. A detective and a crime scene team followed them inside. By now the sun had come up.

They congregated in the living room so Audra could elevate her leg on the couch.

The detective spent a good hour collecting information from them.

"I'll give you the number at the radio station," Audra said. "The manager tapes every program. Tom was the last caller before I went off the air last night, though he introduced himself as Mark.

"The producer will give you the tape. If the call came from a pay phone, that's one thing. But it could have originated from Tom's work phone, his house phone or his cell. Do you want those numbers?"

The detective nodded and jotted them down. He lifted his head and looked at each of them. "Is there anything else?"

"Yes." Pam sat forward. She looked as ill as Audra felt. "One of our big concerns is that the new owner of the ranch, Edwin Torney, was supposed to fly in yesterday with his son, Hal. Because of the tornado, I don't know if they made it to Austin or not.

"I think for the Torneys' welfare, Edwin needs to be made aware of the problem we're facing here."

"Definitely. If we've got someone who's not dealing with reality, they could be a target."

"I've written down Mr. Torney's phone number and address in Cleveland, Ohio." She handed the piece of paper to him.

Clint said, "You've got the number of our attorney, Mr. Cutler. He can provide you with copies of our depositions."

While he was talking, the other officers and crime scene team went back outside. The detective got to his feet. He left a card on the coffee table.

"Call me if anything comes up no matter how trivial it might seem. We'll stay in close touch."

Rick let him out and shut the door before turning to his father. "I think it would be best if Audra slept at the ranch house with you and Pam tonight. Tomorrow you can all drive to Austin and get a hotel room where Nate and Laurel will be staying."

Audra bristled. "I resent being treated as if I weren't even in the room, Rick. The point is, if I'm vulnerable, so are you."

His gray eyes darkened from emotion. "Without you on the premises, I'll be fine."

"You can't stay here," she cried before she realized how upset she sounded.

"If I leave," he retorted in a calm voice, "then Tom has won this round."

"He's right, Audra," Clint concurred.

"I don't care if he wins. Not if it means your life's in danger."

"Danger's my business, isn't that what you've been telling me?"

She looked away, embarrassed for her cousin and Clint to be witness to things better kept private.

"You heard the detective," Rick said. "It will be better if you don't do your show tomorrow night. Let Tom think you've caved in and we've vacated the premises. Your producer can broadcast one of your old shows like he did when you went on tour last year."

Her body froze. "So you'll remain here and wait for the three of them to hurt you or worse?"

His smile had an icy quality. "I won't be alone.

My brother's coming tomorrow morning. The timing couldn't be more perfect. This is the weekend your uncle is moving into his condo, and the boys know it.''

''What does one thing have to do with the other?''

''After the moving van shows up for David's things, we'll arrange for the men to drive over here and pack your belongings, too.''

Her heart dropped to her feet.

This stolen week alone with Rick was over, just like that.

She bowed her head. One shattered window and the boys had brought about a convenient way for Rick to distance himself from her.

Nothing held him here.

What had he said when she'd told him it was just a crush on her part?

I like the way you think.

Of course he liked it. He was a no-strings guy.

Another week and he'd be functioning well enough to get in his car and drive away.

''If the boys are watching,'' he continued, ''they'll congratulate themselves for giving you such a fright you left the bungalow before your cast came off. One of them will listen to your program and find out it's a rerun. That will send another false message.

''Knowing the family will be gone for a big portion of the weekend to help with the move, your cousins won't realize we've set a trap until everything's a fait accompli.''

''What kind of a trap?'' Pam didn't sound any happier about it than Audra.

"I have a plan. Nate will help me. I feel in my gut things are going to go down this weekend. If I'm wrong and nothing happens, we'll work out a different strategy, even if it means hiring you a bodyguard, Audra. The important thing is, if you and Pam are in Austin, the boys won't have access to you this weekend."

Pam studied her cousin with anxious eyes. "Did you get any sleep last night?"

Audra shook her head.

"Then it's settled. I'll come by after dinner and get you."

Rick stared hard at Audra. "Why don't you lie down on my bed right now where you'll be comfortable."

"That's a good idea, honey," Pam agreed with him.

Audra knew she was beyond exhausted or she wouldn't have rejoiced that she wouldn't be leaving Rick until tonight. The prospect of separation from him was too painful to consider.

CHAPTER TWELVE

"HOLT REALTY. How may I help you?"

Clint had just driven off with Pam. Rick stood on the porch of the bungalow and watched until he lost sight of his car.

"This is Rick Hawkins. I'm trying to reach Jed Holt. In case he doesn't remember me, I played golf with him and Brent Marsden a couple of weeks ago."

"He's in a sales meeting. Let me see what I can do, Mr. Hawkins. I'm going to put you on hold."

"Thank you."

After a minute the receptionist came back on the line. "He'll be with you in a moment."

While Rick waited, he went inside the house to check on Audra, who appeared to be asleep at last. Too many shocks since yesterday had taken their toll. He could only hope she wouldn't have a nightmare.

"Rick Hawkins?" sounded an enthusiastic voice. "To what do I owe this great honor?"

A smile broke out on Rick's face. He headed for the living room. "I need a good Realtor. Brent says you're the best."

"You've made my day. Are you calling from Arizona?"

''No. I stopped in Texas to visit my father and ended up in the hospital with a broken collarbone.''

''Uh-oh. How did that happen?''

''A horse fell on me.''

''You wouldn't be joking with me?''

Rick chuckled. ''No.'' After he'd explained about the snake, he said, ''During this period of recuperation, I've had a lot of time to reflect on my career. The bottom line is, I'm due for a change.''

The other man's silence said plenty.

''This is just an idea, mind you, but I'm thinking of establishing a racing school for drivers interested in Formula One, Indy racing. I need a place to put a building, plus an indoor and outdoor track. Somewhere halfway between Copper Mountain and Denver off I-70.''

''What an exciting idea! I know several pieces of property along that route with easy access to the freeway. Let me do some research and I'll get back to you. Give me your phone number.''

Rick complied. ''Do me one more favor?''

''Of course.''

''Don't mention my name to anyone, and not a word of this to Brent.''

''Understood. What time frame are we looking at?''

''ASAP.''

''In that case, expect to hear from me within twenty-four hours.''

''Good. Thanks, Jed.''

''Thank *you*.''

He hung up and went to the kitchen for a cola. With

that phone call, he'd taken his first step away from the world of competition and toward a different realm.

It felt right. He could tell by the sense of exhilaration that swept through him.

While his mind reeled with the exciting prospect of running his own business, he saw a blue Honda Civic pull into the driveway. There was a brunette at the wheel.

It was Sherry, Jim's wife. She'd come alone.

He tossed the can he'd drained into the wastebasket and dashed through the house to intercept her before she rang the bell and wakened Audra.

When he opened the door, he hardly recognized her. She'd been crying. He could tell by her puffy face and swollen lids. One look at him and she didn't try to reach the porch.

"Sherry? What is it you want?"

She shuddered. "I need to talk to Audra."

"I'm afraid she's asleep. Will I do?"

"No." She looked anxious. "This is something between the two of us." She started to turn away, when a familiar voice sounded behind him.

"I'm awake, Sherry. I heard your car pull in. Come inside."

Rick wheeled around in surprise. Their eyes met. "Are you sure you're up to this?"

"Yes."

Once Sherry entered the living room, Rick shut the door. Audra invited her to sit down on the couch.

"Whatever you have to tell me, you can say in front of Rick. We don't have any secrets left. Things have gone too far for that."

Sherry bit her lip. "I agree. That's why I'm here. After dinner last night, Greg called, then Tom. They talked for a long time in secret before Jim left in the truck and never came home.

"When it got to be two-thirty in the morning and he still hadn't shown up, I was frantic. To prevent myself from panicking, I turned on the radio to listen to your program while I waited for him to walk in the door." She paused for a moment before adding, "I've never told you this before but I really love your show. You're so fabulous."

Rick's glance swerved to Audra, whose eyes looked suspiciously bright.

"When I heard Tom's voice—the things he said to you—I was outraged. Especially when I knew you'd asked Uncle David to call all of us to warn us about the storm."

Good for you, Sherry. It's about time.

"I'm ashamed for the boys' behavior, appalled!" Tears poured down her pale cheeks. "When you talked about paying the community back for everything they'd done for you and Jim and the family years ago, it hit me that there's something horribly wrong with all three of them.

"Tom may be the ringleader, but Jim and Greg continue to go along with him. It's got to stop!" She dabbed at her eyes before she poured out the rest of the story.

"I had to make up a reason why Jim wasn't at breakfast this morning so the children wouldn't be upset. He never returned any of my calls. When I arrived at work, I phoned Diane and Annette. They'd left their answering machines on.

"At that point I couldn't concentrate and went back home. Jim was there." She swallowed. "He refused to tell me where he'd been all night. We had a horrible fight. I warned him that if he didn't tell me the truth, I was going to leave him."

"Sherry—"

Audra's compassionate heart was one of the things Rick loved most about her.

"You were right when you accused me of being a fence-sitter. I've been thinking hard about that ever since the other night. I'm so sorry for the way they acted when they heard about Rick's accident."

That was news to Rick. He'd get it out of Audra later.

"I called Mom, and then I called the school to give my permission for her to pick up the kids and take them home with her. When I leave here, that's where I'm going. She's never really approved of Jim. When I told her everything, she said she wouldn't let me go back to him, that I needed an attorney. We're going to find one today.

"If my husband wants to communicate with me, he'll have to do it through a lawyer. For a long time I've told him he needs professional help to get over his anger. He has just ignored me. But he can't ignore me now unless he wants to lose me and the children. I don't want his hang-ups rubbing off on them. He's an angry man. They've already suffered damage because of it.

"Diane had a huge fight with Greg because he refused to take her to Pam's wedding or let her go alone.''

"I didn't know that," Audra muttered. "I'm sure Pam doesn't either.''

"Both Greg and Jim forbade us to say or do anything. They wouldn't even let us go near you when you were in the hospital after your accident, Audra. Because of the children, we've been afraid to move. It's like being in a prison.'' Sherry took a deep breath and wiped the tears from her cheeks with a tissue.

"The children love you and Pam a lot. They don't understand why all of this is happening. That's the reason Diane took her kids and went to stay with her parents in Fort Worth for a week. She knows the boys' treatment of you and Pam and Uncle David is totally sick. I can't speak for Annette, but I believe deep down she's terrified of Tom.''

Audra nodded. "That's what I think, too.''

"I came here to warn you. I can feel the boys are up to something terrible, but I don't know what it is.''

"That's all right,'' Rick interjected. "We've got the police on top of it now.''

Her eyes widened in shock. "The police?''

"Someone shot out the window in Audra's bedroom in the middle of the night.''

Sherry's face crumpled. She stared at her cousin-in-law. "Are you all right?''

"We can thank providence she wasn't in there at the time,'' Rick answered. "I called 9-1-l. While the detective was here, we gave him the names of the parties we feel were responsible.''

"I'm glad,'' Sherry declared. "It looks like the

law's going to be the only way to put an end to their reign of terror.''

''That's what it's been,'' Audra said in a tremulous voice.

Sherry got to her feet. ''If there's anything I can do, anything you need to tell me, just call me on my cell phone. I swear I'll help you any way I can.''

Audra looked up at her. ''There is one thing you can do right now.''

''What's that?''

''Stop at the main house and tell Pam and Clint everything you've told me. It will mean the world to both of them. And when you get to your mom's, phone Uncle David and repeat everything to him?''

''I promise.''

''Sherry?''

''Yes?''

''Thank you. You're very courageous.''

She shook her head in abnegation. ''If I am, I learned that quality from you and Pam. Please be careful, Audra.''

''I will.''

Rick cupped Sherry's elbow. ''Let me walk you outside.'' He opened the front door and helped her to her car. Once she was inside, he said, ''Be expecting a phone call from a police detective later today. He'll want to talk to you.''

''Okay.''

He watched her drive off, then he hurried into the house. Audra stood in the middle of the living room balancing on one crutch. Moisture glazed her cheeks.

Without conscious thought, he put his arm around her and let her cry it out.

"Why is it the children always have to suffer?"

Rick hugged her as close as he could with the sling between them. "You heard Sherry. She's already taking steps to see that the abuse stops."

"I'm proud of her."

"So am I."

She raised her head. Her wet blue eyes held a sadness that wrenched his heart. "My cousins must have had some wonderful traits or their wives wouldn't have married them. How tragic if three couples are forced to divorce because the boys can't or won't be helped."

"There's always hope," he said, but he didn't really believe it in their case.

He kissed her curls. "I think it's time you had something to eat. How about some soup?"

"That sounds good."

They'd barely started for the kitchen, when Rick heard another car pull into the driveway. Maybe Sherry had something else to tell them.

"Walk into the hall while I find out who it is," he said.

In two seconds flat he reached the front door and opened it in time to see a workman from Diamond Glass get out of his truck. Clint had said he'd take care of the repairs. With all the broadcasting equipment, not to mention the expensive harp and soundboard, the room needed to be secured.

Rick showed the man in and introduced him to Audra. While he replaced the window, the two of them ate a late lunch. After he'd gone, she phoned her boss to let him know why she couldn't do the Friday-night radio show.

"Any problem?" Rick asked when she'd hung up.

"None at all. Because we devoted the program to the tornado victims, he'd been listening and got angry when he heard Tom's comments. According to him, the requests for CDs haven't stopped pouring in. We'll be able to send a nice amount of money to the Red Cross. With all our personal problems, I haven't given a lot of thought to the poor people who've lost homes and barns."

"You did last night. People aren't going to forget."

Her gaze flicked to his. "Do you know something? If I were running for office, I'd pick you for my campaign manager. Seriously—" She put a hand on his arm for a brief moment. "I don't know how to thank you for everything."

"Even for breaking into your bedroom?" he teased.

Her lips curved. "Even for that. It's comforting to know that if someone had been attacking me, you would have stopped him."

"You think I could have?"

"With one of my crutches, I have no doubt."

They both chuckled.

"For my own selfish reasons, I don't want you sleeping at the main house tonight."

She toyed with her soupspoon. "I admit it's been fun having you around. I've never had a roommate before."

"Aren't you forgetting Boris?"

"We didn't live together." He sensed her hesitation before she asked the question he knew was coming. "Did you? Live with those three women, I mean?"

He shook his head. "Not in the sense that they brought all their belongings and moved in with me. No—living with you is a first. I like it. I like it a lot.

"For one thing, you're a great cook. Listening to you sing live is better than putting on my Walkman headphones. You're easy on the eyes, and you have the sexiest accent this side of the Continental Divide."

Her eyes were smiling.

"Now it's your turn," he prodded.

"I've already written a song about you."

He cocked his head. "That was your impression of me before you got to know me."

"Well, you put the fear in my cousins the other day when they broke in. That rates high in my book."

"Keep going."

"You honored my uncle's request to stay with me without asking why. When you do something that kind for him, you've done it for me."

"I'll keep that in mind," he drawled. "Go on. You've got to tell me two more things so we're even."

"Two more things…" She rolled her eyes. "You leave the bathroom neat and clean. That's a huge plus."

He grinned. "One more."

"You're a gentleman like your father. It's a trait I

haven't seen in another man except Uncle David, whom I trust with my life.''

''How about something more personal?''

''Oh—so you want to hear I like my roommates tall, dark and handsome? I do, but I also like them with two arms.''

Rick burst into laughter. ''Give me another week.''

''It's okay. This peg leg of mine leaves a lot to be desired, too.''

''With all our handicaps, we managed fine in the culvert yesterday. That's what comes from living together on a twenty-four-hour basis. I'm not sure how I'm going to fare when I'm alone.''

''You told me your brother's coming.''

''My older brother,'' he emphasized. ''He can't cook, he sings off-key and he doesn't have curls like bluebonnet blossoms.''

She looked stunned.

''Hasn't anyone ever told you that before?''

''No,'' she whispered before averting her eyes.

''I've been working on a song about you. One day when it's finished, I'll sing it for you.''

''The music *and* the lyrics?''

''That's right.''

''I can't wait!'' She sounded genuinely excited.

''Not all my talents have to do with speed.''

When he read Audra's mind correctly, a built-in truth mechanism sent a blush over her face and body.

''Next you're going to tell me you strum a mean guitar.''

A slow smile broke the corners of his mouth. ''No.

I appreciate music, I don't play it. One of my interests is golf.''

"I once dated a guy in Austin who tried to show me the fundamentals."

"End of story?"

She laughed quietly. "I wrote a song about it."

"Of course. What did you call it?" He couldn't wait to hear.

"'That's Par For the Bogey Woman!'"

Rick tried to hold back the laughter, but it was impossible. "Brent's got to hear that."

"Who?"

"Nate's brother-in-law. He came close to being a pro golfer. It'll crack him up. Do you have the song on CD?"

"It's in the inventory somewhere."

The package of CDs he'd ordered from the station should have arrived at the main house. He would ask his father to bring it when he came for Audra later.

"Speaking of my stuff, I've got to get busy and sort things for the movers to pack."

"I'll help."

"I'd better start with my instruments. The first thing I need to do is get my harp ready."

He followed her into the first bedroom. "I know nothing about them, but it looks elegant and expensive."

"It's a Venus Grand Concert Model 75 pedal harp. Kind of like your M3."

"Aren't you nervous how the movers will transport it?"

"It has a special case. If you'll tell them to rest it on its column before they strap it, there's no worry."

"Where's the case?"

"In the closet. It's a burgundy color."

"I'll get it."

Rick loved doing things with her, for her. Anything, as long as they were together. When he thought about night coming on, he hated it because she wouldn't be in the house. Audra had changed him until he didn't know himself anymore.

Too soon Pam came for her. He put Audra's suitcase in the trunk, then helped her into the front seat of his car and leaned inside the window. After brushing her lips with his own he said, "Give that kiss to little Becky for me tomorrow. Sleep well tonight."

FRIDAY AFTERNOON. It was time to go.

Clint was driving Audra in Rick's car. Pam followed behind them in the truck.

Strange how Audra had dreaded the day when she would be leaving the ranch she'd lived on all her life. Yet right now every bit of her pain had to do with being parted from Rick.

Last night they'd slept apart. The kiss he'd given her had suffused her whole body with yearnings that had kept her awake all night. It wasn't fair when there were no guarantees she'd be seeing him again anytime soon.

The ranch house looked deserted as they drove away. If the boys came by either house, they would assume there was no one on the premises.

That was the whole point.

She felt Clint's glance. "You'll always have a home with us, Audra."

As long as he didn't know how deeply she loved his son, she would let him go on thinking her tears were for this abrupt uprooting from all she held dear.

Little did anyone know she'd already done her grieving. The boys' cruelty had tainted everything. When she didn't think she could take any more, Rick had come into her life, bringing her more joy and happiness than she'd thought possible.

If this was all she could ever have of him, she would hug the memory to herself forever.

"The boys aren't going to be a menace much longer."

She let out a sigh. "Did Sherry talk to you?"

"Yes. She had Pam in tears before she was through."

"When this is all over, Uncle David and I want to have a wedding reception for you and Pam. I'm sure Sherry and Diane will help. There are so many people who love Pam and would want to honor both of you. We could hold the function at the church in Hill Grove."

He patted her arm. "You spend your whole life worrying about everyone else."

"Don't give me any credit. Pam's the selfless one. In case you didn't know, I'm so thankful she went to Colorado and met you. I had to talk her into going."

"I didn't know that."

"Even though it was her best friend getting married, she hated leaving Uncle David, but I convinced her I could look after him while she was gone. She fell in love with you so fast, my uncle and I walked around the house with huge smiles on our faces.''

''When Anja died, I didn't think it was possible to love again like that. But I hadn't counted on Pam coming into the store. One look in those big brown eyes of hers and I felt a jolt in my heart.

''The more time passes, the more I'm convinced the Jarretts and the Hawkinses were meant to meet.''

She bit her lip. ''I just hope you don't live to regret those words.''

''Stop worrying about the boys. I have every confidence things are going to work out. Why don't you try to sleep until we get to the hotel.''

She closed her eyes and put her head back to humor him, then knew nothing more until they arrived at the hotel.

EVERYONE HAD CONGREGATED in the sitting-room area of Clint and Pam's suite. It seemed while Audra had been asleep in the car, Pam had picked up Uncle David at the Cattlemen's Club. Now they were all together.

''Audra Jarrett?'' Clint said, holding little Becky in his arms. ''I'd like you to meet my son Nate and his wife, Laurel.''

She let go of the crutch handle to shake hands with them. ''I'm so happy to meet you at last.'' Her eyes fastened on their baby. ''Oh, your daughter is adorable.''

''Isn't she?'' Clint beamed at his granddaughter.

Her gaze flicked back to the stunning couple standing before her. Laurel Hawkins was a beautiful blue-eyed woman with glistening black hair, the kind Audra would have killed for in her younger days when everyone called her Red.

Nate, on the other hand, had dark-blond hair and blue eyes, which smiled at Audra as if he knew a secret. In every way except his coloring, he resembled Rick so much she had to discipline herself not to stare. There couldn't be two better-looking men anywhere in existence. Three, if you included their father.

"Sit down and rest your leg, honey." Her uncle patted the seat next to him on the couch.

She walked over and put her crutches against the wall. "I've missed you," she said, giving him a kiss and a hug, which he reciprocated.

Laurel and Nate sat down in the two chairs next to them. Clint and Pam took the other love seat. There was a coffee table in the middle loaded with several trays of drinks and sandwiches Pam had ordered from room service.

Nate reached for one and devoured it so fast, it could have been Rick sneaking food from the kitchen counter before she'd had time to put it on the table.

He treated her to another searching gaze. "My brother sent us something in the mail the other day. We've been listening to your CDs nonstop."

Heat scorched Audra's cheeks.

"You're the most fabulous singer!" Laurel cried. "You compose and play. I can't get over it."

"Neither can I," Nate murmured. "Why aren't you marketed nationally? You're phenomenal."

"No, I'm not, but thank you for your kind words."

"She's a musical prodigy," her uncle spoke up.

"When she plays her harp, it's like having my own little angel around." His eyes glistened with tears.

"Will you all stop?"

By now Pam was cuddling the baby. "Audra could have a film or television career if she wanted. I can't tell you the number of agents who've tried to get her to sign with them and make her a star."

"That's not what I want, Pam. You know it's not. I'm perfectly happy doing my radio show, performing on my harp. Let's not talk about me."

"It's impossible not to," Nate persisted with that same intensity his brother exhibited. He leaned forward. "I want to know when you wrote 'Racetrack Lover.'"

Audra had been afraid of that. She averted her eyes in panic.

"I think I can answer your question," Pam interjected. "It was the night I called her after she'd finished her program. I was worried that she'd overdone it. She was upset with me for hovering when I had a husband who needed his sleep.

"I told her Clint was outside watching for Rick, who was expected any minute. Audra said, wouldn't it be funny if the legendary Lucky Hawkins had gotten lost and was whizzing around the various ranches in the area asking, 'Does my daddy live here?'"

"*Pam!*" Audra couldn't believe her cousin would reveal a confidence like that.

Nate burst into laughter. So did everyone else. The noise startled Becky, but Pam soon got Nate's little girl under control. Laurel didn't know it, but she probably wouldn't get to hold her baby again until she and Nate flew back to Colorado.

If tending Becky didn't convince Pam she needed a child of her own to dote on, nothing else would. Clint was so crazy about his granddaughter, Audra had the strongest feeling he'd love to be a father again.

She felt a nudge and looked at her uncle. More often than not, they were on the same wavelength. Sure enough, the twinkle in his eye meant he was picturing Pam with a baby of her own.

Audra smiled at him.

Maybe her cousin was already pregnant. Wouldn't that be fantastic. Another Hawkins…

CHAPTER THIRTEEN

RICK HAD TOLD Nate the two-story main ranch house had been built in the Queen Anne style. He wouldn't be able to miss it because it looked so out of place against the flat land. The house was completely dark and it gave him a lonely, empty feeling.

The bungalow was supposed to be three miles farther down the road on the right. Another minute and he spied the mailbox out in front of the property where a yellow-sided structure sat back a little ways from the road. There were no lights on here either.

He picked up his cell phone and rang his brother. "It's me. I'm just pulling into the driveway."

"Terrific. Drive around back so no one can see your car from the road. I'll let you in through the side door."

"Will do."

For someone who could only use one arm, Rick's bear hug was almost as bone crushing as their father's. "It's good to see you, bro."

They stood in the darkened kitchen taking each other's measure. Nate shook his head. "How did you and I ever end up on a ranch in this back-of-beyond state?"

"That's the way it appeared to me on the drive

down, but I've discovered Texas has certain things to recommend it after all," Rick replied.

"If you're speaking of Ms. Audra Jarrett, I have to agree with you. That woman's accent sounds positively sexy when she sings. There's only one word for her. Sensational."

Their eyes met. "I'm glad you got the CDs."

"Laurel and I started listening to her songs and couldn't stop."

"Did you meet her?"

"Yes. You were right. She's one attractive redhead. Watching her perform must really be something."

"You don't know the half of it. How did she seem tonight?"

The emotion in Rick's voice, the concern in his eyes revealed everything Nate had suspected. "A little tired, but otherwise all right."

"She's not all right. When Dad drove her away this evening, she realized this was the end of life as she's known it on the ranch all these years. But she hides everything well, just like Pam."

"Let's be thankful she's in Austin now where she's safe."

"Thank God." Rick expelled a deep sigh. "That bullet could have hit her if she'd happened to be standing in the trajectory."

"Don't think about it. When I left the hotel suite, she was holding Becky and loving it. Everyone was having a great time. Dad and David Jarrett seem to be close."

"They are. David's a great man."

Rick was no longer the same brother who'd left Colorado ten days ago heartbroken and lost. And it seemed that Audra Jarrett was the reason for this profound change in him.

For that alone, Nate was prepared to love her. It was worth whatever he had to do to help clear their path.

"Show me the bedroom where her cousin shot out the window."

In a few minutes Nate had been given a tour of the house. "With the threat of a lawsuit, I don't think the boys are going to strike again in the same place."

"I don't either, but you never know for sure," Rick muttered.

"On the drive from Austin I tried to put myself in their shoes. What would I do if I wanted revenge?"

"Light the ranch houses on fire?" Rick supplied. "The possibility of that happening hasn't left my mind."

"That's crossed my mind, too. But something else has occurred to me because of your accident."

"I don't follow."

"Her cousins are angry because they have to board their horses at a neighboring ranch. Didn't you tell me they wanted Audra to leave the bungalow so they could live here while they built a barn in the back?"

His brother nodded.

"Since you thwarted them, what better way to get the women where it really hurts than to lock Marshmallow and Prince in the barn behind the main house and set it on fire?"

"I think you've hit on something," Rick exclaimed. "Those horses are the women's pride and joy. If the boys were to steal them, or do something to injure them so they'd have to be put down, it could be the cause of a lot of grief, fire or no fire."

"Let's check the horses out right now to make sure they're okay," Nate suggested.

"Good idea. After that I'll give you a tour of the main house. Audra left me the keys. Let's go."

Before long they'd reached the other property. Nate drove around the back. He whistled softly. "That's a nice big barn. No wonder the boys are upset."

"Wait till you see inside the ranch house. It's a mansion, the kind they don't build anymore. Between the girls and David, they've kept it in immaculate condition."

Nate looked all around. "It sounds like Dad has really taken to this place."

"That was my impression the evening he took me horseback riding."

Rick unlocked the doors to the barn and they went inside. The smell of hay and warm animal flesh filled his nostrils. He turned on the light. "If Pam had never gone into the ski shop to buy a pair of sunglasses, our father would still be grieving."

"He and Pam are a great match."

"I agree. We can't let anything ruin it for them. He said he wanted to help make her dream for a bed-and-breakfast a reality."

"That may have been true once," Nate interjected. "Now I'm convinced this has become his dream, too."

"Dad always did love a challenge. The higher the stakes, the sweeter the prize."

They walked over to the first stall. "This is Marshmallow. She's as sweet-natured as Pam." Rick rubbed her nose. The mare nuzzled him back.

Nate smiled. "She looks in good shape despite her falling on you."

"Don't remind me." They heard neighing from the next stall. Rick chuckled before walking over to the gelding. "Prince doesn't like being ignored, do you, boy. He's missing Audra."

"Is she as fabulous an equestrian as she is a musician?"

"Probably, but from what I understand, Pam was the women's champion trick rider at the Austin rodeo three years in a row in her twenties."

"I bet Dad loved hearing that."

Rick nodded. "Kind of like winning her own version of the womens' downhill. According to David, she could trick ride like nobody's business and won dozens of trophies at events throughout the state of Texas."

"What's the old saying, still waters run deep? Trust Dad to meet another woman with a competitor's heart."

"That's Pam, but I would never have known it when I was first introduced to her."

"No," Nate agreed.

"Audra confided to me that her cousin was terrified of our reaction to the news that she and Dad were engaged to be married."

"That seems like a century ago."

Rick nodded. "I won't lock the barn yet. When you come back, park the car in here, then lock it."

"Good idea."

He turned off the light and gave Nate a quick tour of the house. Ten minutes later they returned to the bungalow.

Nate had been suitably impressed with the large ranch house. "Their bed-and-breakfast will be the showplace of the entire region when they're ready to receive guests.

"When I drive back there, I think I'll keep a watch from that widow's walk upstairs on the side of the house. It'll give me an uninterrupted view of everything, including the barn."

"That's a perfect spot," Rick replied. "Just so you know, Pam left plenty of food in the fridge when you get hungry. I'll stay outside here tonight and do guard duty."

"As soon as the sun's up I'll come and get you. We'll wait for the movers together."

"Sounds like a plan. Phone me when you're situated. I want to talk to you about something important." Rick got out of the passenger side and shut the door.

Nate leaned his head out the window. "I hope you're going to tell me you won't be heading to Arizona when that sling's removed."

Without waiting for Rick's response, he backed out to the road and headed for the main house. Let his brother chew on that for a few minutes while he called Laurel to say good-night to her.

Cell phones were a wonderful invention. She answered before the second ring. "Nate?"

"Hi, darling. How's everything? How's Becky?"

"She's asleep in her carryall."

"Good. Let's hope she'll give you six hours without interruption."

"Don't I wish! Are you all right? I have to admit I'm nervous about you and Rick being there alone."

"You don't think we can take care of ourselves?"

"Not if someone's shooting at you—" Her voice trembled.

"The boys won't do that again. In any case, they were trying to scare Audra. How was she after I left?"

"She played with Becky until David went back to his club. At that point she gave her up and said goodnight, but I doubt she'll be getting any sleep. You can tell she's worried sick."

"This will soon be over."

"How's Rick?"

"If I didn't know he was my brother, I wouldn't recognize him."

"Oh darling, if you're saying what I think you are—"

"I'll know more in a little while."

"Why? What's happening?"

"As soon as I'm settled at the main house, he wants me to call him so he can talk over something important."

"Phone me when you're through. I have to hear everything."

"You might be asleep. I'd hate to wake you when you need sleep so badly."

"You think I could sleep tonight?" she asked incredulously. "I'm going to watch a movie while I wait for your call."

"Okay, sweetheart. I love you."

"I love you, Nate. Please, please be careful."

"Nothing's going to happen to any of us."

AFTER HIS THIRD TRIP around the bungalow, Rick heard his cell phone ring and he clicked on.

"How goes the watch?"

"All clear for now."

"Same here."

"I found a casserole of lasagna and warmed some. It's better than Laurel's, but don't tell her I said that."

Rick grinned. "When David told me Pam was the best cook in the Hill Country, he wasn't kidding. Audra learned everything from her."

"For someone who's been in the hospital recently, I thought you were looking well fed," his brother quipped. "Was that the important thing you had to tell me?"

Emotion swept through Rick. "You know it wasn't."

"Go on."

"What would you say if I told you I'm thinking of having a racing school built?"

"Where?" His brother's reply came back so fast it stunned him.

Rick's hand tightened on his phone. "Somewhere off I-70 between Denver and Copper Mountain. I've got Brent's friend Jed looking for a piece of property now. Chip could be the manager. In my gut I know Wally would come on board.''

"Does that mean you'd make a permanent home in Copper Mountain?"

"Yes. I can't see myself living anywhere else."

"Neither can I." His brother sounded choked up. "I guess I don't have to tell you what those words mean to me."

"You and Jed are the only people I've told. I want to keep it that way until I've got everything lined up."

"What about Dad?"

"He has enough on his mind right now."

"Rick—"

"I know what it'll mean to him, but nothing's definite yet. I've got to talk to my attorney and my investment broker. When you start to think about all that's involved…

"I've only seen this business from the driving end. It's going to be a whole new experience to put a racing school together."

"No one could do it better than you. When new drivers coming up in the ranks hear they're going to be taught by Lucky Hawkins himself, you'll have to turn away applicants in droves. I think you ought to call it the Racetrack Lover's School of High Performance."

A smile broke out on Rick's face. "You heard that one."

"Laurel and I must have played it twenty times.

That song helped me understand why you said you and Audra were still dancing around each other.''

Rick frowned. "When did I say that?"

"In the hospital."

"What else did I say?"

"Something about bottle rockets and curls that looked like bluebonnet blossoms."

"Jeez."

"Don't worry. My lips are sealed."

"I think she likes me."

"You only think?" Nate mocked. "Then how did you end up living with her at her bungalow?"

"She wanted the protection I could provide. Audra has nightmares."

"How many did she have while you were consoling her?"

"One."

"Is she still dreaming about being trapped in that car with the man who died?"

"No. This time she was trying to rescue me instead of Pete."

There was a long silence. "Well, you know how to fix that in a big hurry."

Rick's eyes closed tightly for a minute. "What if it doesn't fix everything?"

"What do you mean?"

"She's got trust issues."

"Because of the man who broke her heart?"

"Did Dad tell you about that?"

"He intimated she'd had a past relationship that hurt her."

"I found out his name was Boris. He was some

French conductor who couldn't deal with the fact that she was more brilliant than he was.''

''Not too many men could. It takes a man totally confident with himself. A man like you, brother. The guy who's been leaving the competition behind him since he put on his first pair of skis, rode his first bike, built his first go-cart and drove his first race car. You could always do anything. Now you're in the race of your life. You know what I mean?''

Rick knew.

''Just apply some of that famous Lucky Hawkins technique when you know you're so close you can taste victory. You won't fail.''

It took a minute before he whispered, ''Thanks.''

''Anytime. Since nothing's happening around here, tell me more about your plans. I want to hear details.''

''OH NO—there's been a mistake!'' Audra cried to Pam when she saw the movers bring the framed picture of the bluebonnets into her uncle's condo.

Her cousin eyed her with a puzzled expression. ''I gave it to you for your birthday.''

''I know, but it looked so pretty in the blue bedroom it ought to stay at the bungalow.''

''I'm glad Rick told the movers to pack it. With things the way they are right now, who knows if you would have ever seen it again.''

''Ma'am?'' one of the movers approached Audra. ''Would you mind coming out to the truck? We're all finished except for the equipment to be taken back to the radio station. Mr. Hawkins told us to be sure you inspected everything before we leave here.''

Rick. There was no one like him.

"Of course." Adjusting her crutches, she followed the man out the back door to the carport. The two-year-old condos formed a complex of one-floor dwellings with individual patios. Only one occupant had lived in Uncle David's unit. It was in excellent condition, with plantation shutters and neutral walls and carpet that had been recently cleaned.

Both men helped her up the ramp into the back of the truck. Her eyes sought out the Telos zephyr, the mixing board, the plug-in mike and the volume controls.

"All the equipment's here."

The man gave a satisfied nod. "If you'll sign this, we'll go."

She put her signature on the dotted line. With their assistance, she made it to the floor of the carport and swung herself back inside the condo where everyone was still working, even Laurel.

They'd been at it all day.

Never one to be idle, her uncle had spent the last few days buying things for the condo. Several deliveries had come while they were moving in. They now had dishes, pots and pans, bathroom supplies, a dinette set and a bed and dresser for Audra.

Pam and Clint had stepped out long enough to buy groceries. When they returned, they cooked up some Mexican food. The smell of ground beef, onions and corn tortillas cooking gave the condo a lived-in feeling.

Audra was grateful for the help and the company.

She knew her uncle was, too. It made the transition, from one life to another, bearable.

"Is the painting too high, too low?" Clint and David held it against one of the walls in the living room for the women's approval.

"Right there," they cried at the same time.

Clint smiled. "I'll mark it."

In a few minutes the bluebonnets had taken their place as the focal point of the room, which contained all of the furnishings from the parlor of the ranch house.

Her uncle looked around, then glanced at Audra. "This is nice, isn't it, honey?"

She had to give her uncle points for acting as if this was a day like any other. He was the best.

"It's wonderful and familiar. We're going to be happy here."

"You're darn tootin' we are."

"Dinner's ready," her cousin interjected. Pam knew how hard this moment was on their uncle. Audra was sure Pam didn't want him to have time to dwell on the drastic change that had just occurred.

Audra also knew Clint and Pam had begged him to stay on at the ranch until he died if that was his desire, but he wouldn't have any part of it.

If it was true that he really wanted the opportunity to meet a woman, then Audra was going to proceed from here on out with that thought in mind. Otherwise she wouldn't be able to stand what was happening.

When Laurel's cell phone rang, Audra rushed to take the baby from her. All day Audra had been listening for her own phone to ring in the hope it might be Rick. She missed him so much. Not hearing from him or Nate had deepened her anxiety that something was wrong.

From the look on Laurel's face, she was on edge, too. Who wouldn't be, when Audra's lunatic cousins were out doing who knew what?

Laurel didn't talk long before hanging up. "Nate says to tell everyone hi. So far there's been no activity. He and Rick followed the movers out to the highway in case the boys were watching.

"They doubled back and found a hiding place. At the moment they're keeping an eye on things and taking turns sleeping. When it gets dark they'll go back to the same places they were last night. If anything goes on tonight, they'll deal with it."

Though Audra was relieved with that much news, she was afraid that Rick was using this opportunity to distance himself from her.

"Here's a plate for you, Audra."

"Thanks, Pam."

The last thing she felt like was food, but she had to keep up the pretense of being hungry.

"Uncle David? Why don't you get Harry on the phone and invite him and your friends over for a housewarming tonight? I'm sure they're missing you already. You can break in the dinette set with five card stud."

"We bought plenty of food, so you won't run out of things to eat or drink," Pam was quick to join in.

"There's an NBA game on tonight," Audra blurted as an afterthought. "If you call them now, they'll be here in time for the first quarter."

"What about you, honey?" Her uncle looked at her with a neutral expression.

"I'll be busy organizing my bedroom."

"Use my cell phone." Clint handed it to David before helping himself to another couple of tacos.

Her uncle knew exactly what they were doing, but part of him must have realized it would be therapeutic to have friends over tonight. Otherwise, he wouldn't have gone along with Audra's suggestion.

After everyone had eaten and the dishes were done, Clint suggested it was time to get the women back to the hotel. It had been a long day. Heaven knew it was going to be an even longer night while they waited to hear from Rick and Nate.

Laurel was a real trooper. No doubt at a time like this she derived immense comfort from her baby. Audra hated to see the family go, but there was no help for it.

The silence in the condo didn't last long, and she was grateful for this. Henry and two other retired rancher friends showed up and brought the place back to life. She left them dealing cards and went to her bedroom.

The room was a little smaller than the blue room at the bungalow, but it didn't matter. The place had never represented home to her. As for the main house, knowing Pam lived there with Clint made her happy. Hopefully, in time, the thought would bring a certain contentment to her uncle, too.

She rested her crutches against the wall and turned out the light. Suddenly exhausted, she lay down on top of the bed.

Face it, Audra. You've come to the crossroads of your life. It's up to you to make the best of it without Rick Hawkins in the picture.

Things had to get better once her cast came off. If all went well, she'd be free of it by this time next week. What a difference it would make when she could drive the truck again, do her program at the studio.

If it appeared her uncle wanted to be free to invite a woman over, she'd find herself an apartment and start giving harp lessons. Until then she had a project that would keep her busy for a while.

She'd be all right during the days. It was the nights she had to get through, those dark hours when her subconscious brought her deepest longings and fears to the surface.

The sounds of the men's voices in the other room droned on. It was after one in the morning and they were still going strong. That was good. By the time they left, her uncle would be ready for sleep.

Audra needed to get up and brush her teeth. As she started to move off the bed, her cell phone rang. It was on the dresser. She felt sick for fear it was Tom.

After grabbing a crutch, she got up to look at the caller ID.

It was Rick!

With heart pounding, she clicked on. "Hello?"

"Audra? I hope you don't mind me phoning this late. I was listening to your prerecorded radio program tonight and got this urge to phone in on the request line. How about singing something to help me stay awake?"

Rick.

"I take it you're back at the bungalow. Where's Nate?"

"Observing from the widow's walk."

"I haven't been up there in years. You can see the whole property from there."

"That's the idea."

"How long do you plan to keep this up? The boys might not cause any more trouble again for weeks."

"Nate'll keep watch with me through Sunday morning. Then he and Laurel have to fly back to Colorado Springs."

"This has been no vacation for them," she lamented.

"It wasn't intended to be."

"She's amazing. She pitched in all day to help. I know she's exhausted and will probably be up in the night several times to nurse her baby."

"Laurel knew what this visit was about. She wouldn't have come with Nate if she hadn't wanted to. It's given Dad and Pam a chance to be with her and Becky."

"Actually, I think Uncle David spent more time with the baby than anyone else today. He adores that little girl."

"She's a cutie. How's he doing?"

"His friends are still here playing poker."

"That had to be your idea."

"I thought it would help."

"And who's helping you?"

Oh, Rick. Don't ask me questions like that.

"You did when you sent the photograph of the bluebonnets. Thank you for being so thoughtful."

"It does belong to *you*. I thought it might make you feel more at home."

"Yes," she whispered. "We've hung it in the living room as a reminder. But in case you didn't realize, when I was in college I lived on campus during the week. After that, I was gone for two years in France. Living in the city, away from the ranch, is nothing new. Uncle David and I have each other. That's the important thing."

"Audra—"

Her breath caught. "Yes?"

"I'm glad he's there if you should have another nightmare."

She'd thought he was going to say something else. She didn't know what exactly.

"Me, too. Good night, Rick."

THE LINE ON HER END had gone dead. Rick clicked off with a grimace.

She was so damn noble, but he wouldn't want her any other way.

The situation with the boys was so infuriating, he felt as if he was going nuts, especially in this straitjacket he had to wear. Less than a minute passed before his cell phone rang.

"Nate?"

"We've got company."

That was music to Rick's ears. The sooner this business with Audra's cousins was resolved, the sooner he could make plans for a future he'd never thought possible.

"A white half-ton pickup truck just pulled into the driveway."

"That's Greg's. Give me a minute to phone 9-1-1, then call me back."

Rick gave the dispatcher the particulars and the case number on the card the detective had left with him, then he started for the main house at a run.

He slowed down to take Nate's next call.

"Two guys are down there. The one hooking up the horse trailer to the back of the truck is slender. The huskier one has walked to the barn."

"That would be Tom."

Maybe Sherry had gotten to Jim by moving in with her mother. Too bad Greg hadn't seen the light yet.

"As long as Tom's out for revenge, he's mercenary enough to want to make some money off the girls' horses. That's what the boys are after. I'll be there in a minute, Nate."

"I'm going downstairs now. I'll slip out to the front porch to wait for the police."

After clicking off, Rick picked up speed. His adrenaline had kicked in. It felt good to stretch his legs. This was a different kind of high, one he wasn't going to come down from.

Nate met him in front of the house. "You got here fast."

"That's what happens when you're motivated."

"One way or the other, the boys are in for it now."

They didn't have to wait long for the police. If Rick

had set up the scenario himself, he couldn't have planned it better.

Greg had just pulled the trailer as far as the road to make a turn when three squad cars suddenly appeared coming from both directions.

Their lights were flashing and Rick could hear one of the officers telling the boys to step out of the truck with their hands on their heads.

Rick turned to his brother. "Thanks for coming. We do good work."

"I agree."

They waited nearby until the boys had been placed under arrest and driven away, then they spoke with the officer in charge.

It took close to a half hour before their statements had been taken and the horses were led back to the barn.

Nate drove his rental car out of the barn while Rick shut the doors. Tom had broken the lock, but Rick was satisfied nobody would be breaking in before his dad and Pam arrived back at the ranch.

He climbed into the car and shut the door. "Drive me to the bungalow for my things. Then let's head to Austin."

"And then what?" It was a leading question.

"Since the base of Becky's car seat is already in the back of my M3, how would you and Laurel like to drive me to Colorado Springs this morning?"

His brother grinned. "I've been waiting to get my hands on that baby. Dad's going to miss her after we leave."

Rick nodded, momentarily distracted. But his mind

was on other things than his car. "Jed phoned and told me he's found the perfect spot for my business. I thought I'd pay Chip a visit. We'll check out the property. I want his input and Wally's before I make a decision."

A decision that was going to affect his whole life and hopefully Audra's. If she loved him enough....

CHAPTER FOURTEEN

"MY LEG FEELS so strange without the cast."

"That's normal," the doctor said. "My nurse will give you the number for the physical therapy clinic. Make an appointment as soon as possible to get started. It will strengthen that leg and hasten your recovery time.

"Use your crutches when you leave here. Start walking around the house without them when you get home. Your therapist will tell you when you don't need them anymore."

Audra looked him square in the eye. "Give it to me straight, Dr. Tobler. Do you think I'll have a limp?"

"No. The X ray shows your bones have knit together beautifully. I expect you to make a full recovery."

"Really?" she cried out, trying hard to fight back the tears. Last night she'd had a humdinger of a nightmare where she limped so badly she couldn't reach Rick's race car, which had overturned and burst into flames.

"Yes. In a couple of months you'll be able to ride your horse."

"What about driving the truck?"

"Ask your therapist after you've had a few sessions. It's all in how that leg starts to feel to you."

Her heart swelled with gratitude. "Thank you for saving it."

The surgeon eyed her with a solemn expression. "Someone upstairs performed the miracle, not me. He must have something special in store for you."

"My life and leg were spared. That's special enough."

She hugged the doctor, then walked to the waiting room on both feet using her crutches. The second her uncle saw her without her cast, he broke out in a smile and rushed over to her.

"You're walking great, honey."

Audra nodded. "The doctor says I'm not going to have a limp. I should be able to function at the wedding reception for Pam and Clint next Saturday without my crutches."

Now both their eyes had tears.

"Give me a minute. I have to make an appointment with the therapist, then we'll go home."

Except that the condo wasn't home. She didn't have one.

Her heart quaked.

Life as she'd once known it was over. She could never go back. It was all gone. Everything.

Rick was gone.

He'd been out of her life for a week, having left for Colorado Springs with Nate and Laurel. She'd tried to survive without him, but you wouldn't call it living.

Now that the cast had been removed, she was supposed to get back to normal. How?

What was normal when you had no place to go? When the man you adored had moved on to pursue his dreams?

Except that he *was* coming for the reception. At least she'd be able to stand on her own two feet and wish him luck in his future racing endeavors.

But hard as she tried to convince herself that she was strong enough to face him one more time, the truth was, she felt like dying every minute. Clint had told her that until Rick was free of the sling, he'd be spending time at the Pike's Peak Raceway with his buddy Chip.

Of course—Rick lived for racing. Still, next Saturday couldn't come soon enough for her. She needed to see him, look at him one more time before he returned, once and for all, to Arizona. She couldn't think beyond that.

Between plans for the reception, visits to the therapist and doing her radio programs, she filled her week with activity, but nothing could stop the ache in her heart. If there was one good thing, Mr. Cutler had talked with the boys' attorney. Some plea bargaining had gone on before their arraignment in front of the judge.

The charges of breaking and entering, vandalism and attempted burglary would be dropped if the three of them all went into two years of intensive psychiatric counseling by order of the court to get the help they needed. The boys agreed, even Tom.

Shock of shocks, Jim came by the condo with

Sherry and actually apologized to Audra and their uncle. They made another visit to the ranch to see Clint and Pam and tell them the same thing.

After so many years of family turmoil and pain, Audra couldn't have been happier with the astounding turn of events. The family's debt to the Hawkins men just kept growing.

Pam planned to wear the cream-colored suit with the lace trim she'd been married in to the reception. But she insisted on taking Audra shopping for a new dress—something frothy and feminine. Something to match her eyes.

In the end, Audra picked out a simple blue silk dress with cap sleeves and a scooped neck. It might not be frothy, but when she modeled it for her cousin, Pam said it would do fine. She bought of a pair of black, low-slung heels that wouldn't give her leg problems.

The night before the reception, Audra and her uncle went to dinner with the Torneys at the hotel where they were staying. The police had been in touch with them. Now that the threat was over, they wanted to get together for a friendly visit.

Audra knew that Hal had instigated it. Nevertheless, they had an enjoyable time. His parents were very nice people. It turned out Sheila Torney had been raised on a farm in Ohio.

She wasn't a big-city type and she had bad arthritis so the winters were too hard on her. That's why they'd decided to buy ranch property in Texas where she wouldn't freeze in the colder months.

The revelation made Audra a little ashamed of her

blanket criticism of the windshield ranchers gobbling up their state.

On impulse, she invited them to Pam and Clint's reception at the church recreation center in Hill Grove the next day between six and nine o'clock. If they came, they'd get to know some of the ranching families in the area, which might make them feel more at home.

Hal said yes without looking at his parents. She feared he thought she was attracted to him. To be honest, Audra couldn't see the day coming when she'd be interested in any man again, not after Rick.

But she smiled at Hal and his parents, telling them she and her uncle would look forward to seeing them if they could make it.

The next day Audra and her uncle drove out to the church early to start setting things up. The food was being catered, but when the pastor's wife showed up with a lot of friends from the church, everyone had brought casseroles and cakes and a ton of wedding gifts.

Before long, Josie Marshall, the friend whose wedding Pam had attended in Colorado, arrived to help.

Soon Sherry and Diane appeared with their children and half a dozen pies. Everyone hugged and kissed. It was an emotional reunion, but Audra was glad there wasn't time to talk about the past. They'd reserve that for another day.

She'd hired a wonderful band from the University of Austin to play for the occasion. The guests could eat and dance to the music. Audra had worked out a program to appeal to all ages and tastes.

Two of the guys in the group were good friends of hers. She'd given them an arrangement of a little song she'd written for Pam and Clint. Around four-thirty the group came in and set up so she could practice with them before the guests started to arrive.

The idea that Rick would be among them made her feverish with longing.

RICK WALKED through the doors at the rear of the church behind Brent and Julie, who were flanked by their two boys.

His heart raced like the engine of his car as it screamed around the last lap of the track. It felt good to be wearing a tuxedo jacket. No longer a one-armed bandit, he was ready for that 4:00 a.m. truck ride with a certain redhead.

Judging by the vehicles out in the parking lot, a large crowd had already assembled. His dad and Pam stood at the front of the hall greeting well-wishers. Rick and Nate had been assigned to float for the next three hours.

That was fine with him. He could follow Audra around, but first he had to find her. His hungry eyes scanned the room for a head of dark mahogany curls. He didn't have to wait long.

She was a beautiful sight as she came through the double doors leading from the kitchen. The way she moved in that blue dress, you'd never know she'd almost lost a leg.

Since the moment he'd climbed in her window and found her battling nocturnal demons, an ache for her had been growing in his heart. It would not go away until he could make sure there would be no more separations.

He blazed a path through the crowd to intercept her.

"Audra?"

At the sound of her name, she came to a standstill. A mischievous look entered the lovely eyes that lifted to his.

"Uh-oh. One tall, dark, sexy man has just entered the room. Now hear this. All ladies, run for your lives!"

The corner of his mouth lifted. "How come you're not taking your own advice?"

"I already have a crush on you, remember?"

"I'm glad you haven't forgotten."

"That would be impossible. There's only one Lucky Hawkins. He's standing in front of me, and he even has two arms."

"This must be our lucky night. I see you've got your other leg back. How does it feel?"

"Not as weird as it did the day my cast came off. Are you still in pain?"

"No, but I'm not ready to do handstands at the gym yet."

She cocked her head. "Did you ever do them?"

He grinned. "No."

That produced a chuckle.

"What can I do to help?"

"Looking like you do tonight, just continue to circulate. It'll keep the female population happy."

"Even you?"

"Especially me. I'll talk to you later when things settle down."

He let her go, but he was no longer smiling. Rick could tell she was glad to see him. You couldn't hide certain signs. Yet in his gut he felt something was wrong.

Her banter was too pat—as if she was party to a secret he didn't know anything about. It made him nervous as hell. Until he could get her alone, he'd be forced to remain in this anxiety-filled state.

For the rest of the evening he did what Audra had asked of him and made conversation. He was in Texas now. People were dancing and enjoying themselves. No one was at a loss for words.

Many guests had come from all over the region to honor Pam and her new husband. It was a real tribute to her and the Jarrett family.

Audra never came near him, but he hadn't expected her to. She was in charge of the reception, the perfect excuse to stay clear of him. He had to bide his time and simply watch her from a distance.

At ten to nine he saw her walk over to the band and reach for her guitar, resting on a stool. She approached the mike with the kind of poise and ease of a seasoned celebrity. Her beauty made it impossible to look anywhere else. The crowd fell quiet and Audra began to speak.

"Everyone has wished the happy couple well. Now I'd like to add my contribution by singing a little song. This terrific band from the University of Austin is going to back me up.

"Some of you here don't know Pam has always

been my feminine role model. After the tornado struck twenty-three years ago, she was the saint left on earth to help me make it through. I know her well.

''She keeps her feelings locked deep inside. If we were all privy to the secrets in her heart the day she met Clint Hawkins, they would go something like this.''

Then Audra began to sing.

Love came full blown that snowy morn,
In the summertime of my life.
Like the hearty primrose that pushes through
The icy fissures of winter's strife.
I found it waiting, waiting, waiting for me,
In a place far away from the Hill Country.
Where men match their mountains
Yet can be so sweet,
The heart is pierced
With emotions too deep.
Gray eyes warm and tender smiled into mine,
I saw inside a soul so noble and fine,
It made me tremble, it made me cry,
It took my breath, I wanted to die
For the love that came to me that day,
It arrived full blown, it swept me away.
So here I'll linger till I'm old and worn,
With my beloved who on that morn,
Gave me love in the summertime of my life.

The palpable silence that followed her performance was testimony to the power of words sung so exquisitely. Rick couldn't speak, couldn't move. A stillness held the crowd mesmerized. There wasn't a dry eye to be found. Pam had hidden her face against Clint's shoulder.

Rick looked over the heads of the guests and met Nate's intense gaze. He could read his brother's mind. In a time long ago and far away, they'd held a certain conversation, which he knew neither of them could relate to now.

"Since I couldn't reach you, I decided to fly home from London yesterday in order to give Dad an early surprise."

"And?"

"I'm afraid I'm the one who got the surprise. You could say I received the shock of my life."

"You're not about to tell me he's turned to drinking—"

"Sorry. You're not even close."

"Just spit it out."

"When I walked through the house, I found our father *in the kitchen. He wasn't alone…"*

"Rick—"

"He had this woman in a clinch by the sink. They were so far gone, they never saw or heard me. I don't know how I did it, but I managed to tiptoe back to the living room before calling out to Dad that I was home."

"This soon after Mom?"

"It gets worse. After Dad brought her into the living room and introduced us, he announced that they're engaged to be married. They'd gone to Denver to pick out her ring. Dad said he was glad I'd

*decided to come home for a surprise visit because
that saved him having to phone me with the news.''*

"If this woman is someone Mom and Dad knew
before the accident, I don't wa—"

*"Noooo. She's a Texan who came to Colorado a
month ago to attend a friend's wedding reception.
Apparently, she's never been on a pair of skis. While
she was shopping for sunglasses in the ski shop, Dad
challenged her to get out on the slopes and try it. He
gave her a few lessons, and things went from there.''*

"Hey, everybody?" Audra's voice brought Rick
back to the present. "This is a wedding reception not
a funeral wake."

David Jarrett was the first person to start clapping,
then the others followed suit. The band broke into an
old Glenn Miller song and people started dancing
again.

Rick made his way through the crush of people to
reach Audra. He'd waited three hours while she'd
kept the reception running smoothly. Now that she'd
sung a song that must have melted his father's heart,
there was nothing to hold him back.

Except Hal Torney.

Where in the hell had he come from? He'd trapped
her next to the band with a devouring gleam in his
eye.

No way he was going to let that man get in his
way.

Gritting his teeth, Rick kept right on going until
he'd reached them. He put a hand on the other guy's
shoulder so he'd be forced to turn around. "It's Hal,
isn't it?"

The sandy-haired man blinked. "Hey, it's *you!*"

Yes, it's me.

"Looks like you're all better."

It looks like I am.

"I hate to interrupt you two, but Audra's needed in the kitchen on some kind of emergency."

Her eyes widened in surprise. "Excuse me for a minute, Hal."

"Sure. I'm not going anywhere."

No. You're not. But we are.

She moved fast on those shapely legs of hers. No sign of a limp. For her sake he was thankful. After following her into the kitchen, he put his arm around her waist and walked her straight out the back door to the parking lot.

"What are you doing, Rick? I thought you said there was an emergency."

"There is. You and I have a date with the moon."

"Not tonight."

"It has to be tonight. I rented a truck for the occasion. You can't turn me down. I drove it all the way from Austin."

"What?"

"We're going to ride around till four in the morning, remember?"

"I can't leave right now. A lot of work is still ahead of me."

"There must be a hundred people inside, including the catering staff, getting the job done as we speak. Come on. I've missed my roommate. We're overdue some quality time together."

He grasped her hand and started walking toward

his rental truck. His instinct was to grab her and run, but it was too soon considering her cast hadn't been off that long.

When they reached it, she pulled her hand from his. "Rick, we can't do this."

"Why not? It's June."

"What are you talking about?"

"It was May on the night we were lying on my bed kissing each other—with great enjoyment, I might add. You told me that next month or next year we'd be in a different truck with our arms and legs wrapped around each other."

Even in the darkness he could see the color that filled her cheeks. "No. I said we'd be in different trucks with different people." She shook her head. "This is an absurd conversation."

He grimaced. "Not to me."

She avoided his eyes.

Don't pull away. My heart can't take it.

"There's something I want to ask you. We need privacy."

"If it's about going to a Formula One race with you, I've considered your invitation and I'm afraid the answer has to be no."

His body froze. "Why, Audra? It isn't as if watching one race would make your nightmares any worse. I'm hoping the experience will have the opposite effect on you."

She studied him as if he was a challenging calculus problem. "Let me ask you a question. Why didn't you want me to watch the tornado?"

"You know the answer to that," he whispered.

"Then you have your reason why I don't want to attend a car race. There are some things in life where you don't need the experience to know they're not good for you."

"I'm not going to be in it. I'll be a spectator on the sidelines with you."

Her eyes grew suspiciously bright. "Is my going that important to you?"

"Yes."

"Why?" she retorted.

"I want you to get a taste of my world."

"Why?"

"Because I'm in love with you."

Her sad smile devastated him. "For now maybe. We were thrown together under some unusual circumstances.

"Rick—I'm not trying to be cruel or insensitive. I won't lie to you or pretend that the time we spent at the bungalow wasn't some kind of miracle for me. But there were three women before I came along. They weren't what you were looking for. Neither am I. One of these days your equal will show up. Someone strong and exciting in her own right. She'll love you for exactly who you are."

"Are you telling me you don't think you're that woman?"

"I don't think, I *know*," she said with an exaggerated accent.

That dreaded blackness began to steal back into his soul.

"I've observed the Hawkins men at close range for some time now," she said. "You have many traits in common, but there's one you've developed to such a high degree, you've mistaken it for love. It's your protective instinct.''

Audra, Audra. Where's this all coming from?

''While Laurel was helping me unpack at the condo, she told me how close you were to your mother. I understand you two shared many things, including a love of skiing. She said you took her death especially hard.

''I have the strongest impression you've been trying to save me and my family because you couldn't save her. I believe your feelings are mixed up and confused.

''Don't forget, I saw your face the day I told you about the tornado. I didn't know it then, but I know it now. You relived your mother's death that day, and your grieving heart viewed me as poor little Audra who needed saving. That's why you leaped to my rescue during one of my bad dreams.

''This isn't a criticism of you, Rick, or anything like it. I've grown to love you for the person you are. Talk about my own Sir Galahad, ready to defend me against the evil princes of the realm. No one ever had a better champion.

''You and I will always enjoy a closeness because of Pam and Clint. But your self-imposed obligation is over. I set you free, Sir Knight, to fight and win new battles.

''One day in the future you'll wake up and realize you've worked your way through your grief. When that happens, you'll find your destiny.''

She glanced at her watch. ''We've been out here

too long. I've really got to go inside. I still have to pay the band and the caterers." She started backing away from him.

"Good luck at the track. Don't y'all be a stranger now, you hear?"

NATE BROUGHT IN the last of the wedding presents from the back of David's truck. Brent and his boys had been helping him.

"This is everything," he said to the happy group assembled in the living room of the main house where Pam had been urged to start opening their mountain of gifts.

Everyone would be staying over.

Everything in Nate's world was just about perfect.

Before the hour was out, his brother would be walking in the house with Audra sporting a diamond on her ring finger. Then there was going to be a wild celebration on the Jarrett Ranch tonight!

Laurel's eyes met his with a private message of love. Julie, who was beginning to show her pregnancy, was just as bad as her sister when it came to keeping a secret like this.

The champagne was in the fridge, ready to be popped open. Hopefully, David and Nate's dad and Pam were still on such a high, they hadn't picked up on the excitement coming from everyone else.

Pam turned to Clint. "Don't you think we ought to wait until Audra and Rick get here?"

"I don't think Uncle Rick's coming," eight-year-old Joey piped up.

"He'll be here pretty soon," Nate murmured. "He's helping Audra clean up the reception hall."

A grin broke out on his face. He could picture it now. Mr. Domestic, willingly hog-tied and chained for life.

"No, he won't," Joey insisted.

By now all eyes were focused on Brent and Julie's youngest boy.

Tension lines bracketed Brent's mouth. "Do you know where he is?"

"He got in his truck and took off like he was driving his race car."

Nate felt as if he'd just been kicked in the gut. "Was Audra with him?"

"No. I think they had a fight."

"Come here, honey." Julie beckoned her son, who walked over to her. "Why do you say that?"

"Because I was outside with some of the boys looking for the skunk that made such a bad smell. While we were creeping around, I saw Uncle Rick talking to her by his truck. He had this real sick look on his face before he got in it."

"It's true, Mom," ten-year-old Mike informed her. "When she came back in the kitchen, she looked as if she'd been crying. Some guy named Hal had been looking for her. She asked me to tell him she was too busy and would talk to him another time."

Out of the mouths of babes.

What in the hell could have gone wrong?

Nate excused himself and went into the hall to call Rick on his cell phone, but his brother had turned his off.

Jeez.

He heard a noise behind him and wheeled around in time to see Audra slip inside the door carrying her guitar.

"Hi."

Her head flew back. "Hi," she said in a soft tone when she saw him standing there.

This was honesty time. "Who brought you home?"

"Jim and Sherry."

"Where's Rick?"

Her eyes closed tightly. "I don't know."

"But you have an idea."

"H-he's probably in Austin by now. That's where he said he'd rented the truck."

"Is he planning to come back?"

"I'm not sure."

"Joey said you had a fight."

"Did he?" She turned her head away.

"Audra? Talk to me. My brother's been living for tonight. He's only had one thought on his mind, and that was to be with you. What happened?"

She drew her composure around her like a cloak and faced him. "Nothing. He asked me to go to a Formula One race with him and I turned him down."

Wait a minute... Something wasn't right here.

"That's why you're not together now?"

"It's part of the reason, but not all."

"My brother's more fragile than you know. Did you tell him you weren't in love with him? I'm not asking that out of any other reason than concern for him."

"I believe you, but my being in love with him has nothing to do with anything."

She *was* in love with him.

"I don't understand."

"Rick thinks he's in love with me, but there were three other women before me, and I'm sure there'll be someone else as soon as he's back on the Mayada team. He needs more time to get over your mother's death."

Nate blinked.

Audra was afraid.

She reminded him of Pam, who'd been terrified their father would wake up after the wedding and decide he didn't want to be married after all.

She and Pam had been close for so many years, she'd internalized her older cousin's fears.

That song she'd sung tonight had sprung out of her love for Rick, but she'd masked it to look as if those were Pam's feelings. It was all making sense.

Unfortunately his brother hadn't proposed first. That's where he'd made his big mistake, probably the first ever. Now he was hurting.

If he knew Rick, he'd turned the truck in at the airport. Either he was waiting to board the next flight back to Denver, or he'd rented a car so he could get out of the state of Texas as fast as possible.

This was something Nate needed to talk over with his father before they went to bed.

CHAPTER FIFTEEN

IT WAS THREE in the morning when Audra heard a knock on the bedroom door. This was the room she'd grown up in. She doubted anyone but her cousin would be walking around right now.

"Pam?"

"Yes, honey. Can I come in?"

"Of course."

Audra dashed the tears from her face with the sheet. Her cousin slipped in quietly and hurried over to the bed. She sank down next to Audra.

"After that wonderful reception, I haven't been able to sleep, and figured you couldn't either."

"I hope it made you and Clint happy."

"It was wonderful." She put her arms around Audra and rocked her. "Thank you for one of the most beautiful nights of my life. Did you see Jim gave me a kiss?"

"No. I can't believe it!"

"Neither could I. He looked like he was about to cry when he told us he hoped Clint and I could forgive him. Do you know what that remarkable husband of mine said?"

"I can guess. Something about helping him build a barn?"

"Yes, and sharing ours until it's ready."

"That sounds like Clint. Diane says Greg's got a ways to go but she's confident that breaking away from Tom's influence will change everything with time."

"I agree," Pam murmured. "It's Tom I'm worried about. Annette called me before we left for the reception to apologize for not coming. Things aren't good. She talked to the psychiatrist who's going to be working with him.

"After she'd given him a little history, the doctor said he suspects Tom had a mental break, or a brain freeze as they call it, at the time of the tornado. He was at a vulnerable age and simply shut down. In cases like his, there's only so much therapy can do, but Annette's trying to be optimistic."

"Then we will be, too." But Audra didn't want to think about sad things right now. "Did you like my song?"

"Very much. There's only one problem. You were singing it to the wrong couple. That beautiful love song was meant for Rick. When you two are married, you'll have to sing it to him. The only line you need to tweak is the one that says, in the summertime of my life. Change it to springtime, and it's perfect."

"We're not getting married—" Audra blurted in shock.

"You're not?"

"No." She lowered her eyes. "He hasn't asked me."

"I wonder what's holding him up."

"H-he came close to getting married to three different women."

"Only three?"

"Pam—"

"Well, you're the one who labeled him the Racetrack Lover."

"I admit I was too judgmental in the beginning. Deep down he's terrified of commitment to a needy woman. The problem is, all women are needy when they're in love, and since his mother died, his feelings are even more confused."

"In what way?"

"He doesn't know the difference between loving someone and being protective of her. They're two different things."

"Oh. I see."

"Rick stopped by here to visit his father and ended up trying to protect all of us. He's good at rescuing people."

"He's a Hawkins. They come by it naturally. Have you ever thought he's afraid you've been comparing him to Boris?"

"That's absurd and he knows it."

"Sometimes the things that seem so plain to us are anything but to someone else."

Pam was sounding cryptic. "Are you saying Rick's afraid I'll turn him down if he asked me to marry him?"

"Would you? Turn him down, I mean?"

"Yes. Not because of anything to do with Boris!"

"His career then."

She bit her lip. "I don't want to go there."

"Is that why you two quarreled earlier tonight?"

"How did you find out?"

"Joey happened to be in the parking lot and saw you."

"I'll have to remember that he's a tattletale in the future."

"Does it really matter? All this family cares about is your happiness. What happened?"

Audra took a shuddering breath. "Rick's hoping that if I see a race, I'll get over my fear."

"I think he's hoping for a lot more than that."

"What do you mean?"

"You need to ask him, not me. If you'd met Rick halfway tonight, you would already have your answer." Pam gave her another hug and got up from the bed. "I'll see you in the morning." She disappeared from the room.

You need to ask *him,* not me.

Like a mantra, those words went around in Audra's head for the rest of the night.

Finally, the first rays of pink and yellow came through the window. She got dressed and slipped out of the house to the barn to curry Prince and give him some oats. At one point she pressed her cheek against his neck.

"Pam was trying to tell me something earlier. She never does that without a good reason."

"Were you talking to me?"

She spun around to discover Nate was in the barn. "I—I didn't know you were here," she stammered.

"Last night I promised Dad I'd check on the

horses. Dad and Pam shouldn't have to worry about anything today.''

''I ought to have offered to tend the baby so you and Laurel could sleep in, too.''

He smiled. ''That's very sweet, but with Becky nursing, I'm afraid we don't have a normal schedule anymore. Of course, that's due to change in a few months.''

''It will.'' Her heart was racing so fast she felt ill. ''Nate? When are you going back to Colorado?''

''Today at four-thirty.''

''I've been thinking about everything and realize I need to talk to Rick. It can't be over the phone. This has to be in person. But he was so upset when he left for Austin, I'm not sure he'll give me the chance.

''If I flew back with you, do you think you could help me? I don't want him to know I'm coming or he might be more put off than he already is.''

Nate's eyes gleamed. ''Leave everything to me.''

''I'D BETTER GO. I told Jackie I'd be home by nine.''

''You shouldn't have stayed this long.'' Rick walked Chip to the front door. ''Thanks for coming to my rescue today.''

''I owe you for all the times you had to listen to me moan about my problems with Jackie.'' After a slight pause, ''Rick, I know things look bleak to you right now because of Audra. Just don't let it get you down too far.''

''Easy advice to give. Impossible to heed.''

His buddy shook his head. ''What an irony. Just

when Jackie and I are starting to put our lives back together, you—''

''I don't want to talk about it anymore,'' Rick muttered. ''Wally's flying in tomorrow morning. I'll let you know what time to meet us at his hotel.''

Chip nodded. ''If you find you can't stand your own company later, drive to Denver and crash with Jackie and me.''

''That's the last thing you two need, but I appreciate the offer. I've got plenty of work to do on the computer tonight.''

His friend scrutinized him for a minute. ''Why don't you follow me home now? You know damn well you're just going to lie around here and sink deeper.''

''We don't have any secrets left, do we, Chip?''

''Nope.''

Rick rubbed his jaw. He hadn't bothered to shave this morning. Now he was regretting it. ''If my demons get worse, I'll call you.''

''No, you won't, so I'll be phoning *you* later. Better turn your cell back on. Otherwise, people will think you died. Good night, Rick. I'll see you tomorrow.''

He watched his friend drive off before he shut and locked the door.

Now he was alone in this house he loved.

It had always been his refuge, but since that nightmarish moment in the church parking lot when Audra had sent him packing, he could find no comfort anywhere.

He'd wanted her so much he'd refused to understand what should have been clear to him all along.

The Jarrett family had sustained too many losses. Audra was terrified of loving him for fear she'd lose him. All the talk about his confusion and protective instincts was just camouflage.

She'd been in a car crash with a friend who'd died. Pam was married to a man who'd secretly feared Rick would die on the racetrack. Audra had known all about his father's fears for Rick before she'd ever met him.

Even if she'd given him the chance to tell her his days of competition were behind him, she'd probably hate the idea of his school.

He wandered into the study and turned on the CD player. She'd composed dozens of songs. He flung himself down on the couch to listen to them. Nate would tell him he was a masochist.

Tears stung his eyes when he listened to "You Should Have Asked Your Mama." Audra's mother had been taken away in the whirlwind. Literally swept away in the kind of funnel cloud Rick had seen at close range. His body shuddered. Audra had only been five. She never got the chance to know her mother. Rick still had a hard time comprehending it.

His gaze fell on the photograph of his mom in her wedding dress. She'd been there for him every second of his life growing up. Audra had been forced to turn to Pam when she was in pain. Pam was a loving woman but no one can take the place of your real parents.

Pam had known her own mother well. Who knew how deep the pain went when she never returned from church…

How had David found the strength to deal with his own grief and still raise five children who weren't his?

Unable to stand his torturous thoughts another minute, he levered himself from the couch and turned off the music. To his surprise, the doorbell was ringing. He wondered for how long.

The last thing he needed was company.

If people wanted to see him, they should have called first. Then he remembered his phone was turned off. Hopefully the person would give up and go away.

When they kept ringing, he stole over to the window and peeked out. Nate's car was in the driveway behind his M3. He must have just come back from Austin.

If his brother was this anxious to talk to him, why didn't he just let himself in with the key?

Unless he didn't have it on him.

"Hang on, Nate. I'm coming!" He hurried to the front door and opened it. That's when his heart crashed into his ribs.

"Audra—"

While he stood there in shock, she stepped past him with her suitcase. The last thing he saw before shutting the door was his brother's car going down the street.

"Last night you said you had something important to ask me. I assumed you were talking about us watching a race together, but Pam said there was a lot more to it than that." She sought his gaze. "Was she right?"

The courage it took to ask that question was as telling as the little wobble in her voice.

He reached for her and crushed her body against his. Finally they could meld together in a seamless line. She clung to him with a fierceness that satisfied him to the depths of his soul.

"Marry me, Audra. I can't live without you."

"Why didn't you say that to me last night?" she cried softly into his neck.

He buried his mouth deep in her curls. "I wanted to give you a romantic evening in the truck first."

"That's very sweet. I'm sorry I ruined it with all my fears."

By now his body was trembling with excitement and desire and so many emotions, he was afraid he'd burst.

"Does this mean you don't have them anymore?"

"No," she replied with predictable Jarrett honesty. "But you're the love of my life—the only man I want for my husband, the one I want to be the father of my babies.

"If you crash and die before we have the chance to grow old together, then so be it. I'll take whatever is offered for as long as it's offered because I can't live without you either."

She threw her arms around his neck and kissed him, revealing a longing, a hunger for him he would remember all the days of his life. Their passion drove him to carry her up the stairs to his bedroom. There was a tiny velvet box he needed to get off his dresser.

"This was burning a hole in my pocket yesterday," he murmured after he'd set her down on his bed.

"There's something you need to know before I put it on you.

"Meeting you has changed my life. I'm no longer going to be racing cars. I've already purchased property about forty-five minutes from here in order to build a racing school."

"Rick!"

Her cry contained all the happiness and joy he could have hoped for.

"I love the sport, but the thrill of competition isn't there anymore. It hasn't been there for the last year. I'm excited to mentor new drivers. The beautiful part is, we can live right here. We'll make this our home.

"With Nate and Laurel in Colorado Springs, and the Marsdens and Warners in Denver, we'll be surrounded with family and friends.

"This house has room for your uncle. He can live with us part of the year if you think he'd like it. We'll fly down to Texas all the time so you won't get too homesick.

"I'm sure with a few inquiries you could have your own radio program in the Denver area. Maybe they'd let you broadcast from the house like you did at the bungalow." He paused, having given her a lot to think about in a very short period of time. But he couldn't wait, he needed her answer.

"What do you think?"

She gazed at him out of lustrous blue eyes. "I love you with all my heart and soul, Rick Hawkins."

"I knew that while you were singing to Dad and Pam. It was *our* love song, sweetheart."

Audra nodded. "While you and I were living together, I learned that home is where you are. I found it when I found you. I don't feel lost anymore. I'm so full of love for you, there isn't room for anything else.''

Feelings had welled up inside him, so he couldn't speak. He knelt on the floor, then reached for her left hand and slid the diamond on her ring finger.

''I chose a solitaire because it looks like the top of a bluebonnet,'' he said before kissing her fingertips and hands. In the next breath he followed her down on the mattress.

She was here in his arms, waiting for him with a love in full bloom. He'd found his woman of fire in the last place he would have expected. Now she'd followed him home to Copper Mountain.

Here they would stay.

Life was glorious once more.

EPILOGUE

"BY THE AUTHORITY vested in me, I now pronounce you, Audra Sealey Jarrett, and you, Richard Soderhielm Hawkins, husband and wife from this day forth, for as long as you both shall live."

I'm his wife.

Audra couldn't believe it. The three weeks of endless waiting for this day to come were over.

"Before Rick kisses his lovely new bride, he wants to present her with something."

Audra couldn't imagine what it was. He'd already made her the happiest woman alive.

His gray eyes seemed to glow with a secret. She watched him look out over the congregation assembled in the church where his parents and his brother had been married.

He cleared his throat. "Today I believe my mother is here in spirit. She's the one who instilled the love of music in me. On my way to the Jarrett Ranch I was listening to a fabulous female vocalist out of Austin and fell in love with her voice, her music, her words.

"Little did I know it was Audra...

"I wrote a song to tell her how I feel about her.

I'd like to sing it now without accompaniment.'' He grasped both her hands.

> My love was born in a Texas meadow,
> Plucked from a waving sea,
> Now she's planted in my heart,
> Where she was always meant to be.

> I came across my bluebonnet,
> Lying helpless on the ground,
> A wind had carried her far off course,
> She didn't make a sound.
> Tears glazed my cheeks that one so fair,
> Could simply blow away,
> I kissed the blossoms of her hair,
> Before I took her home that day.

> My love was born in a Texas meadow,
> Plucked from a waving sea,
> Now she's planted in my heart,
> Where she'll always be with me.

''Darling—that was so beautiful, it hurts,'' Audra cried before their mouths met and clung.

Until the pastor asked the congregation to rise while Mr. and Mrs. Hawkins walked down the aisle, she'd forgotten they had an audience.

The second they reached the garden where their reception was being held, her uncle was there to hug her. ''You're my little bluebonnet, too,'' David said in a choked-up voice. ''I love Rick for making you so happy.''

She hugged him back. "After our honeymoon we'll come and see you."

Clint grabbed her next. "I guess I don't have to tell you what you mean to me. My son didn't get nicknamed Lucky for nothing. Welcome to the family."

"I love your family."

"So do I," Pam chimed in. She drew Audra to the side and put her arms around her. "Can you stand any more happiness today?"

Audra pulled back so she could look into her cousin's brown eyes. They brimmed with joy. She was pregnant!

"Don't say anything. I haven't told Clint yet, but I couldn't keep it a secret from you, not when you're going to be in San Francisco for the next week."

"What are you two whispering about?"

"Last-minute pointers," Audra quipped before hugging Nate and Laurel.

He burst into laughter. "You and my brother are so crazy about each other, you don't need any. After his performance in the church, you're going to have to call your radio program the *Red and Rick Show*."

"I heard that." Rick grinned. "Today was a one-time-only deal."

"Hey, Rick?" Nate said. "Have you told your wife what you're naming your new business?"

"I'll get around to it."

"I want to know now." She kissed her husband.

"It was Nate who came up with the idea. Go ahead. You're dying to tell her anyway."

"The Racetrack Lover's School of High Performance."

"You're kidding!" Her chuckle grew into laughter. "I love it—it's perfect!"

Her husband drew her into his arms. "I'm glad you approve. Now, let's finish greeting our guests. I can't wait much longer to take you on that truck ride until four in the morning. You know the one I mean."

Audra knew the one he meant. This ride was going to last a long time past four in the morning.

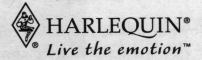

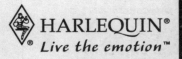

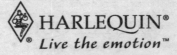

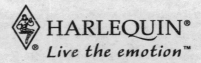